'Mr Ogilvy tells me you play a good game.'

Greer glanced around the room, smiling broadly. 'Good enough to have beaten most of the gentlemen present on more than one occasion. He has compelled me to come and defend men everywhere.' He gave the chalk on his cue tip an efficient blow, looking entirely likeable.

'Hear, hear,' came a few cries from the back of the room.

The dratted man was going to steal her crowd if she wasn't careful. Usually she admired Greer's ease, how people *wanted* to cheer for him. She wasn't admiring that trait at the moment. Beneath his aura of bonhomie he was primed, a veritable powder keg, and the fuse was lit. He was going to ignite this room and she'd get caught in the explosion.

She hadn't lost the room yet. And she wouldn't. She'd beat Greer and give these boys a show they

Mercedes met G   h
of the table, eye   r,
her mouth a per   A
gentleman or two sighed when she chalked up
and raised the cue to her lips in her trademark
g   ld get
th

From the fabulous Bronwyn Scott
comes a wickedly naughty and sensational
new duet

LADIES OF IMPROPRIETY

Breaking Society's Rules

Practised gambler Mercedes Lockhart
takes on the big boys—and the irresistible
Captain Barrington—in England's billiards clubs
in
A LADY RISKS ALL
July 2013

Elise Sutton is a lady in a man's world
when she finds herself fighting for her family's
company at London's Blackwell Docks—
but that doesn't mean she can't show the
roguish privateer Dorian Rowland who's boss
in
A LADY DARES
August 2013

Two scandalously sexy stories.
Two alluringly provocative ladies
who dare to flout the rules of the *ton*—and enjoy it!

Also, don't miss out on the seductive Lucia Booth,
proprietor of Mrs Booth's Discreet Gentleman's Club
and former spy, in
A LADY SEDUCES
coming July 2013
to Mills & Boon® Historical *Undone!*

A LADY RISKS ALL

Bronwyn Scott

First published in Great Britain 2013
by Mills & Boon, an imprint of Harlequin (UK) Limited.
Harlequin (UK) Limited, Eton House, 18-24 Paradise Road,
Richmond, Surrey TW9 1SR

© Nikki Poppen 2013

ISBN: 978 0 263 89836 1

Harlequin (UK) policy is to use papers that are natural, renewable
and recyclable products and made from wood grown in sustainable
forests. The logging and manufacturing process conform to the
legal environmental regulations of the country of origin.

Printed and bound in Spain
by Blackprint CPI, Barcelona

Bronwyn Scott is a communications instructor at Pierce College in the United States, and is the proud mother of three wonderful children (one boy and two girls). When she's not teaching or writing she enjoys playing the piano, travelling—especially to Florence, Italy—and studying history and foreign languages.

Readers can stay in touch on Bronwyn's website, www.bronwynnscott.com, or at her blog, www.bronwynswriting.blogspot.com—she loves to hear from readers.

Previous novels from Bronwyn Scott:

PICKPOCKET COUNTESS
NOTORIOUS RAKE, INNOCENT LADY
THE VISCOUNT CLAIMS HIS BRIDE
THE EARL'S FORBIDDEN WARD
UNTAMED ROGUE, SCANDALOUS MISTRESS
A THOROUGHLY COMPROMISED LADY
SECRET LIFE OF A SCANDALOUS DEBUTANTE
UNBEFITTING A LADY†
HOW TO DISGRACE A LADY*
HOW TO RUIN A REPUTATION*
HOW TO SIN SUCCESSFULLY*

And in Mills & Boon® Historical *Undone!* eBooks:

LIBERTINE LORD, PICKPOCKET MISS
PLEASURED BY THE ENGLISH SPY
WICKED EARL, WANTON WIDOW
ARABIAN NIGHTS WITH A RAKE
AN ILLICIT INDISCRETION
HOW TO LIVE INDECENTLY*

†*Castonbury Park* Regency mini-series
*Rakes Beyond Redemption trilogy

And in M&B:

PRINCE CHARMING IN DISGUISE
(part of *Royal Weddings Through the Ages*)

**Did you know that some of these novels
are also available as eBooks?
Visit www.millsandboon.co.uk**

AUTHOR NOTE

Billiards is just about as English as horse racing. References note that by the seventeenth century there wasn't a village in England that didn't boast at least one billiards table in an assembly hall or tavern. Here are some fun facts about Greer and Mercedes's story:

1838 is part of the 'gateway' period of billiards as it moves closer to the modern pool game.

John Thurston is a real historical figure and has a cameo appearance early in our story. In 1799 he established the House of Thurston in London, and is credited with new inventions for the table such as his 1835 rubber cushions, the use of warming pans to keep the cushions supple and replacing wood table beds with slate (c.1826). The table Greer mentions from his time in Greece is based on a true story.

1838 also sees the introduction of the 'run' style of today's pool game. The run is first officially mentioned by Game Master Hoyle, in association with 'the French following game' in an 1845 edition of game rules. It crosses the Atlantic to America in 1857.

I should also take a moment to mention Alan Lockhart. He is modelled after the nineteenth-century billiards champion Edwin Kentfield.

I hope you enjoy this first of two stories in my *Ladies of Impropriety* duet. Stay tuned for Elise Sutton's story. In the meanwhile, stop by my blog at www.bronwynswriting.blogspot.com for forthcoming news.

DEDICATION

This one is for my dad, who kept asking me when was 'that billiards book' coming out. Here it is, finally, with much love.

Chapter One

Brighton—March 1837

There was nothing quite as exhilarating as a man who knew how to handle his stick. Mercedes Lockhart put an eye to the discreet peephole for a second glimpse, separate trills of excitement and anxiety vibrating through her. Rumour was right, he *did* have an amazing crack.

Outside in the billiards hall, that crack would sound like a cannon. But here in the soundproof peeping room, she could only watch and worry about what his presence in her father's club meant.

There's someone I want you to meet. The phrase rang through her head for the hun-

dredth time. When fathers said that to their
daughters it usually meant one thing: a suitor.
But those fathers weren't billiards great Allen
Lockhart. He was more likely to bring home
a gem-studded cue than a suitor. Perhaps that
was the reason she'd been so surprised by the
summons. 'Come down to the club, there's
someone I want you to watch,' he'd said. It
had been a long time since he'd needed her
in that way. She didn't dare refuse. So, here
she was, ensconced in the 'viewing room', eye
riveted to the peephole, taking in the player at
table three.

He was a man she'd have noticed even without her father's regard. Most women would.
He was well built; broad shouldered and lean
hipped, an observation made inescapable by
the fact he was playing with his coat off. At
the moment, he was bent at the waist and lev-
elling his cue for the next shot, a posture that
offered her a silhouette of trim waist and tautly
curved buttock, framed by muscled thighs that
tensed ever so slightly beneath the tight fawn
of his breeches.

Her eyes roamed upwards to the strong
forearms displayed tan against the rolled back
cuffs of his white shirtsleeves, to the taper of
lean fingers forming a bridge through which

his cue stick slid effortlessly, expertly as he made his shot.

He straightened and turned in her direction, accepting congratulations on the shot. He pushed back the blond hair that had fallen over his face. Mercedes caught a glimpse of startling blue eyes; a deep shade of sapphire she could appreciate even at a distance. He was confident, not cocky in the way he accepted the congratulations of others. There was no doubt he handled his cue with ease, his playing strategy sound but straightforward, his use of the 'break' progressive and in line with the new style billiards was starting to take.

But Mercedes could see immediately there wasn't a lot of finesse in it. It was understandable. A player with his skill likely didn't see the need for finer machinations. That was something that could be improved upon. Mercedes halted her thoughts right there. Why? Why should she improve him? Is that what her father wanted her opinion for? What interest did the legendary Lockhart want with a handsome young billiards player? The anxiety that had plagued her trilled again. Was he a suitor for her? A protégé for her father?

Neither option sat well with her. She had no intentions to marry although she was aware of her father's ambition for her to wed a title. It would be the final feather in his cap of self-made glory—Allen Lockhart's daughter married to a peer of the realm! But she had other goals and neither a suitor nor a protégé was among them.

Mercedes stepped back from the peephole and scribbled a short note to her father, who sat in the main room in plain sight. There was no skulking in private viewing chambers for him, she thought with no small amount of frustration. It hadn't always been like this: spying through peepholes and pretending she didn't exist. It used to be that she had the run of the place. But she'd grown up and it was no longer seemly or prudent, as past events had proven, for her to roam the halls of Lockhart's Billiards Club, no matter how elegant the setting or how skilled the player. The bottom line was that men didn't like to be beaten by a woman. Thus had ended her career of playing in public. For now.

This was why the thought of a protégé met with her disapproval. If there was to be one, it *should* be her. She'd honed her own skill at her father's side. When she'd shown some aptitude for the game, he'd taught her to play as only a professional can. She'd learned his secrets and developed her own until she was on par with the best. Then she'd committed the crime of turning seventeen and her freedoms had been curtailed; in part by society and in part by her own headstrong judgement.

It was something of a curse that the one thing she was good at—no, not merely good at, excellent at—was a talent she did not get to display. These days she practised for herself, alone in the privacy of their home and she waited, forever ready if the chance to prove herself came her way.

Mercedes folded the note and sent it out to her father. She bent her eye to the peephole one last time, a thought occurring to her as she watched the man pot his final ball. Maybe he was her chance. Her earlier excitement started to hum again. She'd been waiting five years for her opportunity, alert for any possibility. In all that time, she'd never thought her chance would come in the form of a handsome Englishman—she'd had her fill of those. But if her father could use him, perhaps she could too.

Slow down, she cautioned herself. A good gambler always assessed the risk and there *was* risk here. If her father intended him to be a protégé and she assisted with that, she could effectively cut herself out of the picture altogether. She would have to go carefully. On the other hand, it would be a chance to show her father what she could do in a situation where he would be unable to deny her talent.

It was a venture that could see her exiled or elevated, but she was nothing if not her father's daughter; a gambler at heart who knew the risks and rules of any engagement and chose to play anyway.

Gamblers of any successful repute generally acknowledged the secret to luck resided in knowing three things: the rules, the stakes and when to quit. No one knew this better than English billiards legend, Allen Lockhart. He couldn't remember a time when the stakes hadn't been high—they always were when all one had to risk was a reputation. As for quitting—if there was a time to quit, he hadn't discovered it yet, which was why the usual ritual of a brandy with long-time friend and partner, Kendall Carlisle, did not fill him with the usual satisfaction on this dreary March afternoon.

Normally this time of day was his favourite. It was a time when he could sit back in one of the club's deep chairs and savour his domain. *His domain.* Carlisle managed the place, but it had been *his* billiards money that had built this and more.

Across from him, oblivious to his restless observations, Carlisle took a swallow of brandy followed by a contented sigh. 'This is the life, Allen. Not bad for two junior boot boys.'

Allen smiled in response. It was a well-loved reminiscence of his. The two of them had done well over the years kowtowing to the rich gentlemen in the subscription rooms of Bath for shillings. They'd watched and they'd learned, eventually establishing their own small empire. Now *they* were the rich gentlemen. Now *they* ran the subscription rooms, not in Bath, but in more lucrative Brighton. They earned much more than shillings from customers these days. At the age of forty-seven, Allen Lockhart took great pride in having used the rules of billiards to rise above his poor beginnings.

From their grouping of chairs by the fire, Allen could hear the quiet snick of ivory balls on baize, the unmistakable sounds of lazy-afternoon billiard games going on in the room beyond him. Later in the evening, the club would be crowded with officers and gentlemen, the tables loud with the intensity of money games.

Allen felt his hand twitch in anticipation of the games to come. He didn't play in public often anymore, not wanting to tarnish his image by making himself vulnerable to defeat. A legend couldn't be beaten too often without damaging the illusion of being untouchable. But the desire was still there. Billiards was in his blood. He was the legendary Allen Lockhart, after all. He'd built this club on his fame. People came here to play, of course, but also to see him. It wasn't enough to be good at billiards; one also had to be a showman.

He knew the power of a well-placed word here, a timely stroke tip there. It was heady stuff to think people would talk about a single sentence from him for months in London. 'Lockhart says you have to hit the ball from the side' or 'Lockhart recommends African ivory for balls'. But lately, the usual thrill had faded. Such excitement had become *de rigueur*. He was restless.

The resounding crack of a hard break shattered the laconic atmosphere of the room. Allen briefly acknowledged it with a swift glance towards table three where a young officer played before turning back to Kendall.

'I hope you're coming up to the house tomorrow for the party.'

'I wouldn't miss it. I'm looking forward to seeing the new table.' Carlisle raised his glass in a toast. 'I hear Thurston has outdone himself this time.'

Lockhart grinned broadly like a proud first-time father. 'Slate tables with rubber bumpers are the way of the future. They're fast, Kendall.' Another loud break from table three interrupted. This time Lockhart spared the table more than a passing glance. 'Good Lord, that lad's got some power.' He chanced a look in the direction of the secret viewing room and wondered what Mercedes would make of it. Kendall hadn't lied when he'd said the lad could play.

Their chairs were angled to take in the expanse of the elegant club if they chose. Both men fell silent, focusing on the game, looking out into the well-appointed billiards floor. Long windows let in enormous amounts of light for quality shots. Subtle forest-green wallpapering with matching floor-to-ceiling curtains gave the room the air of a sophisticated drawing room. This was no mean gambling hall. This was a place meant to invite a higher class of gentleman to engage in the noble sport of billiards and right now table three was heavily engaged.

The 'lad' in question was not a boy at all, but a blond-haired officer with the broad-shouldered build of a handsomely put-together man. A confident man too, Lockhart noted. Effortless charm and affability poured off him as he potted the third ball and proceeded to run the table. Affable and yet without any feigned humility.

'He reminds me of you back in our salad days,' Carlisle murmured after the officer made a particularly difficult corner shot.

'How old do you think he is?' Kendall would know. Information gathering was Kendall's gift. His own was using it. The combined talent had been invaluable to them both over the years.

'Mid-twenties. He's been in a few times. His name's Barrington. Captain Barrington,' Kendall supplied as Lockhart had known he would.

At that age, he and Kendall had been living on the road, Lockhart thought wistfully. They'd played any money game they could find in just about every assembly hall between Manchester and London. They'd run just about every 'angle' too—plucking peacocks, two friends and a stranger and a hundred more.

'He's bought a subscription,' Kendall volunteered.

'On half-pay?' Any officer in town these days with time for billiards was on half-pay. But on that salary, a subscription to his fine establishment was a luxury unless one had other resources.

Kendall shrugged. 'I cut him a fair deal. He's good for business. People like to play him.'

'For a while.' Lockhart shrugged. Barrington would have to be managed. If he was too good, players would tire of getting beaten and that would be just as bad for business. He didn't want that to happen too quickly.

'With the big championship coming up in July, I thought he might generate some additional interest,' Carlisle began, but Lockhart's mind was already steps ahead. Perhaps the Captain could be taught when to lose, perhaps he could be taught a lot of things. Carlisle was right. The young man could be very useful in the months leading up to the All England Billiards Championship. The old thrill began to course.

'Thinking about taking a protégé?' Kendall joked.

'Maybe.' He was thinking about taking more than a protégé. He was thinking about taking a trip. For what reason, he wasn't sure yet. Perhaps the urge was nothing more than a desire to walk down memory lane one more time and relive the nostalgia of the old days. Perhaps he wanted more? His intuition suggested his restlessness was more than nostalgic desire. There were bigger questions to answer. At forty-seven, did he still have it? Could the legend make a comeback or was the 'new' game beyond him?

'Is that all you're thinking?' He felt Kendall's shrewd gaze on him and kept his own eyes on the game. It would be best not to give too much away, even to his best friend, if this was going to work. A footman approached with a folded note. Ah, Mercedes had announced her verdict.

Lockhart rose, flicking a cursory glance at the simple content of Mercedes's note and made his excuses, careful to school his features. Kendall knew him too well. 'I've got to go and see about some business.' Then he paused as if an inspiration had struck suddenly. 'Invite our young man up to the house

tomorrow night. It might be fun for him to see
the new table and I want him to meet Mercedes.'

If he was going to try this madcap venture
at all, he would need her help. She'd already
consented to the first bit by coming down
today. The hard part would be convincing her
to try it all on. She could be deuced stubborn
when she put her mind to it. With any luck,
he wouldn't have to do the convincing. He'd
leave that to a certain officer's good looks,
extraordinary talent with a billiards cue and
a little moonlit magic. He knew his daughter.
If there was anything Mercedes couldn't resist
it was a challenge.

Chapter Two

Captain Greer Barrington of the Eleventh Devonshire had seen enough of the world in his ten years of military service to know when the game was afoot. It was definitely afoot tonight, and it had been ever since Kendall Carlisle had offered him an invitation to the Lockhart party. There seemed little obvious logic in a man of Lockhart's celebrity inviting an anonymous officer to dine.

Greer surveyed the small assemblage with a quick gaze as Allen Lockhart greeted him and drew him into the group of men near the fireplace, a tall elegant affair topped with a mantel of carved walnut. Suspicions confirmed. First, the small size of the gathering meant this was a special, intimate cohort of friends and professional acquaintances. Second, Allen Lockhart lived finely in one of the forty-two large town houses that comprised Brunswick Terrace. Greer had not been wrong in taking the effort to arrive polished to perfection for the evening, and now the buttons on his uniform gleamed appreciably under the light of expensive brass-and-glass chandeliers.

'You know Kendall Carlisle already from the club, of course.' Allen Lockhart made the necessary introductions with the ease of a practised host. 'This is John Thurston, the man behind the manufacture of the new table.' Greer nodded in the man's direction. He knew of Thurston. The man ran a billiards works in London and a billiards hall off St James's.

'John,' Lockhart said with great familiarity, 'this is Captain Greer Barrington.' Lockhart had a fatherly hand at his shoulder and Greer did not miss the reference. Either Lockhart was a quick study of military uniforms or he'd done his research. 'The Captain has a blistering break—sounds like a cannon going off in the club every time. He ran the table on Elias Pole yesterday.'

Ah, Greer thought. So Lockhart *had* been watching. He'd thought he'd sensed the other man's interest in his game. Appreciative murmurs followed with more introductions.

Talk turned to billiards until a young woman materialised at Lockhart's side, stopping all conversation—something she would have done without saying a word. 'Father, dinner will be served shortly.'

This gorgeous creature was Lockhart's daughter? Whatever game was afoot, Greer mused, he'd gladly play it and see where it went if she was involved. There was no arguing her beauty. It was bold and forthright like the flash of a smile she threw his direction.

'Captain, you haven't met my daughter, Mercedes,' Lockhart said affably. 'Perhaps I could persuade you to take her in to dinner? I believe she's seated you with her at the one end.'

'It would be my pleasure, Miss Lockhart.' Yet another pleasant addition to the evening. This invitation was turning out splendidly. Mercedes Lockhart was a stunning young woman with dark hair and wide grey eyes framed with long lashes. But there was an icy quality to that perfection. Beautiful and cold, Greer noted. Greer was confident he could change that. He smiled one of his charming smiles, the one that usually made women feel as if they'd known him much longer than they had.

She was less than charmed. Her own smile did not move from that of practised politeness, her sharp grey eyes conducting a judicious perusal of their own. Greer stepped back discreetly from the group, drawing her with him until he had space for a conversation of his own.

'Do I pass?' Greer queried, determined to make this haughty beauty accountable for her actions.

'Pass what?'

'Inspection is what we call it in the military.'

She blushed a little at his bluntness and he took the small victory. She looked warmer when she blushed, prettier too if that was possible, the untouchable coldness of her earlier hauteur melting into more feminine features.

'I must admit more than a passing curiosity to see the man who beat Elias Pole. My father talked of nothing else at supper last night.'

There was a fleeting bitterness in her tone, some of her hard elegance returning. Provoked by what? Jealousy? The defeat of her champion? Elias Pole was a man of middle years, not unattractive for his age, but certainly he wasn't the type to capture the attentions of a young woman.

Greer shrugged easily. 'I am flattered I aroused your curiosity. But it was just a game.'

Her eyebrows shot up at that, challenge and mild disbelief evident in her voice. 'Just a game? Not to these men. It would be very dangerous to think otherwise, Captain.'

Ah. Illumination at last, Greer thought with satisfaction. Now he had a better idea of why he was here. This was about billiards.

Dinner was announced and he took the lovely Mercedes into supper, her hand polite and formal on the sleeve of his coat. The dining room was impressive with its long polished table set with china and crystal, surrounded by the accoutrements of a man who lived well and expensively: silver on the matching sideboards and decanter sets no doubt blown in Venice.

Greer recognised the subtle signs of affluence and he knew what they meant. Allen Lockhart aspired to be a gentleman. Of course, Lockhart wasn't. Couldn't be. Lockhart was a billiards player, a famous billiards player. But fame could only advance a man so far.

That was the difference between Lockhart's shiny prosperity and the time-worn elegance of Greer's family estate. Greer's father might not be wealthy by the exorbitant standards of the *ton*, but he'd always be a gentleman and so would his sons. No amount of money could change that. Nevertheless, Greer knew his mother and sisters would be pea-green with envy to see him sitting down to supper in this fine room. He made a mental note to send them a letter describing the evening *sans* its circumstances. His father would be furious to think any son of his had sat down to supper with a gambler, even if the son in question wasn't the heir.

Greer pushed thoughts of family and home out of his mind. Those thoughts would only make him cross. Tonight he wanted to enjoy his surroundings without guilt. He had delicious food on his plate, excellent wine in his goblet, interesting conversation and a beautiful woman in need of wooing beside him. He meant to make the most of it. Life in the military had taught him such pleasures were fleeting and few, so best to savour them to the fullest when they crossed one's path. Life had been hard these past ten years and Greer intended to do a lot of savouring now that he was back in England.

'Where were you stationed, Captain?' A

man to his right asked as the fish course was served.

'Corfu, although we moved up and down the peninsula with some regularity,' Greer answered.

Corfu caught John Thurston's attention. 'Then you may have played on the table we made for the mess hall there.'

Greer laughed, struck by the coincidence. 'Yes, indeed I did. That table was for the 42nd Royal Hussars. I wasn't with that regiment, but I did have the good fortune of visiting a few times. The new rubber bumpers made it the fastest game to be had in Greece.'

John Thurston raised his glass good-naturedly. 'What a marvellously modern world we live in. To think I'd actually be sitting down to supper with a man who played on one of my tables a thousand miles away. It's quite miraculous what technology has allowed us to do. To a smaller world, gentlemen.'

'My sentiments exactly.' Greer drank to the toast and applied himself to the fish, content to let the conversation flow around him. One learned a lot of interesting things when one listened and observed. Mercedes Lockhart must think the same thing. She was studying him once more. He could feel her gaze returning to him time and again. He looked in her direction, hoping to make her blush once more.

This time she was ready for him. She met his gaze evenly, giving every indication she'd meant to be caught staring. 'They're wondering if they can take you, you know,' she murmured without preamble. 'There will be games after dinner.'

Was that all they wanted? A game against the man who had beaten Elias Pole? Greer managed a nonchalant lift of his shoulders. 'Elias Pole isn't an extraordinary player.'

'No, but he's a consistent player, never scratches, never makes mistakes,' Mercedes countered.

He raised a brow at the remark as if to say 'is that so?'. The observation was insightful and not the sort of comment the women he knew made. The gently reared English women of his experience were not versed in the nuances of billiards. But Mercedes was right. He knew the type of player she referred to. They played like ice. Never cracking, just wearing down the opponent, letting the opponent beat himself in a moment of sloppy play. Yesterday that particular strategy hadn't been enough to ensure Pole victory.

'And now they know your measure. Pole has

become the stick against which you are now gauged,' she went on softly.

'And you? Do you have my measure now?' Greer gave her a private smile to let her understand he knew her game. 'Is that your job tonight—to vet me for your father?'

'Don't flatter yourself.' She gave him a sharp look over the rim of her goblet. 'The great Allen Lockhart doesn't need an agent to preview half-pay officers with shallow pockets for a money game.'

There was no sense in being hurt. The statement was true enough. There was no advantage *to* fleecing an officer. He had no source of funds *to* fleece. Even his subscription to the club had been bought on skill and a politely offered discount from Kendall Carlisle. Lockhart had to know. Whatever someone at this table managed to win from him would hardly be more than pocket change.

Greer dared a little boldness. 'Then perhaps you're in business for yourself.'

'Again, don't flatter yourself.' Mercedes took another sip of wine. To cover her interest? Most likely. She was not as indifferent to him as she suggested. He knew these discreet signs: the sharp comments meant to push him away in short order; the pulse at the base of her bare neck, quickening when his gaze lingered overlong as it did now.

This room displayed her to perfection. Greer wondered how premeditated this show had been. In the drawing room, she'd merely looked like a lovely woman. In the dining room, she might have been posed for a portrait. Her blue gown was a shade darker than the light blue of the walls. The ivory ribbon trimming her bodice, a complement to the off-white wainscoting and moulding of the room, acted as an ideal foil for the rich hues of her hair, which lay artfully coiled at her neck. Greer's hand twitched with manly curiosity to give the coil a gentle tug and let its length spill down her back.

But he could see the purpose of the demure coil. It drew one's attention to the delicate curve of her jaw, the sensual display of her collarbones and the hint of bare shoulders above the gown's *décolletage*. It was just the work of another skimming glance to sweep lower and appreciate what was *in* the gown's *décolletage*, that being a well-presented, high, firm bosom. Mercedes Lockhart was absolutely enticing in all respects.

She would be stunning regardless of effort, but Greer couldn't shake the feeling that this had all been engineered, right down to the colour of Mercedes's gown for some ulterior purpose he had yet to divine. He understood the basic mechanics of the evening well enough. This dinner party was about business.

Under the bonhomie and casual conversation, there was money to be had. Lockhart, Carlisle and Thurston were in it together. Thurston wanted to sell tables. He'd likely promised Lockhart and Carlisle a commission for the advertising. Each of the other gentlemen at the table owned billiard halls, some in Brighton, a few others from nearby towns. Purchasing a table would be good for their businesses in turn. They understood the favour Lockhart did them by letting them be the first to place orders. It was all very symbiotic. He alone was the anomaly. No one would mistakenly assume he'd be purchasing a table on tonight's venture.

Mercedes took up an unobtrusive spot in the large second-floor billiards room and plied her needle on an intricate embroidery project. She knew she looked domestic and that was the point. Billiards was a man's domain. The men gathered around the new Thurston table would not dream of her joining their game.

But as long as she looked utterly feminine and devoted herself to her embroidery, her presence would be acceptable. They would see her as the indulged only child of Allen Lockhart, a daughter so loved, her father could not bear to let her wander the house alone while he entertained close business acquaintances. Under those circumstances, what could really be wrong with her joining them as long as she stayed quietly placed in her corner?

Mercedes pulled her needle through the linen and surreptitiously scanned the men. They had finished talking business. Rubber bumpers, warming pans and all the latest technologies to keep the table fast had been discussed. Now it was time for action, time to see what the table could do. It was time to play, the one thing the men had been yearning to do all night.

Her father passed around ash-wood cues from a rack hung on the wall. The two men from the other Brighton billiards halls had the honour of the first game. But her eyes were on the young captain, Greer Barrington. Up close, he did not disappoint. He was precisely as she'd seen him from behind the peephole: tall, blond, broad shouldered and possessed of an easy charm that had no limit. Those blue eyes of his were captivating, his flirtations just shy of obvious, but that was part of his charm. He was not one of London's sleek rogues with deceitful agendas, even though he possessed the unmistakable air of a gentleman.

Mercedes watched him laugh with Thurston over a remark. Instinctively, she knew he was genuine. Honest in his regard. Yet many would mistake that quality for naïveté, to their detriment. That could be a most valuable commodity if she could tame it. He was no gullible innocent. He'd spent time in military service. He'd seen men die. He'd probably even killed. He knew what it meant to take a life. He knew what it meant to live in harsh circumstances even as he knew what it meant to be comfortable amid luxury.

The opulence of her father's home had not daunted him. This was where her father was wrong. He saw a young man with no purpose, a half-pay officer at loose ends with few prospects outside the military. Mercedes disagreed.

Greer Barrington was a gentleman's son. She'd lay odds on it any day. He didn't have the beefy build of a country farm-boy, or the speech of a lightly educated man. That could be sticky. Gentlemen's sons didn't take up with billiards players mostly because gentlemen's sons had better prospects: an estate to go home to, or a position in the church. Her father, whatever his intentions were, wasn't counting on that.

Captain Barrington stepped up to the table. The prior game was over and her father was urging him to play one of the men who'd come over from nearby Hove. Carlisle spoke up as the two players chalked their cue tips. 'You're a good player, Howe, but I'll lay fifty pounds on our Captain to take three out of five games from you.'

Mercedes's needle stilled and she sat up a bit straighter. Fifty pounds wasn't a large bet by these men's standards, merely something small and friendly, but big enough to sweeten the pot. But fifty pounds would support a man in Barrington's position for half a year. There was a murmur of interest. To her father's crowd, the only thing better than playing billiards was making money at billiards.

Howe chuckled confidently and drew out his wallet, dropping pound notes on the table. 'I'll take that bet.'

'Captain, would you care to lay a wager on yourself?' her father asked, gathering up the bets.

Barrington shook his head without embarrassment. 'I don't gamble with what I can't afford to lose. I play for much smaller stakes.'

Her father laughed and clapped him on the back. 'I've got a cure for that, Captain. Don't lose.'

But he did lose. Captain Barrington lost the first two games by a narrow margin. He won the third game and the fourth. Then Carlisle upped the wager. 'Double on the last game?'

Howe was all confidence. 'Of course. What else?'

Mercedes wondered. Was this a set-up? Had Carlisle and her father arranged this? Were they that sure of Barrington's skill and Howe's renowned arrogance? If so, it would be beautifully done. Howe wasn't the best player in the room, but he thought he was and that made all the difference. If Barrington beat Howe, the others would be tempted to try, to measure their skill.

Barrington had the lay of the table now. He'd made adjustments for the speed of the slate and the bounce of the rubber bumpers. He won the break and potted three balls to take an early lead. But Howe wouldn't be outdone. He cleared three of his own before missing a shot.

Mercedes leaned forwards in her chair. Barrington's last two shots would be difficult. He stretched his long body out, giving her an unadulterated view of his backside, the lean curve of buttock and thigh as he bent. The cue slid through the bridge of his fingers with expert ease. The shot was gentle, the cue ball rolling slowly towards its quarry and tapping it with a light snick, just enough to send it to its destination with a satisfying thud in the corner pocket while the cue ball teetered successfully on the baize without hazarding. Mercedes let out a breath she'd been unaware she held.

'Impossible!' Carlisle exclaimed in delight. 'One shot in a million.'

'Think you can make that shot again?' Howe challenged, not the happiest of losers.

Her father shot her a look over the heads of the guests and she mobilised into action, crossing the room to the table. 'Whether or not he can must wait for another time, gentlemen.' She swept into the crowd around the table and threaded an arm through Captain Barrington's. 'I must steal him away for a while. I promised at dinner to show him our gardens lit up at night.' Whatever her father's reasons, he didn't want Barrington challenged further. As for her, she had suddenly become useful for the moment.

Chapter Three

~~~~~~~~~~~~~~~~

'So this is what billiards can buy.' Barrington looked suitably impressed as they strolled the lantern-lit paths of the garden, which must have been what her father intended. The gardens behind their home were well kept and exclusive.

'Some of it is.' Mercedes cast a sideways glance up at her companion. He was almost too handsome in his uniform, buttons winking in the lantern light. 'My father invests.'

'Let me guess—he invests in opportunity, like tonight.' His insight pleased her. Barrington was proving to be astute. Would such astuteness fit with her father's plans? 'Tonight's party was about selling tables.'

He'd guessed most of it. Her father *was* selling tables tonight, but he was also attempting to buy the Captain. Perhaps her father meant to use him to drum up business for the All England Billiards Championship.

'That doesn't explain what I'm doing here. I'm not in the market for a table and your father knows it.'

Too astute by far. Mercedes chose to redirect the conversation. 'What *are* you doing here, Captain? Any plans after you leave Brighton? Or do you await orders? We've talked billiards all night, but I haven't learned a thing about you.'

'I thought I'd wait a few months and see if I am recalled to active duty. If the possibilities are slim, I'll sell my commission.'

'You like the military, then?'

Captain Barrington fixed her with a penetrating stare. 'It beats the alternative.'

They'd stopped walking and stood facing each other on the pathway. There was seriousness in his eyes that hadn't been there before and she heard it in his voice.

Her voice was a mere whisper. 'What's the alternative?'

'To go back and run the home farm under my brother's supervision. He's the heir, you see. I'm merely the second son.'

She heard the bitterness even as she heard all the implied information. A man who'd experienced leadership and independence in the army would not do well returning to the constant scrutiny of the family fold. A little thrill of victory coursed through her. She'd been right. He was a gentleman's son. But he was staring hard at her, watching her for some reaction.

'Are you satisfied now? Is this what you brought me out here to discover? Had your father hoped I might be a baron's heir, someone he might aspire to win for your hand?' His cynicism was palpably evident.

'No!' Mercedes exclaimed, mortified at his assumptions, although she'd feared as much earlier, too. Her father had tasked her with the job of unearthing Barrington's situation, but hopefully not for that purpose. If not that, then what? An alternative eluded her.

'Are you sure? It seems more than billiards tables are for sale tonight.'

'You should ask yourself the same thing, Captain.' Mercedes bristled. He'd put a fine point on it. She'd stopped analysing her father's motives a long time ago. Mostly because being honest about his intentions hurt too much. She didn't like thinking of herself as another of his tools.

The comment wrung a harsh laugh from the Captain. 'I've been for sale for a long time, Miss Lockhart. I just haven't found the highest bidder.'

'Perhaps your asking price is too high,' Mercedes replied before she could think better of the words rushing out of her mouth. She had not expected the charming captain to possess a streak of cynicism. It forecasted untold depths beneath the charming exterior.

'And your price, Miss Lockhart? Is it too high as well?' It was a low, seductive voice that asked.

'I am not for sale,' she answered resolutely.

'Yes, you are. We all are.' He smiled for a moment, the boyish charm returning. 'Otherwise you wouldn't be out here in the garden, alone, with me.'

They held each other's gaze, blue challenging grey. She hated him in those seconds. Not hated *him* precisely—he was only the messenger. But she hated what he said, what he revealed. He spoke a worldly truth she'd rather not recognise. She suspected he was right. She would do anything for her father's recognition, for the right to take her place at his side as a legitimate billiards player who was as good as any man.

'Are you suggesting you're not a gentleman?' Mercedes replied coolly.

'I'm suggesting we return inside before others make assumptions you and I are unlikely to approve of.'

Which was for the best, Mercedes thought, taking his arm. She wasn't supposed to have brought him out here to quarrel. Of all the things her father had in mind, it wasn't that. Perhaps her father thought they might steal a kiss, that she'd find the Captain charming; the Captain might find her beautiful and her father might find that connection useful. She could become the lovely carrot he dangled to coax Barrington into whatever scheme he had in mind.

The garden had not been successful in that regard. Not that she'd have minded a kiss from the Captain. He certainly looked as if he'd be a fine kisser with those firm lips and mischievous eyes, to say nothing of those strong arms wrapping her close against that hard chest. Truly, his manly accoutrements were enough to keep a girl bothered long into the night.

'Shilling for your thoughts, Miss Lockhart.' His voice was deceptively close to her ear, low and intimate, all trace of cynicism gone. The charmer was back. 'Although I dare say they're worth more than that from the blush on your cheek.'

Oh, dear, she'd utterly given herself away. Mercedes hazarded part of the truth. 'I was thinking how a quarrel is a waste of perfectly good moonlight.'

He'd turned and was looking at her now. 'Then we have discovered something in common at last, Miss Lockhart. I was thinking the same thing.' His blue eyes roamed her face in a manner that suggested she had the full sum of his attentions. His hand cupped her cheek, gently tilting her chin upwards, his mouth descending to claim hers in a languorous kiss.

She was aware only of him, of his other hand resting at the small of her back, intimate and familiar. This was a man used to touching women; such contact came naturally and easily to him. Warmth radiated from his body, bringing with it the clean, citrusy scent of oranges and soap.

It wasn't until the kiss ended that she realised she'd stepped so close to him. What distance there had been between their bodies had disappeared. They stood pressed together, her body fully cognisant of the manly planes of him as surely as he must be of the feminine curves of hers.

'A much better use of moonlight, wouldn't you agree, Miss Lockhart?'

Oh, yes. A much better use.

'Will you help me with him?' It was to her father's credit, Mercedes supposed, that he'd waited until breakfast the following morning before he sprang the question, especially given that breakfast was quite late and the better part of the morning gone. The men had played billiards well into the early hours, long after Captain Barrington had politely departed and she'd gone up to her rooms.

Mercedes pushed her eggs around her plate. 'I think that depends. What do you want him for?' She would not give her word blindly; Barrington's remarks about being for sale were still hot in her ears.

Her father leaned back in his chair, hands folded behind his head. 'I want to make him the face of billiards. He's handsome, he has a good wit, he's affable and he plays like a dream. For all his inherent talents, he needs training, needs finishing. He has to learn when it pays more to lose. He has to learn the nuances of the game and its players. Billiards is more than a straightforward game of good shooting between comrades in the barracks. That's the edge he lacks.'

'Playing in the billiard clubs of Brighton won't give him that edge—they're too refined. That kind of experience can only be acquired...' Mercedes halted, her speech slowing as realisation dawned. 'On the road,' she finished, anger rising, old hurts surfacing no matter how deeply she thought she'd buried them. She set aside her napkin.

'No. I won't help some upstart officer claim what is rightfully mine. If you're taking a protégé on the road, it should be me.' She rose, fairly shaking with rage. Her father's protégés had never done her any good in the past.

'Not this again, Mercedes. You know I can't stakehorse a female. Most clubs won't even let you in, for starters.'

'There are private games in private houses, you know that. There are assembly rooms. There are other places to play besides gentlemen's clubs. You're the great Allen Lockhart—if you say a woman can play billiards publicly, people will listen.'

'It's not that easy, Mercedes.'

'No, it's not. It will still be hard, but *you* can do it. You just choose not to,' she accused.

'I'm as good as any man and you choose to do nothing about it.'

They stared at each other down the length of the small table, her mind assembling the pieces of her father's plan. He wanted to take Barrington on the road, to promote the upcoming July tournament in Brighton.

'Maybe he's not interested.' Mercedes glared. What would a gentleman like Barrington say to being used thusly? Maybe she could make him 'uninterested'. There were any number of things she could do to dissuade him if she chose. A cold shoulder would be in order after the liberties of last night.

'He'll be interested. That's where you come in. You'll make him interested. What half-pay officer turns down the chance to play billiards for money and have a lovely woman on his arm?' So much for the cold-shoulder option.

'One who has other options. He's a gentleman's son, after all.' Of course it was a wild bluff. She knew how Captain Barrington felt about his 'options'. 'Even if his options are poor, no family of good birth is going to let their son go haring about the country gambling for a living.'

That comment struck home. Her father had always been acutely aware of the chasm between himself and his betters. No amount of money, fame or victory could span that gap. 'We'll see,' he said tightly. 'Men will do all variety of things for love or money. Fortunately, post-war economies do much for motivating the latter.' Mercedes feared he might be right on that account.

'I need you on this, Mercedes,' he pleaded. 'I need you to travel with us, to show him what he needs to know. I'll be busy making arrangements and setting up games. I won't have near enough time to mould him.'

'I'll think about it.' She was too proud to surrender easily, but in her heart she knew it was already done. It was the only offer she was likely to get and she was her father's daughter. She'd be a fool not to invest in this opportunity. On the road, she could show her father how good she really was, how indispensable she was to him. Perhaps they could recapture some of the old times. They could be close again, like they'd been before her tragic misstep had driven a wedge between them. Anything might happen on the road. Even the past might be erased.

'Well, don't think too long. I'm sending a note to Captain Barrington inviting him to dinner. If this proposition succeeds, I want to leave within days.'

Yes, anything might happen, especially with weeks on the road with the attractive Captain and his kisses. Damn his blue eyes. His presence would make the trip interesting once she decided if she should love him or hate him. He was both her golden opportunity *and* the fly in her ointment. He was the man stealing her place beside her father, but, in all fairness, the place hadn't been hers to start with. She didn't possess it outright and hadn't for years. She merely aspired to it, as much as the admission galled her. Then there were his kisses to consider, or not. She had to be careful there. Kisses were dangerous and she wasn't about to fall in love with her father's protégé. She knew from experience such an act would dull her sensibilities, make her blind to the job that needed doing. But perhaps one could just have the kisses. She'd be smarter this time.

All in all, going on the road was an offer she couldn't afford to refuse. Perhaps Barrington would say she'd just found her price.

Greer sat at the small writing desk in his lodgings, sorting through the dismal array of post. At least he had an 'array' of it. He should take comfort that the world had not forgot him even if it had nothing pleasing to send.

He slit open the letter from the War Department. It was his best hope for good news. A friend of his father's with higher rank and influence had enquired about a new posting on his behalf. Greer was eagerly awaiting a response. He scanned the contents of the letter and sighed. Nothing. It was something of an irony that the goal of the military—to maintain peace and order—was the very thing that made the military a finite occupation. In peace, there was no work for all the aspirants like himself.

Greer set aside the letter. It was becoming more evident that his military options were coming to a close. Of course, he could stay on half-pay as long as he liked, but with no re-posting imminent, it seemed a futile occupation.

The second letter was from home and he opened it with some dread. He could predict the contents already: news of the county from his mother and a directive to return home from his father. As always, a letter from home filled him with guilt. He should *want* to go back. But he didn't. He didn't want to be a farmer, and he didn't want to be a countryman. His father was a viscount, but a poor one. The title had come with only an estate four generations ago, and money had always come hard for the Barringtons. He did not want a life full of expenses he could barely meet and responsibilities he was required to fulfil. His older brother was better suited to that life. To what he himself was suited for, Greer did not yet know.

He reached for the third letter, surprised to see it was from Allen Lockhart. The short contents of the note brought a smile to his face. *Mercedes and I would like to invite you to a private supper this evening to become better acquainted.*

The sentiments of the note might be Lockhart's, but the firm, cursory hand that had penned it was definitely Mercedes's. Greer could see Mercedes penning the note with some agitation, her full lips set in an imperious line, in part because she didn't want to see him again and in part because she did. He was quite cognisant that Mercedes had no idea what to do with him—kiss him, hate him, or something in between if that was possible.

Mercedes.

She'd stopped being Miss Lockhart the moment he'd taken her in his arms. Their kiss had been far too familiar, far too intimate to think of her any longer on a last-name basis. In his arms, she'd been alive, warm and far more passionate than the sum of her cold hauteur had indicated at dinner. It had been the most pleasant surprise in an evening full of surprises. Therein lay the rub.

Had it been a surprise? Greer thumbed the corner of the heavy paper in contemplation. The kiss had seemed completely spontaneous at the time. They'd been quarreling. He'd thought the moment for stealing a kiss had passed and then suddenly the moment had returned.

He'd done the kissing. He distinctly remembered making what might be termed as the 'first move'. But Mercedes had supplied the motivation. She knew very well what she was doing with her reference to moonlight. Was the flirtation contrived? Had it been her last effort to comply with some secret plan of her father's for the evening? Had she realised that quarrelling with a coveted guest was not constructive? The note he held in his hand certainly suggested as much. There had to be a reason for getting 'better acquainted'. And yet the kiss itself did not seem contrived in his memory. Instead, it seemed very much the honest product of curious passion.

And now there was to be a private dinner. Greer was aware there was more to it than a simple dinner, but even so, he was looking forward to it a great deal. There would be good food, good wine and the intriguing Mercedes would be there. That alone was enough to secure his acceptance.

Chapter Four

The atmosphere at dinner was decidedly different than it had been the prior evening—less orchestrated, less of a show—but no less impressive because of it, and Greer found he was enjoying himself immensely.

The three of them dined informally in a small, elegantly appointed room done in subtle shades of gold designed expressly for the purpose of holding more intimate entertainments. Even the mode of eating reflected that intimacy. They dined *en famille* on juicy steaks and baby potatoes, helping themselves to servings from the china bowls in the centre of the round table and pouring their own rich red wine from glass decanters, thus removing the need for hovering footmen.

Greer had lived with the deprivations of military life long enough to fully appreciate the little luxuries of the moment, and man enough to appreciate the woman across from him.

Mercedes Lockhart glowed in the candlelight, dressed in a copper silk trimmed in black velvet, a gown so lovely it would have driven his sisters to violence. Her hair shone glossy and sleek, the flames picking out the chestnut highlights winking deep within the dark tresses. Tonight, she wore those tresses long, their length furled into one thick curl that lay enticingly over the slope of her breast, a most provocative cascade to be sure and a most distracting one. He nearly missed Lockhart's next question.

'What are you doing in Brighton, Captain?' Lockhart poured wine into his empty glass. 'Our sleepy little resort town must be tame by comparison to the military.'

Greer picked up his newly filled goblet. 'Waiting for the next adventure.' Brighton wasn't all that different in that regard than the military. There'd been plenty of waiting in the army as well. Hurry up and wait; wait to live, wait to die. He was still waiting, only the scenery had changed.

'Will there be one? Another adventure?' Lockhart probed in friendly tones but Greer sensed he was fishing for something, looking for some piece of information. He'd discussed his situation with Mercedes last night but she'd apparently not chosen to pass the details on to her father. He shot Mercedes an amused glance. Why? To prove she wasn't her father's agent as he'd accused?

'Well, that's the question.' Greer saw no reason to dissemble. His life was a fairly open book for those who cared to read it. Open and relatively dull, if the truth was told. 'A family friend is making enquiries on my behalf, but I am not alone in my desire for a posting.'

'I expect not these days,' Lockhart replied with a knowing nod. 'There are a lot of officers looking for work. Half-pay is a hard way to live. It's not enough to support a wife or start a family.' Lockhart offered him a smile that bordered on fatherly. 'No doubt those things are on your mind at your age.'

'Eventually, I suppose, sir.' Greer thought the question a bit too personal on such short acquaintance. Lockhart was still fishing, but this time Greer chose not to bite. Lockhart was not put off by his cool response.

'Sir?' Lockhart laughed good-naturedly.

'The military has trained you well, but there will be none of that here. We are not so formal as that, are we, Mercedes?'

'Of course not, Father. We're very friendly here,' Mercedes said. She spoke to her father, but she was looking at him, something sharp and aware in her eyes as she studied him.

'Call me Allen.' What was going on here? Greer was instantly suspicious. The request was friendly enough, to borrow Mercedes's word, but far too familiar. His father had raised him to be wary against such easily given bonhomie.

'Allen' leaned forwards. 'Have you considered that you don't need the military to provide the next adventure?'

Ah, things were getting interesting now. Very soon, all would be revealed if he played along. 'Forgive my lack of imagination; I'm hard pressed to think of another outlet.' What would a man like Lockhart have in mind? Did he want to make a salesman out of him? Have him sell Thurston's tables? Wouldn't that rankle his father? A viscount's son hawking billiards tables. It might be worth doing just to stir things up.

'Come on the road with me. I need to drum up business for the All England Billiards

Championship in July. Why don't you come along? I'll pay all expenses, give you a cut of whatever money we hustle up along the way, and the best part of it is, I am not asking to put your life on the line for a little fun and adventure.' *Unlike the military* came the unspoken jab at his other alternative. And he could bet with surety they wouldn't be sleeping in the mud and the rain or eating bread full of weevils and spoiled beef.

'What would I do?' Greer questioned. He'd have to do *something* to earn his keep; his pride wouldn't let him accept a free ride around England.

Allen shrugged, unconcerned. 'You play billiards. Kendall tells me people like to play you. Your presence will be good for business, help people think about making their way to Brighton when summer comes.'

It sounded simple, simple and decadent—to make money doing something he was so very good at. But something philosophic and intangible niggled at him, likely born of the conservative life-lessons his father had instilled in him. Lockhart was right: he wasn't risking his life. But he might well be risking something more. His very soul, perhaps. 'The offer is generous. I don't know what to say.' This was not the 'gentleman's way'.

Lockhart smiled, seemingly unbothered by his lack of immediate acceptance. 'Then say nothing. Take your time and think about it. I like a man who isn't too hasty about his decisions.' He set down his napkin and rose. 'I must excuse myself. I have some last-minute business to take care of at the club tonight.'

Greer rose, understanding this to be his cue to leave as well, but Lockhart waved away his effort. 'Sit down, stay a while, talk it over with Mercedes.' Lockhart winked at Mercedes. 'Persuade him, my dear,' he chuckled. 'Tell him what a fabulous time we'll have on the road, the three of us bashing around England. We'll hit all the watering holes between here and Bath, catch Bath at the end of their Season, and turn north towards the industrial centres.'

Greer raised a brow in Mercedes's direction. 'The three of us?'

Mercedes gave a small, almost coy smile, her eyes fixed on him knowingly as if she understood her answer would seal his acceptance. 'I'll be going, too.'

She was daring him with those sharp eyes. Was he man enough to go on the road with her? Or had he had enough after last night? Was he brave enough to come back for more? More of what? Greer wondered. Her tart tongue or her sweet kisses? Potent silence dominated the room as they duelled with their eyes, each very aware of the thoughts running through the other's mind.

Allen Lockhart coughed, a thin, near-laughing smile on his lips as he reached into his coat pocket. 'In all the excitement, I almost forgot to give you this.' He handed a thick envelope to Greer. The flap was open, revealing pound notes.

'What is this for?' Greer stared at the money. It would keep him for quite a while in his drab rented room. Perhaps he could even send some home. His father had mentioned the roof needed fixing on the home farm. *Stop*, he cautioned himself. This wasn't his money. Not yet.

Lockhart's smile broadened. He looked like someone who has taken great pleasure in pleasing another with a most-needed gift. 'It's yours, from last night's winnings.'

Greer shook his head and put the envelope down on the table. 'I didn't wager anything.'

'No, but I did. I bet on you and you worked for me last night. This is your cut for that work, your salary, if you prefer to think of it that way.'

It was so very tempting when Lockhart put it that way. 'I can't take it. You wouldn't have billed me if I'd lost.'

Lockhart nodded in assent. 'I understand. I respect an honest man.' He scooped up the envelope and tossed it to Mercedes who caught it deftly. 'See if you can't find a good use for that, my dear.'

'What shall it be?' Mercedes gathered up the ivory balls from their pockets around the table. 'The losing game? The winning game? Colours? Name your preference.' She'd brought the Captain to the billiards room after her father had left. Another look at Thurston's table wouldn't be amiss. Nothing persuaded like excellence.

'You play?' She could hear Barrington's chalk cube stop its rubbing, a sure indicator she'd stunned him into silence.

Mercedes set the balls on the table and fixed him with a cold smile designed to intimidate. 'Yes, I play. Why? Does that surprise you? It shouldn't. I'm Allen Lockhart's daughter. I've grown up around billiards my whole life.' Mercedes selected a cue from the wall rack, watching the Captain's reaction out of the corner of her eye. To his credit, he didn't follow up his surprise by stammering the usual next line, 'B-b-but you're a woman.'

Captain Barrington merely grinned, blew the excess chalk off his cue and said, 'Well then, let's play.'

They played the 'winning game', potting each other's balls into various 'hazards' for points. Mercedes played carefully, a mix of competence and near-competence designed to draw Barrington out, expose his responses. Would he play hard against a woman? She potted the last ball into the hazard with a hard crack. 'I win.'

She gave him a stern look, suspecting he'd purposely let up towards the end of the second game. 'I shouldn't have. You gave up a point when you missed your third shot.' It had been a skilful miss. An amateur would have noticed nothing. Near-misses happened; tables were full of imperfections that could lead to a miscalculation. But she'd noticed. 'Are you afraid to beat a woman?'

He laughed at that—a deep, sincere chuckle. 'I've already beaten you once tonight. *I* won the first game, if you recall?'

'I do recall, and I suspect you were too

much of a gentleman to win the second.' Mercedes was all seriousness.

This was the type of thing her father wanted her to ferret out and destroy. Chivalry was anathema on the road. She supposed his idea of chivalry didn't stop at women, but extended to poor farmers who'd come to town on market day and stopped in to play a game, or to men seemingly down on their luck, or to men, unlike him, who wagered with what they couldn't afford to lose. Such chivalry stemmed from the code of *noblesse oblige* that gentlemen were raised with and it would definitely have to go.

'Such fine sentiments will beggar you, Captain.' Mercedes flirted a bit with her smile, gathering up the balls for another game.

Barrington shrugged, unconcerned. 'Manners beggar me very little when there's no money on the line. We were just playing.'

'Is that so?' Mercedes straightened. *Just playing?* Her father would blanch at the idea of 'just playing'. There was no such thing in his world. She reached for the envelope where she'd laid it on a small table. She tossed it on to the billiards table. 'I want your best game, Captain. Will this buy it?' She'd known precisely what use her father meant for the envelope. She was to buy the Captain with it.

'Are you serious?' His eyes, when they met hers, were hard and contemplative, not the laughing orbs that had not cared she'd accused him of going easy on her.

'I am always serious about money, Captain.'

'So am I.'

She knew it was the truth—the calculation in his eyes confirmed it. This was a chance to rightfully win what her father had offered earlier. He'd desperately wanted that money; she'd seen the delight that had flared in his eyes ever so briefly. Only his honour had prevented him from taking it. 'You're on, Captain. Best two out of three.'

She won the first game by one point, earned when he barely missed making contact with his ball, legitimately this time.

He took his coat off for the second game and rolled up his sleeves. Was he doing it on purpose to distract her? If so, it wasn't a bad strategy. Without his coat, she could see the bend and flex of him clearly outlined by his dark-fawn trousers, and there was something undeniably attractive about a man only in waistcoat and shirt, especially if the man in question was as well proportioned as the Captain.

He was handsomely turned out tonight in a crisp white shirt and fashionable, shawl-collar waistcoat of burgundy silk, showing off those broad shoulders. His blond hair had fallen forwards, the intensity of their play defeating the parting he wore to one side. Now, all that golden perfection fell forwards, hiding his eyes from her as he concentrated on his next shot.

It was a sexy look, an *intense* look—a crowd would love it, a woman would love it, looking up into that face, that hair, as he moved over her, naked and strong. Mercedes pushed such earthy thoughts away. She had a game to lose. This was no time to be imagining the Captain naked and in the throes of love-making.

Barrington won the second game, just as she'd planned. His honour ensured it. He'd promised her his best game and he could be counted on to keep his word, his honour making him blind to any dishonour in another. It would prevent him from seeing her game as anything other than straightforward and perhaps his bias would, too. No matter what a man said, a man never believed a woman was a real threat until it was too late. She didn't think the Captain was any different in that regard. It was the nature of men, after all, to believe in their infallible superiority.

'This is it. Winner takes all.' Mercedes set her mouth in a grim line of determination. Whether anyone knew it or not, there was just as much pressure to lose well as there was to win. But Barrington was nearly untouchable in the third game, potting balls without also hazarding his cue ball, and it made her job easier. He was starting to smile, some of the intensity from the second game melting away, overcome by his natural assurance and confidence.

'Look at that,' he crowed good-naturedly after making a particularly difficult shot, 'just like butter on bread.'

Mercedes laughed too. She couldn't help it. His humour was infectious. *This must be why people like to play him*, she thought. Even if you were losing to him, you wanted him to win. His personality drew you in, charmed you. *That* would have to be saved. She added it to the mental list in her head: chivalry, no, personality, yes. She wondered if she could change the one without altering the other? Without altering *him*? Because Greer Barrington was eminently likeable just the way he was. She had not bargained on that. She lined up her last shot and took it with a little extra force to ensure the slip. She would make her shot—he would be suspicious if she didn't—but her cue ball would hazard and that would decide the game in his favour.

Mercedes thumped the butt of her cue on the floor with disgust. 'Devil take it,' she muttered on her breath for good, compelling measure, her face a study of disappointment. 'I had that shot.'

Barrington laughed. 'You're a bad loser.' He said it with a certain amount of shock as if he'd made a surprising discovery. He shifted his position so that he half sat on the edge of the table, his eyes alight with confidence and mischief. But Mercedes already knew what was coming. Part of her wanted him to take the money and be done with it. If he was smart, he'd pocket that envelope, walk out of here and forget all about the Lockharts. His blasted chivalry was about to work against him.

'I'll give you a chance to win it back. One game takes all, I'll wager *my* envelope against—'

She interrupted. 'The road. Your envelope against the road. I win, you take my father's offer.' *Don't do it. The wager is too much and you should know it.*

Barrington studied her for a moment. 'I was going to say a kiss.'

'All right, *and* a kiss,' Mercedes replied coolly. But she wasn't nearly as cool as she let on. This wouldn't be like the previous set of games where she'd been entirely in charge of the outcome. She'd decided who'd won and it had been easy to control things simply by losing. She wouldn't have that control here. Her only option this time lay in complete victory.

She chalked her cue and watched Barrington break one of his shattering breaks in the new style becoming popular in the higher-class subscription rooms. She studied the lay of the table and took her shot. On her next shot, Mercedes carefully leaned over the table, displaying her cleavage to advantage where it spilled from the square neckline of her gown. If he could take off his coat, she could make use of her assets, too. She looked up in time to catch Barrington hastily avert his gaze, but not until he'd got an eyeful. She smiled and went back to her shot. 'Like butter on bread,' she said after it fell into a pocket with a quiet plop.

Barrington shot again. 'Like jam on toast.' He raised a challenging eyebrow in her direction. His shot had been an easy one and he had the better lay of the table. None of his remaining shots would require any particular skill or luck. If she didn't do something now, he'd outpace her and win. The shot she was looking for was risky. If she missed, it would assure Barrington's victory and she'd have some explaining to do to her father. But if she didn't try she would likely end up losing anyway.

She bent, eyeing the table. Unhappy with the angle, she moved, bent, sighted the ball and moved again. Finally pleased, she aimed her cue. 'I find jam a bit sticky.' She shot, the cue ball splitting the pair she'd sighted perfectly, each one rolling smoothly to their respective pockets.

The Captain favoured her with a sharp look. 'Impressive. I think you may have been holding out on me.'

Mercedes lifted a shoulder in a shrug. 'A lady must have her secrets, after all.'

Two shots later she claimed victory. Her risky shot had paid off.

Barrington settled his cue on the table, a not entirely happy look on his face. 'You win. The road it is.'

Mercedes came around the table and stood beside him, guilt threatening to swamp her. She'd goaded him into this. She'd directed the evening towards this very outcome. Perhaps it hadn't been fair. 'You'll like it. You can play billiards all day, all night, and my father will introduce you to a lot of people. You'll have opportunities.' She pressed the envelope into his hands. 'And you'll have your money. You won't have to take up the home farm for a while.' She tried for a laugh, but it fell flat.

'I lost.'

'I don't recall asking for the envelope if I won.' Mercedes smiled up into his face. She hoped he saw that smile as one of friendship. She'd been hard on him tonight, whether he knew it or not. But they were in this together now. He was her chance. His successes would be her successes, at least for a while, at least until she decided he'd served his purpose as he had tonight.

She boldly took the envelope from his hands and put it inside his waistcoat. His body was warm through his shirt where her hand made contact with his chest. She tucked the envelope securely into an inside pocket.

'You don't mind the road all that much, do you? I was fairly sure last night you didn't have any plans.' Mercedes was gripped by another bout of conscience. She hoped she hadn't ruined anything for him.

'No. I'm looking forward to it, actually.' Barrington gave a fleeting smile, perhaps designed to appease her guilt. 'I was merely wondering what my father would make of all this.' Ah, the sainted Viscount with his empty coffers.

'Sometimes fathers don't always know best,' Mercedes answered softly. 'Especially if what they want for us is holding us back. Our paths can't always be theirs.'

He gave her a look that held her eyes and searched her soul. Before he could ask some difficult, probing and personal question, she stretched up on her tiptoes, put her arms about his neck and kissed him hard on the mouth.

He answered it; the evening had been too intense not to use the outlet the kiss offered, a place to spend the energy. His tongue found hers, duelled with it as their eyes had duelled over dinner, sending a trail of goosebumps down her arms. He unnerved her, excited her. It wasn't that she'd never been kissed, never been physically courted by a man before. She was not one of the *ton*'s innocent débutantes. It was the sheer strength of him.

He pulled her close, that strength apparent where his hand rested at her waist, a reminder that this man exuded strength everywhere—physical strength, mental strength. He was a veritable font of it: strength, honour, and self-control. A lesser man would have devoured her mouth by now, swept away with his own base lust. Not Captain Barrington.

He released her, unwilling to make her a party to his baser urges right there on John Thurston's billiards table. Not because he didn't have them, but because it was what a gentleman did. That was a bit disappointing. Captain Barrington unleashed would be a sight to behold. 'What was that for?' It was not said unkindly.

Mercedes stepped back, smoothing her skirts, in charge of her emotions once more. 'It's your consolation prize. Go home and pack your things, Captain. We leave Thursday.'

Chapter Five

Thursday morning found Greer sitting opposite Mercedes in an elegant black travelling
coach complete with all the modern conve-
niences: squabs of Italian leather, under-the-
seat storage for hampers and valises, a pistol
compartment, large glass-paned windows with
curtains for privacy when passengers tired of
the scenery outside. Even his proud father
would feel some envy at the sparkling new
coach.

That didn't mean his father would approve.
Coveting did *not* equate with approval where
his father was concerned. A gentleman might
quietly desire his neighbour's fine coach, but
a gentleman would never lower himself to ac-
quire it by working for it. A gentleman had

standards, after all. Standards, Greer was acutely aware, he had violated to the extreme on several occasions in the last week.

'Your father certainly knows how to travel in style,' Greer commented appreciatively, trying to make conversation, anything to push speculations of his father's reaction to his latest undertaking out of mind.

Mercedes shrugged, unconcerned with the wealth and luxury surrounding her, or perhaps just less impressed. 'He likes the best.' That was all she said for a long while. Mercedes proceeded to pull out a book and bury herself in it, leaving him to the very thoughts he was trying to avoid.

It was just the two of them at the moment. Lockhart had chosen to ride outside along with the groom overseeing Greer's own mount, another circumstance with which his father would take umbrage—an unmarried woman alone in a carriage with a man. Or, in this case, an eligible bachelor alone in a carriage with entirely the wrong sort of woman, the sort who might take advantage of said bachelor in the hopes of marrying up.

Very dangerous indeed! Greer fought back a wry smile. It was laughable, really. He was an officer in his Majesty's army. He could handle one enticing female. If Lockhart had intended anything to happen, such a ploy was obvious in the extreme.

Greer gave in to the smile, imagining all nature of wild scenarios. If Mercedes was to compromise him, how would she do it? Would she leap across the seat, provoked by the slightest rut in the road, and tear his shirt off? Would she be more subtle? Maybe she'd stretch, raise those arms over her head in a way that thrust those breasts forwards and exclaim over how hot she was.

His thoughts went on this way for a good two miles. It was a stimulating exercise to say the least. He had her halfway undressed and fanning herself before he had to stop. A gentleman had to draw the line somewhere. If Mercedes knew what he was envisioning, she might have chosen to engage him in conversation instead.

But since she didn't and since he'd taken his thoughts as far as he ought in one direction, Greer spent the better part of the morning taking them in the other, most of which involved contemplating how it was that he'd packed up his trunk and his horse, the only two items of any worldly worth in his possession, and left town all for the sake of a beautiful woman.

It was definitely one of the more rash things he'd done in a long while. The military was not a place where unwarranted gambles were rewarded. An officer must always balance risk against caution and he was no stranger to the charms of beautiful women: the lovely *señora* in Spain, the mysterious widow in Crete. But looking at Mercedes Lockhart engrossed in her book, their loveliness paled for the simple reason that Mercedes's beauty was not found in the sum of her features: her exotic eyes with their slight uptilt, the high cheekbones and the full sensuous lips that seduced every time she smiled. Nor was it that she knew how to enhance those physical qualities with the styling of her hair and expensive gowns.

No, the core of Mercedes's beauty lay in something more—in her very being, the way she carried herself, all confidence and seduction. She wasn't afraid of her power or her ability to wield it. Mercedes Lockhart was no blushing, *ton*nish virgin or even a woman who affected false modesty in the hopes of appearing virtuous. His father would not approve of Mercedes Lockhart any more than he'd approve of the reasons Greer was in the coach. Both were scandalous adventures for a man of Greer's birth and station.

However, his father would be wrong, Greer thought, if all he saw in Mercedes was a woman of loose scruples. Woe to the man who mistook her for no more than that. What she was was potent and alluring and quite possibly deadly to the man who fell for her. The French had a term for women like Mercedes. *Femme fatale.*

Well, he'd faced worse in battle than one beautiful woman. Greer settled deep into his seat and smiled, deciding to play another secret little game with himself, one that left her better clothed than the previous. How long could he stare at her before she looked up at him? Thirty seconds? One minute? Longer?

At thirty seconds she started to fidget ever so slightly, trying desperately to ignore him.

At forty-five seconds, she was taking an inordinately long time to finish reading the page.

At one minute she gave up and fixed him with a stare. Greer grinned. His *femme fatale* was human, after all.

'*What* are you looking at?' Mercedes set aside her book.

'You,' Greer replied. 'We're to be together for an indefinite period of time and it has occurred to me as I sit here in *silence*, watching the morning speed by...'

'Watching *me*,' Mercedes corrected.

'All right, watching *you*,' Greer conceded. 'As I was saying, it has occurred to me that I've set out on a journey with two strangers I hardly know even though my immediate future is now tied to theirs.'

Mercedes favoured him with one of her knowing smiles. 'Perhaps you're more of a gambler than you thought, Captain.'

Greer considered this for a moment. 'I suppose I am. Although we don't have to remain strangers.'

'What do you propose?'

'A little Q and A, as we call it in the military.' Greer stretched his legs, settling in to enjoy himself. 'Question and answer.'

'Or a consequence,' Mercedes supplied with a smug little smile. 'I know this game, Captain. You're not so terribly original.'

'No. No consequence,' he explained, watching Mercedes's smug smile fade. 'There is no choice to *not* answer. Question asked, answer given. There is no option to refuse.' Greer folded his hands behind his head. 'Ladies first. Ask me anything you'd like.'

'All right then.' Mercedes thought for a moment. 'Have you always wanted to be a soldier?'

'I was raised to it, ever since I can remember,' Greer replied honestly, although he was cognisant of the omissions that answer contained. 'How about you? Were you always good at billiards? Born with a cue in your hand?'

The beauty of the game was that it allowed the participants to ask directly what they'd never dare give voice to in polite conversation over dinners and tea trays. They traded questions and answers over the dwindling hours of the morning, his knowledge growing with each answer.

Greer learned she'd travelled with her father until she was eleven and he'd sent her off to boarding school. After that she'd come home on holidays and wandered the subscription room, watching and studying the game around which their lives were centred.

He learned her mother had died from birthing complications, that her name was Spanish for mercies—although in Latin it meant pity—quite apropos for a baby girl left to the tender sympathies of a single father, a gambler by trade, who could have just as easily have abandoned her to distant relatives and never looked back. But Lockhart hadn't. He'd taken her, cradle and all, on the road and continued to build his fame and his empire until his baby girl was surrounded by all the luxuries his ill-gotten gains could buy.

Those were the facts and when Greer had accumulated enough of them, he did the thing that made him so valuable to the military: he took those singular facts and coalesced them into a larger whole. In doing so, he saw quite well all the fires that had forged Mercedes Lockhart, that were still forging her—this incredible woman of refinement and education and emotional steel.

Was she doing the same to him? Her questions, too, had dealt only in basic, general curiosities—did he have a large family? What were his parents like? What did he like to read? To do in his spare time? Was she taking all those pieces and digging to the core of him? It was an unnerving prospect to think she might see more than he wanted to reveal. But that was the risk of the game—how much of oneself would one end up exposing?

As the game deepened, the questions moved subtly away from generally curious enquiries about each other's family and history and towards the private and personal. 'Who is the first girl you ever kissed?' Mercedes flashed him a mischievous smile as she added, 'And how old were you?'

'Oh, it's multiple questions in a single shot now, is it?' Greer quipped good-naturedly. He didn't mind. The question was harmless enough.

'A first kiss is only a good question if age is attached. It adds perspective,' Mercedes replied, willing to defend her ground in good fun.

'Well, it was Catherine Dennington,' Greer recalled with a fond smile. 'I was fourteen and she was fifteen. Her father was the village baker and she was plump in all the right places.' He feigned a sigh. 'Alas, she's married now to the butcher's son and has two children.' Greer winked at Mercedes. 'How's that for perspective?' He studied her with the exaggerated air of an Oxford professor. 'Speaking of perspective, Miss Lockhart,' he said in his best mock-academic voice, 'It's only fair, if you want to talk about kisses, that you tell me about your first intimate encounter.'

He'd asked mostly out of spirited mischief. She couldn't stoke the fire and then run away. Even with the intended and obvious humour behind the question, Greer had half expected her to scold him for such impertinence and he'd let her wiggle out of her obligation to answer. He'd not expected her to answer it.

She narrowed her catlike eyes and returned his studied stare, making sure she had the whole of his attention. 'Dismal. It was a wet, messy foray into adolescent curiosity. He was in and out and done before it really began for me. And yours, Captain? Better or worse?'

The fun disappeared, replaced by something far more serious. They weren't talking about kisses any more. But Greer matched her with a succinct answer of his own. 'Better, much better.' But it was more than an answer. It was an invitation, one no sensible gentleman would have issued and they both knew it.

'Well played, Captain.' Mercedes leaned back against her seat, impressed. He hadn't been frightened off. Instead of being embarrassed for her, he'd gone on the offensive with a self-assured disclosure of his own. She could choose to take him down a notch with a sharp comment about the natural arrogance of men when it came to estimating their sexual prowess. But such a rejoinder merely led down a tired road of well-worn repartee.

'Now we know each other's secrets,' Greer

said quietly in a manner that fit their newfound solemnity, 'what's next?'

Mercedes peered out the window, buying some time to put together an appropriate answer. The coach began to slow and she couldn't resist a smile. Perfect. 'Lunch. That's what's next.' She couldn't have timed it better herself. The stop would bring their game to a close and with it an end to any awkward probes into her past. The things in her past were best left there. She'd made mistakes, trusted too freely. She didn't want to create the impression such a thing would happen again. It wouldn't do to have Captain Barrington entertaining any untoward notions.

She knew what those notions would be: to get her into bed, have a dalliance and leave her when the differences in their stations became too obvious to go unremarked. Sons of viscounts could offer her no more than a bit a fun. It was not that she'd mind an affair with the Captain. He'd already demonstrated a promising propensity for bedsport and he was certainly built for it. But such a venture would have to be on her terms from beginning to end. Mercedes fanned herself with her hand. Was it just her or was it getting hot in here?

It felt good to get out of the carriage and

stretch her legs. The morning mist had cleared, giving way to a rare, sunny April day. The spot her father had found was delightful: a place not far off the road, and populated by wildflowers and a towering oak with a stream nearby for watering the horses.

Mercedes took herself off for a few moments of privacy, letting the coachman and the groom have time to take care of the horses before she began setting out the food. But when she came back, she saw she was too late. Someone had taken charge and set up 'camp' without her. A blanket was spread beneath the oak tree. The hamper was unpacked and the man most likely responsible for all this activity stood to one side of the blanket, his blond hair falling forwards in his face as he worked the cork free on a bottle of wine with a gentleman's dexterity, a skill acquired only from long practice.

It was yet another reminder of the differences in their stations. Her father had never quite mastered the art of uncorking champagne on his own. He always laughed, saying, 'Why bother when I have footmen paid to do it?' Her father had come late to the luxuries of a lifestyle where champagne was considered a commonplace experience. Not so with

Greer. He could talk all he wanted about the hardships of the military and the lack of wealth in his family. The indelible mark of a gentleman was still there in the opportunities that surrounded him. Boot boys from Bath hadn't the same experiences.

Greer looked up and smiled when he saw her, the cork coming out with a soft pop. He poured her a glass and handed it to her. 'It's still chilled.'

The wine, with its light, fruity tang, was deliciously cold sliding down her dry throat. At the moment, Mercedes couldn't recall anything tasting better. It wasn't until Greer had poured his own glass and had gestured for her to sit down that she realised they were completely alone—the servants off at a discreet distance, her father peculiarly absent. 'Where's my father?'

'He decided to ride on ahead. Apparently there's a spring fair in the village an hour or so up the road.' Greer began fixing a plate from the bread, cold meats and cheese spread out on the blanket. 'He wants to make sure we have rooms at the inn.'

Likely, he wanted more than that. He wanted to see the billiards situation, what kind of people were in town, which inn had a table, who was the big player in the area. He'd have the lay of the land and a new 'best friend' by the time they arrived.

Mercedes glanced overhead at the sky. It was noon. They'd be in the village by two o'clock at the latest. There would still be plenty of time to stroll around the fair and enjoy the treat. They could have all gone together. An hour wouldn't have cost her father anything. But he'd wanted to go alone. There was a reason for that. She'd have to be cautious and not acknowledge him unless he wanted her to. Perhaps he wanted them to appear to be strangers. He and Kendall had done that sort of the thing in the old days.

'Mercedes, your plate.' Greer had finished assembling the food and, to her surprise, the plate he'd been concocting had been for *her*. Of course it was. It was what a gentleman did and Greer did those things as effortlessly as he uncorked wine. She wondered how he would respond to the kinds of confidence games her father liked to play? The kind of games where the limits of honesty were grey areas?

'Thank you.' She settled the plate on her lap and watched him put together his own plate, long, tapered fingers selecting meats and cheese with purpose.

'I was thinking you might like to ride this afternoon since the weather turned out to be nice,' Greer offered. 'I noticed both you and your father brought horses.'

It would be perfect. The afternoon was far too fair to be cooped up in the carriage. It was the ideal conversational offering as well.

They spent lunch talking about riding and horses, something she didn't know half as well as she knew billiards. She liked listening to Greer talk about his stallion, Rufus, and other horses he'd owned. He had a face that came alive when he spoke, and an easy manner that was fully engaged now. She'd caught glimpses of it before; when they'd played billiards and this morning in the carriage, but always somewhat tempered by the side of him that never forgot he was an officer and a viscount's son.

This afternoon, sitting under the oak, he was quite simply *himself.* And she had been quite simply herself, not Allen Lockhart's daughter, not always planning the next calculated move. It was nice to forget and she *did* forget right up until the flags of the fair came into view and it was time to remember what they were there for.

'Should we find your father?' Greer asked,

looking for a place to leave the horses until the carriage and servants caught up to them.

Mercedes smiled and dismounted. 'I think we'll let him find us. Meanwhile, you and I shall enjoy the fair.'

Chapter Six

This was pure recklessness, Mercedes privately acknowledged as they tethered the horses on the outskirts of the fairground. She was inviting all sorts of trouble being alone with the Captain. Not the usual kind of trouble. She was too old to need a chaperon and the Captain wasn't likely to take advantage of her. Her danger lay in mixing business with pleasure. She was on this trip to groom him, introduce him to the world of professional billiards. She was *not* here to picnic under trees, or walk fairgrounds, or to play parlour games in coaches with him.

Those all led to perilous places where business became confused with emotions. But she was not ready to let go of the afternoon. That would happen soon enough. Her father would have plans for the evening that would demand it. But not yet. For now, the afternoon was still hers.

They browsed at the booths, smelling milled soaps from France and laughing when a few of the little cakes were reminiscent of cloying old ladies. They admired the bolts of fabric at the cloth merchant's, the vendor mistaking her for Greer's wife as he tried to convince her to buy some chintz for recovering seat cushions in her sitting room.

She had blushed furiously over the mistake, but seen no way to rectify it. Greer had politely steered them on to the next booth, taking the remark in his stride. The booth contained various blades and he soon became engrossed with the owner in a discussion of blades and hilts. Mercedes moved on to a display of ribbons. She'd been debating the merits of the green or the blue ribbon with the vendor, a woman of middle years, when Greer stepped up behind her. 'She'll take them both,' he said with a laugh, passing over the shillings. 'They're too pretty to choose just one.'

'You have a good husband, ma'am.' The woman smiled, pocketing Greer's coins with a wink in his direction. 'Knows how to spoil his wife properly. You'll have a long marriage, I think.'

'You shouldn't have done that,' Mercedes hissed once they'd moved away from the booth.

'Why not?' Greer teased. 'Don't you like people thinking we're together? Am I too ugly for you?'

She shook her head with a laugh. It was impossible to stay angry with him. 'You know you're not. That woman was rather disappointed you were so devoted to your "wife."'

'Aye, she was likely hoping I might be devoted to her later this evening. But alas, my heart is claimed elsewhere.'

'Stop it,' Mercedes insisted with little vigour. 'You're being ridiculous.' But she was laughing too.

They'd reached the perimeter of the fairground. Their horses weren't far off and the crowd had thinned, leaving them alone. Greer took out the blue ribbon from his coat pocket. 'Will you permit me?' He didn't wait for an answer. He moved behind her, but instead of putting the ribbon in her hair, he slid it about her neck and when she looked down, a tiny silver charm in the shape of a star dangled from the ribbon. She recognised it immediately. She'd stared at it overlong at the jeweller's booth. It had been of surprisingly good worksmanship and Greer had noticed. It had not been cheap either.

'You shouldn't have,' Mercedes began quietly, settling her hair.

'Shouldn't have what? Shouldn't have commemorated this glorious day?' Greer argued in equally soft tones. He turned her to face him. 'I haven't had many nice days like this for a while. As you can imagine, there aren't picnics and fairs in the military. And for once, I don't have anything pressing to worry about. There's no one shooting at me, there are no worms in my food. Life has definitely improved since I've met you.'

She felt guilty. She wanted to tell him she wasn't worth it, that she'd been brought along to tame him, to turn him into something that could make her father money. But she let him have the moment. He'd been a soldier, he'd faced death and delivered it too. He worried for his family and over their finances, and finally he'd had a day where there was fair weather overhead, money in his pocket that bills couldn't claim, and a pretty woman by his side. She could not bring herself to steal that from him. Taking that from him meant taking that from her, too, and she couldn't do it.

Mercedes gave up the fight and said simply, 'Thank you, Greer.' Her hand closed over the charm where it rested against her skin. She would treasure it always, as a reminder of the day a gentleman had treated her like a lady. She stepped closer, her head tilted up in encouragement. Perhaps he'd like to seal the day with a kiss. And he might have if he'd got the chance.

'There you two are!'

Her father approached, his spirits high. Mercedes stepped back, putting more space between herself and Greer. If her father was in a good mood, things must have gone well in town. 'We thought you'd find us when you were ready.' Mercedes offered as an explanation for their truancy.

'You thought right, my smart girl.' He chucked her under the chin playfully. 'I've got rooms at the Millstream Inn, but the billiards table is at the Golden Rooster.' He rubbed his hands together. 'Two inns! Not bad for a sleepy little place. We'll have some fun tonight. Everyone hereabouts is in town with money to spend after a long winter. Are you ready to play, Captain?'

Her father inserted himself between the two of them as they walked back towards town, horses in tow. Behind her father's back, Greer caught her eye and gave her a grin. Mercedes smiled, swallowing her disappointment. The afternoon was officially over.

Bosham was a pretty fishing village at the east end of Chichester Harbour. A Saxon stone church sat neatly on the High Street not far from their rooms at the Millstream Inn, and Greer would have liked time to tour the town with Mercedes. She'd been a game sightseer at the fair and he would have enjoyed exploring the town's countless legends about King Harold and Canute with her.

There would be no time for such an indulgence. Lockhart had not only found them rooms at the comfortable inn, he had already bespoke a private parlour for dinner and was eager to get down to the business of playing billiards.

'We'll go over to the Golden Rooster,' Lockhart said between bites of an excellent seafood stew. 'I want to see what you can do, what your natural inclinations are, how badly you want to win.' Lockhart winked and handed him some funds. 'That should get you started.'

Lockhart rubbed his hands together, the gleam of excitement in his eye. 'There's money to be had in this little town tonight. People are happy, they've made money today, they've been drinking and thinking they've got a bit extra in their pockets.'

Greer cringed inwardly at Lockhart's implication. A single walk through the streets had shown him these were simple people: merchants, farmers and fishermen, some of whom depended on seasonal fairs to last them through the year. The thought of taking their money sat poorly with him, souring the rich stew in his stomach.

Mercedes was watching him. He must have reflected his distaste for the venture in some small way. Quickly, Greer tore off a chunk of bread and dipped it into his bowl, looking busy with eating to mask any other telltale signs of reluctance. Her eyes slid away towards her father.

'I'll be there too.'

'No, I think you should stay here,' Lockhart corrected. 'Relax, spend the night by the fire, enjoy some needlepoint.' He smiled kindly at his daughter, but Greer didn't think Mercedes would fall for the expansive gesture.

She saw right through it. 'I'll come,' she

said with the same brand of feigned politeness her father had used. 'I'm not tired. It will take only a moment to change. Shall I wear the maroon gown?' Greer's lips twitched, suppressing a smile as he watched the two of them play with one another. Would Lockhart be so easily managed?

Lockhart rose and held Mercedes's arm. His voice was low and firm, more fatherly when he spoke this time. Greer recognised it as the tone his own father took when he was younger and he and his brother had pushed the limits of their father's patience with a jest or prank. 'I prefer you remain here. The Golden Rooster is no gentleman's club. With the fair in town, who knows what kind of element will find its way out tonight?'

Mercedes's eyes narrowed. 'I cannot help him if I cannot watch him. By the time we get to the big towns it will be too late to coach him. If he has a flaw, we need to fix it while we're in the villages.'

Greer raised his eyebrows. 'I am still here.' He didn't like being talked about as if he were a thing to be studied and fixed. Mercedes spared him the briefest of glances before turning back to her father.

Lockhart shook his head, his tone softening. 'Please, Mercedes, a tavern is no place for you. When there are subscription rooms or private billiards parlours, you'll be able to join us then. Please, besides, your clothes will give us away. Your gowns are much too fine for the Golden Rooster.' He swallowed and dropped his gaze, arguing softly, 'I would not have you treated less than you deserve, my dear. You know what the men there will think.'

That was the end of it. The last argument seemed to carry some weight. Mercedes acquiesced to her father's better sense with moderately good grace and what could pass as a warning. 'Just for tonight. But don't think I'll sit idly by again. We'll have to find a way to make my presence acceptable long before we get to Bath.'

'Fair enough.' Lockhart kissed his daughter's cheek and turned to Greer. 'Are you ready, then?'

The Golden Rooster was at the other end of town, closer to the fairground than the quay like the Millstream Inn, and the fair crowd had definitely gathered there. At the back of the room was the billiards table. Greer and Lockhart parted ways, Lockhart heading for the bar and Greer for the table with Lockhart's advice in his ear: watch first, then play slow and easy, nothing fancy.

Watching helped settle his nerves and misgivings. These were regular men, not all that different from those he played in the army. They seemed cognisant of what they were doing and the attenuate risks. For a while, players came and went, the winner of a match earning the right to stay at the table and play the next challenger and the atmosphere was congenial. Then, a cocky braggart of a man stepped up and won a few games. He was not a kind winner and Greer felt his blood starting to rise. He wanted to beat this man. When the chance came to play, he took it, hefting the ash cue in his hand with grim determination.

He didn't stay grim for long. It felt good to play and in spite of the worn condition of the table, the balls rolled predictably. He played the braggart again and again, defeat egging the man on until he had to withdraw, his ego and coins spent. The crowd around Greer had grown with a rising raucousness, spurred on by Greer's victories against a disliked opponent. He caught a glimpse of Lockhart shouldering his way into the crowd.

'Who else will play?' Greer called out in friendly tones. Now that the braggart had been routed, they could get back to the business of fun. The crowd parted and a young man, younger than he, emerged. He was tall and sturdily built. His face was tanned, his eyes merry, shoulders broad and thick from hauling nets. A fisherman, a local. A few men clapped the young man on the shoulder and Greer surmised from the comments that the young man was something of a town favourite, newly married with a baby on the way. His name was Leander and he blushed ever so slightly and proudly when the men teased him about Ellie. 'Finally let you out of the house, has she?' they joked.

Leander brushed off the comments. 'Never mind them,' he said good-naturedly to Greer. 'They're just jealous I'm married to the prettiest girl in town.' Most definitely a town favourite, Greer thought as the men laughed.

And a decent player too, Greer amended a few games later. They'd played four games, each winning two and money exchanging hands on an equal basis. Lockhart was frowning in the crowd. Greer would have to step up his game. It would be too much for Leander. If Leander was smart, he'd recognise the superior skill and walk away. At this point, Leander wasn't out any serious money and he could stop whenever he wanted.

Conscience subdued momentarily, Greer took the next three games. Leander was getting frustrated. Greer hoped the young man would stop and call it a night. Instead Leander said, 'Double or nothing on the next game.' There were a few cautious murmurings from the men beside him, warning him to reconsider.

'You played well, Leander, let it be,' one man suggested with an arm about his shoulders, hoping to lead him away. But Leander was young and typically hotheaded where his pride was concerned.

'Think about Ellie and the baby,' another said. 'You'll need that money for the doctor later.'

If it had been up to him, Greer would have put down the cue and walked away, claiming tiredness, but it wasn't up to him. Lockhart was standing there, wanting him to go on and Leander would not back down. Between them, they'd taken away one choice, leaving Greer with only one other avenue of recourse. Three shots in, he scratched, potting the cue ball along with his own and forfeited the game, followed by what he hoped was a sincere show of disbelief.

Greer put down the cue and handed the money over to a beaming Leander. 'Go home to your wife,' he said in low tones, and he was sure the men present would make that happen. Some of them clapped him on the back, as he made his way to the front. Others offered to buy him a drink, but he refused. Lockhart had gone on ahead and would be waiting outside. He wouldn't be pleased and Greer needed to face him.

'You had him,' Lockhart began as they walked back to the Millstream. 'You were doing brilliantly. You ousted the braggart, showed yourself worthy of playing the local best, got the local favourite to come out and play, worked him up to where he offered double or nothing and then you let him go. What were you thinking?'

'I was thinking he didn't have the money to lose.' Greer didn't back down from his choice. 'He's a fisherman with a pregnant wife at home.'

'Maybe.' Lockhart shrugged in the darkness. 'Perhaps they're all in it together and that's the story they tell outsiders.'

Greer grimaced. He hadn't thought of that, probably because it seemed a bit ludicrous. 'I doubt it.'

'Still, no one put a gun to his head,' Lockhart argued.

Greer passed him the original sum Lockhart had given him earlier that night. 'What do you care? Your stake is intact and a little more. You didn't lose anything tonight. My choice cost you nothing.'

'Not yet.' Lockhart sent him a dubious sidelong glance. 'Lord save me from do-gooders.' He took the money and tossed Greer a half-sovereign when they reached the entrance to the Millstream. 'There's your take of the winnings tonight: ten whole shillings, barely the price of a bottle of Holland's Geneva.' Lockhart gave a derisive chuckle. Greer understood the insult. Holland's Geneva was a popular, but not high-quality, drink, definitely not the drink of a gentleman used to a superior claret or brandy.

'Certainly not enough to keep a woman like Mercedes in trinkets and silks,' Lockhart added astutely as they stepped inside.

'I'm not looking to keep a woman like Mercedes or any other. I believe I've mentioned as much before,' Greer growled.

'Really? You could have fooled me today.' Lockhart chuckled. 'Well, no matter. She's in the parlour, remaking a dress if I am any judge of character.' Lockhart nodded towards the private room they'd used for dinner where a light still burned. 'I'm for bed. We'll head out in the morning and try again tomorrow.'

Chapter Seven

Gentlemen were the very devil with their principles and codes! Lockhart stretched out on his bed, hands behind his head and stared at the ceiling, his mind assessing the events of the day. The Captain had lived up to his suspicions, or down to them depending on how one looked at it. Barrington had gone soft at the critical moment.

It wasn't the money he minded losing. These stakes had been small. But what if they hadn't been? What if Barrington chose his conscience over him when real money was on the line? Mercedes would have to be the one to fix that particular flaw. Barrington had not been receptive to his own words of wisdom on that point tonight. Perhaps Mercedes would have more luck.

There was no 'perhaps' about it. He'd seen the way the Captain had looked at Mercedes from the start. Mercedes would be his insurance on this. What the Captain wouldn't do for him, the man would do for Mercedes. When it came to charms, he simply couldn't compete with his daughter where the Captain was concerned. That was one area Mercedes had an advantage on him.

He did wonder how reciprocal those charms were. To what degree did Mercedes return the Captain's attentions? He'd seen the two of them at the fair, strolling the booths arm in arm and that telling moment by the horses at the end. If he'd interrupted a little later there would have actually been something to interrupt. And that bauble. Sheer genius on the Captain's part.

Oh, *that* had been nicely played, although in all probability the Captain had likely meant whatever sentiments went with it. Men like him usually did. Lockhart chuckled in the dark. A gentleman's principles might be sticky wickets when it came to billiards, but they could be useful things indeed when it came to a lady's honour. There were worse people who could court his daughter. He'd seen them and not one of them was good enough for Mercedes with her hot temper and passions.

Mercedes would have to be careful. It would be too easy to fall for a man like the Captain, all handsome manners and good breeding, the very best of English manhood. But she would never fit into Barrington's world and he would make her unhappy in the end. In the interim, it wouldn't do to have Mercedes pick the Captain over him. There could be no running off with the Captain on the grounds of false promises the Captain had no intention of keeping. Of course, she could marry the Captain. He wouldn't stand in the way of that, but he would tolerate nothing less.

Mercedes could be managed. He'd saved her from the consequences of her impetuous nature once before and that deserved her loyalty. He would remind her of that if need be. Still, he wasn't worried. Mercedes had been down that road before. She'd be wary about trusting the Captain outright.

Lockhart laughed out loud. If he and Mercedes played their cards right, he'd come out of this with a protégé and a son-in-law. He'd give anything to be a fly on the wall in that parlour right now. If Mercedes was smart, she'd give the Captain a piece of her mind and then a piece of her heart.

Mercedes knew something had gone wrong the moment Greer stepped into the parlour. 'What happened?' She could guess what it was, though. Her father's competitive streak had run into Greer's principles. Nonetheless, she tucked her needle into the fabric and stilled her hands, giving Greer all her attention.

'This is not what I signed on for—fleecing locals.' Greer fairly spat the words at her in his frustration.

'You were warned,' she said evenly. 'The night we played for the road, you said you were always serious about money. I thought you understood what that meant.' In moments like this, she was convinced men were just overgrown boys, squabbling over principles instead of toy boats. A woman was a far more practical creature. A woman had to be.

Greer pushed a hand through his hair. 'Since when has "come bash around England and generate interest in the billiards tournament" been synonymous with taking money off unsuspecting local players who don't have any idea who they're up against?'

Mercedes set down her sewing and rose.

'Listen to me. If you'd come down off your moral high horse, you'd see the wisdom of it. *You* need to practise. You can't simply walk into an elite subscription room in Bath, or a gentleman's private home, and expect to be perfect without practice. A real player knows "practice" means more than shooting balls around the baize. It means knowing how to work the room to maximum advantage. Places like Bosham are where we practise that skill *before* we try it out for real in places that count, places that don't give you a second chance.'

Greer glared at her. 'What an absolute delight you are. You really know how to cut a man down.'

'Because you came looking for sympathy and I gave you truth?' Mercedes stood her ground. His words hurt, especially after the fun of the afternoon and the flirting in the carriage that morning. But she had a job to do, for her father and for herself. Neither job involved making friends with Greer Barrington, no matter how enticing that option appeared on occasion.

'Lesson one, Captain, is to separate your feelings from your pocket. A good gambler is not emotional about money.'

'I'm not,' he snapped. 'You know very well I don't wager what I cannot afford.'

'Your money *or* theirs,' Mercedes amended. 'Emotions go both ways. Your problem is that you get emotional about *their* money.' She paused, letting the words sink in. 'And maybe you should,' she added.

'Maybe I should what?' Greer challenged.

'Maybe you should play with what you can't afford to lose. You might try harder to win.' Mercedes held his gaze, refusing to back down. He had to learn this most primary of lessons before they could move on. A player who could not set himself apart from the money would never reach his potential. She'd seen it happen too many times.

Greer blew out a breath and she had the sense she'd pushed him too far. 'I can't believe you're siding with him.'

The words sliced her as surely as any blade. If he only knew! She wasn't on her father's side. She wasn't on Greer's side. She was simply on *her* side, trying to make a place in a world that insisted there wasn't one for a female. Her own anger began to spill. 'I'm not siding with him. I'm trying to save you from yourself. Or maybe you don't care. Not all of us have the home farm waiting for us if this doesn't work out.'

Damn him and his high-road principles. She didn't want to need him, but the reality behind all her bravado about emotional detachment was stark and simple. *He* was her chance. Her success was tied to his although she dare not tell him that.

'I must apologise.' Greer clicked his heels together and executed a stiff bow, his tone just as rigid. 'I've taken my frustration out on you. You are merely the messenger of un-pleasant news.' He reached out and covered the star charm where it lay against her neck. His hand was warm on her skin, the gesture intimate, his fingers achingly near her breast. He smiled. 'We're in this together.'

Until it's time not to be. Mercedes masked the self-serving thought with a smile. She needed to exit the room. The atmosphere be-tween them was charged with a new emotion more reminiscent of their unfinished business from the fairground.

'We're not meant to be at each other's throats,' she offered by way of acknowledging his apology. If she didn't leave soon, this con-versation would veer into territory best left un-explored for the moment until she could make her mind up about the handsome officer—was he to be more than a protégé to her? But her feet stayed rooted to the ground.

'Oh, I don't know about that.' He raised a hand to the back of her head, trapping her, drawing her closer, a secret smile on his lips. 'Being at each other's throats isn't all bad.' He took her mouth in a hard kiss, letting his lips wander along her jaw and down the length of her throat, teasing her with a flick of his tongue here, a nip of his teeth there, until he captured her mouth again, challenging her to a heated duel of tongues.

'Or being in them,' she managed between kisses. This was new territory indeed! Usually *she* was the aggressor. It was what she preferred. It reduced the opportunity to be taken by surprise. More importantly, it let her drive the encounter. But it was very apparent that Greer was driving this one.

Her hands anchored roughly in the thick depths of his hair. This was not a gentle exchange and she roused to it, revelling in the feel of his hands at her hips, hard and strong as they held her, the thrill of his lips pressed to her neck, to her mouth.

She sucked at his ear, her teeth taking sensual bites of his lobe until Greer gave a fierce growl of pleasure, but she couldn't completely shake the thought that had taken up residence in the back of her mind. She'd use Greer, use this chemistry between them until he and it had served their purpose. Then she'd cut him free. She'd *have* to.

Such an assumption had always been an underlying tenet of her plan. She was turning out too much like her father. She'd not meant to be. It was a rather sobering revelation and one she was definitely not proud of.

Chapter Eight

'What are the rules to a good hustle?' Mercedes all but barked across the table in yet another small inn in yet another middling, nameless town. Good Lord, the woman was driving him crazy on all levels.

Greer gave her a steely look across the billiards table. If she asked him how to hustle one more time he was going to walk out of this room. Every morning in the carriage it was the same drill: 'Tell me the best place to aim a slice, the proper way to split a pair, what are the best defensive shots.' Every afternoon, it was practice, practice, practice until he could execute the strategies in his sleep. At least he could when he wasn't dreaming of her.

Since Bosham she'd managed to torture him

by day as well as night; the temptress that had sucked his ear lobe to near climax in the Millstream parlour had taken up residence in his dreams, leaving him waking aching and hard. But that temptress became a termagant in the morning.

'Well? What are the rules to a good hustle?' Mercedes prompted when he met her questions with silence. 'Aren't you going to answer?'

Greer put down the cue stick and folded his arms across his chest. 'No, as a matter of fact, I am not.' Then he did as he'd promised himself. He walked past Mercedes and out the front door of the inn into the glorious spring afternoon.

'Greer Barrington, come back here. I have asked you a question.'

Oh, that did it. He was *not* going to acquiesce, not before he gave her a piece of his mind. He didn't stop until he'd reached the town green though he was aware of her behind him every step of the way, her anger palpable as it chased him across the street. Greer turned and faced her, fixing her with a hard stare. 'Can you leave me the hell alone for once? What is it you want? "How do you shoot a slice, how do you split a pair, how do you compensate for angles?" It never stops!'

His voice was too loud, but he didn't care. It felt good to let out the frustrations, sexual and otherwise, that he'd carried for days.

Mercedes answered him evenly, unfazed by his harsh words. 'I like the best, Captain. That's what I want. And if you want what I want, you'd better be the best because I don't have time for anything less.' Nothing got to her. Just once he'd like to see something get under her skin.

'You did in Bosham. You had time for a picnic, time to stroll around the fair.' Greer made a wide gesture to indicate the park around them. 'Spring is passing you by while you're penned up in a dark inn shooting slices and teaching hustles.'

Something shifted in her grey eyes and her gaze lost its hardness. Her anger was fading. For a fleeting moment he thought he saw something akin to sadness in them, then it was gone, replaced by something more stoic, more like the Mercedes he'd come to know. 'If I am, it will be worth it. I can enjoy next spring. Chances don't come my way very often, Captain. I have to take them when they do, spring notwithstanding.'

'Greer, please. No more "Captain." You only call me "Captain" when you're angry.'

Greer gave up the last of his anger, intrigue overriding his frustration. 'What opportunity is that, Mercedes?'

'To be on the road with my father,' she said simply but tersely, and Greer sensed this was not a direction she'd willingly take the conversation. Her relationship with Lockhart was a touchy subject and, quite frankly, the relationship seemed a bit odd to him. It was nothing like the relationship his sisters had with his father. Mercedes and Lockhart were more like partners than a father and daughter.

It was strange, too, to think the indomitable Mercedes would yearn for time with her parent like any other child. He'd spent his childhood lapping up any crumb of attention from his father's table, treasuring those rare moments when his father came out of his office to take him riding. Even now, he knew he still craved his father's approval. He'd wanted to make his father proud of his military career.

Greer gave Mercedes a considering glance as they walked; she was so beautiful and proud it was hard to imagine she harboured the same wants as the rest of them. But she'd no more admit to it than he would, if asked. The conversational angle was played out. She would let

him go no further with it. All he could do was
tuck her arm through his and change the topic.

'Have I ever mentioned how much you remind me of my superior officer, Colonel Don-
ald Franklin? We had a secret nickname for
him.'

Mercedes favoured him with a tolerant
smile, the kind reserved for belligerent six-
year-olds. 'And what was that name? I'm sure
you're going to tell me whether I want you to
or not.'

'Drill book Donny or sometimes Old Prissy
Pants.'

'I'm sure you want to tell me what he'd done
to earn such lovely monikers.'

'He never relented. Buttons, boots, hilts—
he'd have as big a fit over them not being polished to perfection as he would over something
important like messing up manoeuvres.'

'Little things matter,' Mercedes said defi-
antly, taking the Colonel's part. He'd known
she would even if it was just to be stubborn.
He understood that. It was better to be stubborn than vulnerable. 'Besides, he brought you
back alive didn't he? His lessons couldn't have
been that useless.'

He didn't miss the subtle analogy. *She* could
bring him back to life, give him the spark his

life was missing if he'd just listen to her. Still, for the sake of argument, he had to respond. 'Buttons and boots can't get you killed.'

'I disagree. Buttons, boots, manoeuvres— they're all part of acquiring discipline. In fact, it was one of the first things I noticed about you: your well kept uniform. It spoke volumes about the kind of man you were.'

'What kind of man is that?' He was enjoying this now. They were good together this way—walking and talking, sharing insights the polite people of the *ton* would consider too bold between a man and a woman.

'A man who can be relied on to follow the rules.' She tossed him a coy smile. 'There was no Colonel Franklin to insist on polished buttons that night in Brighton and yet they were. No matter how much you may rail against his rules, you will follow them.'

Greer gave a growl of dissatisfaction. He wasn't sure the analysis was all that complimentary. 'You make me sound like a milksop, as if I can't think for myself.'

'Not at all. I've never once thought you were weak. Following rules makes you a man of discipline. It makes you reliable. I find that a very attractive quality.' She smiled again, a smile made for bedrooms and the dark, not public parks in the brightness of the afternoon.

She was flirting overtly with him now, the first time since Bosham. Greer felt himself go hard. Did she have any idea what sort of fuse she was lighting? She was by far the most intriguing woman he'd ever encountered. She called to him body and mind. The very physicality of her sensuality beckoned in wicked invitation while her mind fascinated him with its insights on human nature. To truly know her would be a heady prize, one he doubted any man had yet to capture. But one, he was sure, many men had failed in the attempting.

'Circe,' he said softly, letting the air charge between them and the afternoon be damned. If she wanted to play this game, who was he to deny her? He was confident enough in his abilities. Perhaps he'd be the one to claim the prize.

'I beg your pardon?'

'You,' Greer drawled. 'You're Circe, the siren from Homer's *Odyssey*.'

She tossed her head, tiny diamond studs in her ears catching the light, an entirely seductive movement that drew the eye to her face. 'Tell me, did Circe play billiards?'

Greer laughed. 'No, she was, and I quote directly from Homer, "the loveliest of all immortals." She enticed men, but when they failed to win her, she turned them into animals.'

Mercedes cocked her head to one side, giving him a smouldering stare of consideration. 'Do you think I'm in the habit of reducing men to their baser natures? I think men do that quite well on their own without any help from me.'

'I think, Mercedes, you know exactly how you affect a man.' They'd come to an old, wide oak that hid them from the view of others in the park. It would be the most privacy they'd have. The game was getting dangerous now. How far did he dare take it? How far would Mercedes allow him to take it?

'And Circe? Did she know or was it the type of curse where she was doomed to attract men? I must confess, I wasn't all that good with the classics at school.'

He could imagine that. Mercedes was the practical sort; the classics wouldn't hold any appeal for her unless they held the secrets to turning metal into gold. 'What were you good at?'

Mischief flickered in her eyes. 'Palm reading. Would you like me to read yours?' She took his hand and turned it palm up between them.

'They taught palmistry at your school?' This must have been an interesting school indeed.

'No,' Mercedes said without looking up, all her attention riveted on his palm. 'The gypsies did and they camped near the school every spring.'

'And you ran off to visit them?' At least he hoped her gaze didn't drop any lower. There was an impressive show going on in his ever-tightening trousers. He'd have to get it under control before they started walking again.

'Of course.' She did look up briefly, then, her eyes dancing. 'And no, my father doesn't know.'

He should have known. Greer chuckled. 'Well, go on, tell me what you see.' *Besides a full-blown erection just inches from your skirts.* He was going to have to start wearing his darker trousers. A man couldn't hide anything in fawn. Inexpressibles. Hardly. They were more like *expressibles.*

'For starters, you have an air hand. That means you have long fingers and a squarish palm.' She traced the outline of his hand with a slow finger. 'I noticed your long fingers right away that first night.'

'An air hand? Is that good or bad?' He didn't really care, he just liked the feel of her fingers tracing the lines of his palms.

'Neither. It simply describes characteristics. You like intellectual challenges. You are easily bored. That would explain your enjoyment of the military and your eagerness to avoid the home farm, don't you think?'

Once more they skirted a truly personal issue. This time it was he who shied away from it. He caught her looking up at him from beneath her dark lashes. He chose to play the cynic. 'It would if I hadn't already told you that. How do I know you're not just putting pieces of fact together and making this up to suit?'

'You have to trust me.' She spread his fingers and studied them each in turn. 'Look at that.' Mercedes licked her lips, looking entirely wanton and very much like a gypsy. He was positively rigid now. Her next words just about did him in. She caressed the flat of his palm. 'You are a sexual creature who excels in the intimate arts.'

'Be careful, Mercedes,' Greer warned in low tones. He was about to 'excel' right there.

'Or what? I'll find my skirts up and my legs wrapped around your waist? Is that a promise?' Mercedes gave a throaty laugh. The image she painted was a potent one but this was not the time or place for such a demonstration.

Greer grabbed her wrist none too gently. 'That's enough.' She needed to be taught a lesson about toying with a gentleman's sensibilities. 'I will not play the animal to your Circe in the middle of a public park.'

She shot him a hard look and yanked her wrist away from the shackle of his grip. 'Of course you won't. In the end, you'll always abide by the rules.'

It was said mockingly. She was daring him and he was almost tempted to prove her wrong, that he *would* break those rules and take her right there. Goodness knew it was what his body wanted.

'Is that what you want?' Greer asked tersely. 'Do you want me to take you here in this most uncouth fashion?' He could feel the closeness between them evaporating.

'What I want is for you to concentrate on tonight,' Mercedes snapped. Just like that the termagant was back. For a few moments they'd been something more than travelling partners. The lines that defined their association had blurred ever so briefly. He was coming to recognise Mercedes was very good at such blurring, especially when it helped her get something she wanted.

Damn her.

It all became crystal clear: *the best target is someone whose ego is greater than their skill. Give up a bit early, let them think they've got the upper hand, then raise the stakes and win the game. Always quit while you're ahead.* Greer blew out a breath and had the good grace to laugh. 'Are you hustling me, Mercedes?'

She smiled, wicked and knowing, a finger trailing lightly down his shirt front. 'I don't know, Greer. Tell me again, what are the rules to a good hustle?'

Chapter Nine

'There he is. That's your mark,' Mercedes whispered at his ear a few hours later. The quiet inn had been transformed into a noisy crowd of people. It was a Friday and wages had been paid out. Men jostled at the bar for tankards of ale and the activity was brisk around the billiards table. Even a few women were present, although none were as stunning as Mercedes.

Tonight she wore a tight-fitted gown of deep-blue satin, trimmed in black lace and cut shockingly low, shoulders bared, the star pendant hanging from a black satin ribbon at her neck. Looking as she did, Greer was almost ready to forgive her for hustling him that afternoon. Almost.

He kept a hand at her back, ushering her through the crowd to an empty space near the billiards table where they could watch the games. 'Him?' Greer nodded towards a tall man in his early thirties playing at the table. The man in question had been winning.

Mercedes nodded, but he noticed her gaze kept moving about the room, always landing on one man in particular, a handsome auburn-haired fellow who boldly returned her attention. 'Greer, why don't you get me a glass of wine, if they have any?' she said absently.

Greer questioned the wisdom of leaving her. Every man in the room had noticed her by now, Mr Auburn-haired included. When he hesitated, she laughed up at him and he had no choice but to go in search of wine. 'I'll be fine. But it is sweet of you to worry.' He was going to end up fighting someone over her tonight, he just knew it.

By the time he had returned, hard-won glass of wine in hand, he could see his suspicions weren't far off. The auburn-haired man had moved to her side in his absence and men hovered around Mercedes. Worst of all, that little minx was encouraging it.

'Your wine, my dear.' Greer elbowed Auburn Hair at her side with a little more force than necessary.

She took the glass from him with a smile and a laugh. 'There you are, I thought you'd got lost.' Then she addressed the group around them. 'This is Captain Barrington. He's a fair billiards player, too, like your Jonas Bride there.' Impressive, Greer thought. She had the name of the mark already.

She batted her eyelashes at Auburn Hair. 'Do you think my Captain can take him, Mr Reed?' Her hand idly fiddled with the star charm where it lay against her bare neckline. Every man's eyes were riveted on that bare expanse of skin, especially Mr Reed's. Mr Reed's eye might be a bit darker for it too.

Mr Reed shot him a cocky glance men everywhere have understood for centuries. *I can take her from you.* To Mercedes he said, 'Shall we see?'

Mercedes reached into her cleavage and pulled out pound notes with a graceful gesture while half the room sucked in their breath. Good Lord, she was putting on a show. Even knowing that, Greer couldn't help but feel the first stirrings of desire. Then Greer understood. The mark wasn't Jonas Bride, not really, not unless he chose to make the man his personal mark. The real mark was Mr Reed and she'd been drawing him to her since she'd walked in the room. *Find someone who likes to bet beyond their ego.*

Reed called over to Jonas Bride and a game was quickly established. Mercedes blew him a kiss, the signal to lose. *Give up a bit, build the opponent's confidence.* This would be for both of them should he choose to engage Jonas Bride. It was what Mercedes was waiting for, his test for the evening. Would he personally engage in a hustle? Would he be able to win when he needed to, unlike in Bosham?

'Bride, care for a wager between us?' Greer offered, the affront to his own pride goading him into it. He'd show Mercedes he could play this as well as she could.

Greer lost the first game good-naturedly. Mercedes passed her pound notes to Reed and tossed her dark head. 'Shall we go again?' she said coyly, drawing more money from her bosom. Reed practically salivated. She blew him another kiss. And another.

Reed was standing too close to her, staring too much by the time she gave the signal to win. Greer doubled his own wager with Mr Bride, who gladly took it, seeing it as a chance for easy money. He'd just won three straight games.

Greer broke and won, careful to win just barely. There was no sense in making Bride look foolish. Reed bent over Mercedes's hand and kissed it lavishly before he surrendered the funds, his eyes lingering on her breasts.

It's just a game, Greer reminded himself, watching money pass back and forth between them. She's playing with Mr Reed, working him out of his money. It's you she likes. It's you whose ear she sucked into oblivion; it's you who she kissed in the parlour at Bosham, *really* kissed. You kissed her first and she kissed you back.

But it was hard to remember that when Reed had his hands on her, his mouth possessively close to her ear as if he had any right to Mercedes. And that cocky stare of his! He positively gloated every time he caught Greer looking at them.

Looking at them was proving costly. Reed slid a hand along Mercedes's leg and Greer shot a poorly aimed slice that nearly caused him to scratch. Mercedes laughed and slid a hand inside Reed's waistcoat. Greer clenched his jaw and tried to focus on the game. He should split the pair and make the table difficult for Bride. It was what Mercedes would recommend.

'Don't miss, Captain,' Reed called out. 'I'd hate to have to console your lady if you lost again.'

Greer looked up. Lucifer's balls, Mercedes was in his lap, her mouth at Reed's ear. That was it. No defence, no strategy. He was going to clear this table, take his winnings and his woman and get the hell out.

Greer aimed and aimed again, the shots coming in rapid fire. He saw only the table, only the balls until he'd potted them all.

'I think that might have been the fastest game ever played,' a man breathed somewhere in the crowd. Greer didn't care.

'I'll take my money, Bride.'

'And give me no chance to win it back?' Bride was disappointed.

'No,' Greer said tersely although he could see the answer was not popular with the crowd. Bride had lost a considerable sum. Greer stuffed the money in his pocket. 'Mercedes, we're leaving.'

Mercedes shot him a disapproving look, but he was done. He wasn't going to stand by and watch her flirt with another, especially when he didn't know exactly where he stood with her. It was time to stake that claim.

'Maybe she doesn't want to go, *Captain*,' Reed sneered, deep in his cups by now.

'The lady is with me.' Greer planted his feet shoulder width apart and flexed his hand.

'Is she?' Reed drew Mercedes to him, but she was too quick. A small blade flashed in her hand, coming up against Reed's neck.

'I am.' Mercedes's eyes glinted with the thrill of the hunt.

Reed released her. She moved backwards to his side and Greer felt a profuse sense of relief to have her with him. Ale had made Reed slow, but his sluggish brain was starting to work it all out. 'Hey, that's not fair. You made me believe—'

He couldn't complete the thought before Mercedes interrupted. 'You're right. I made you believe and you fell for it.' She slipped the blade into the hidden sheath in her bodice and gave Reed a wink. 'The last rule of a hustle is to quit while you're ahead. Adieu.'

Greer grimaced. He wished she hadn't said that. Reed wasn't drunk enough to ignore the slight, but he *was* drunk enough to fight. It didn't take a genius to know who he'd be swinging at. It wasn't going to be Mercedes.

Reed lunged. Greer was ready for him. His arm came up, blocking the punch while his other fist found Reed's jaw, laying him out in one staggering blow. Cries of injustice were rising. This was going to get ugly. He and Mercedes were woefully outnumbered. It was past time to get out.

Greer shoved a bench or two in the way to slow down pursuers and pushed Mercedes ahead of him with one word of advice. 'Run!'

But the patrons were unfortunately bored or game or both. And they were happy to give chase. At the door he needed his fists to secure an exit and still they followed them into the streets. He had Mercedes by the hand as they ran through dark streets, winding through alleys until the mob gave up the pursuit.

'Alone at last!' Mercedes gasped, half panting, half laughing as she bent over to catch her breath. Her hair had come down and her face was flushed. Greer thought he'd never seen anything lovelier. Until he remembered. He was supposed to be angry with her.

'You almost got us killed back there!' he panted.

'Beaten up, maybe.' Mercedes laughed, dismissing his concern.

'Easy for you to say. You weren't the one

they were going to punch.' Greer felt his anger slipping away. It was deuced hard to stay mad at her. But he could stay mad at Reed.

Mercedes leaned against the brick wall of a building, her breathing slowing. 'You're looking at me strangely.' She raised a hand to her face. 'Do I have dirt on my cheek? What is it?'

'This.' Greer braced his arm over her and bent his mouth to hers, adrenaline surging through them both, the kiss hard and bruising, its unspoken message was clear. 'You are mine.'

This was a dangerous kiss. All of his kisses were. But that didn't help her resist. Mercedes fell into the kiss, the thrill of the chase finding a new outlet in this physical release. They had kissed before, just as hard and just as furiously. Tonight, it wasn't enough. In the moments of escape, she wanted more and so did Greer. Desire and adrenaline fairly rolled off his body. His hips pressed into her and she could feel the extent of his want, pulsing and hard as his mouth devoured her. Why shouldn't they have more? Why shouldn't they celebrate this moment? Why did it have to mean anything beyond now?

Mercedes reached for him, finding his hard

length through the fabric of his trousers. She stroked it, firm and insistent, moulding the cloth about its rigid form until she felt the tiniest bit of dampness seep through. Greer groaned, sinking his teeth into her throat, his bite an intense mix of pain and pleasure against her skin. His hand too, was not idle. He cupped her breast, thumbing her nipple into erectness beneath the satin of her gown, creating an exquisite friction against her skin. A moan escaped her, swallowed up by his mouth. He was branding her with his kisses, with his touch. She ought not to let him. She belonged to no man. And there could be no future in belonging to this one, only disappointment. But, her body chimed in, not until after great pleasure. Greer would be a matchless lover, their passion unequalled.

Her skirts were up, the evening air cool on the heated skin of her body, her leg hitched around the lean curve of his hip, the decadence of their position fuelling their ardour. They were in a public place. Technically, anyone could come along at any time. It was a naughtily delicious thought to imagine being caught with this man. Even she had not dared so much in such a place before. Greer's hand slipped inside her undergarments and found

her cleft, stroking, teasing her into unquench-
able flames, his own breathing coming ragged
and fast.

Mercedes fumbled in haste with the fastenings of his trousers. 'Come on, get that out
here to play.' Her own voice was hoarse with
want as her fingers groped for access to that
most male part of him. Almost! She almost
had it. That was when she heard it: the sound
of horse harness and carriage wheels. They
were about to be discovered by, 'My father!'

Mercedes tugged at her skirts, giving Greer
a shove into action and pushing him away
from her just as the Lockhart coach stopped
in front of the alley entrance, travelling lanterns lit. A dark figure jumped nimbly down
from the coach box. 'I heard there was a little
commotion at the inn and thought you might
be looking for a ride.' Her father strode forwards looking at ease.

They *did* need a ride, but damn the man, he
was showing up at the worst times. First at the
fair, now this. How in the world was she ever
going to get Greer into bed at this rate? After
tonight, that was precisely where she wanted
him and the consequences be hanged.

She could feel Greer at her side, his hand
warm at her back, his body emanating unsat-

isfied heat. 'This is not over,' he growled for her ears alone.

'It certainly isn't,' Mercedes replied *sotto voce*. No one passed up a lover of this calibre no matter what the circumstances.

'Am I interrupting anything?' Her father grinned. 'Celebrations, perhaps? I heard someone cleaned out a particular Mr Reed tonight and a Mr Bride. I am assuming it was you two?' He elbowed Mercedes good-naturedly. 'Everyone is talking about the woman in the blue dress. Good job, my dear.'

Normally, she would have basked in his praise, but tonight her mind was too full of Greer to spend more than a passing moment on the acknowledgement. At the carriage, Greer handed her up and followed her in, her father choosing to ride up on the box with the coachman and take in the mild evening. But the damage had been done. There would be no resuming of the alleyway. The recklessness of the moment had passed, but it would come again.

She and Greer were headed towards consummation. It was only a matter of time. Still, a foregone conclusion was not without its own delicious torture. A waiting game had been invoked tonight. When would it come? Where and how? Would it be fast and hard and decadent like the alleyway? Would it be a dilettante's pleasure—a slow fire building towards a raging inferno by degrees? He would be capable of both.

Mercedes studied Greer in the lantern light, the blue eyes and the strong set of his jaw. He'd fought for her tonight, kissed the living daylights out of her in an alley. Of course they were headed to bed.

But what then? How long could she keep such a hero? Well, she wouldn't think about that tonight. There were other more pleasant things to ponder, such as how Greer might take her. And less pleasant things, too, such as how she was going to convince her father to let her play. They were nearing Bath where her father wanted to make a considerable stand and she was no closer to earning his public approval than she had been before they left Brighton.

Greer reached below the seat and pulled out the blankets kept there. He handed her one with a smile. 'Go to sleep, Lady in Blue.'

She took the blanket. 'You were jealous tonight.'

Greer nodded, not shying away from the

truth. 'I was. I didn't like seeing Reed's hands all over you.'

Mercedes smiled softly as she spread out her blanket. 'Well, try not to punch anyone else. I'd hate for you to ruin your hands before the tournament. It is just a game, Greer.' She settled her head against the cushioned walls of the carriage.

'My shoulder might be more comfortable,' came Greer's low tones. He didn't wait for a response. Perhaps he sensed forcing a direct answer from her would be too much of a commitment.

Greer slid over to her seat and wrapped an arm about her, drawing her close. She could smell the sandalwood of his soap mingled with the sweat of the evening and clean linen, a comforting, masculine smell of a man who knew how to take care of himself and of others. She was used to hard kisses and fast-spent passions in her associations with men. She was not used to this: the sense of being protected and cherished. She'd not been prepared for the Captain to turn out to be a man who was strong and passionate with a capacity for tenderness. Before she drifted off to sleep she thought she heard the whispered words, 'You're not a game, Mercedes, not to me.' Her

heart cried out one last futile warning. Here
was a man who could ruin her.

Here was a woman who could ruin him.
Greer stayed awake long after Mercedes had
fallen asleep against him. In the moonlight and
lanterns she looked harmless enough, a peace-
ful sleeping beauty to the unsuspecting con-
noisseur. But he knew better, far better than
she knew. He was living on borrowed time
and every mile they drew closer to Bath, more
sand drained from the hour glass.

Bath would be full of people, *his* kind of
people—barons and viscounts who were there
before moving on to London or back to their
estates for summer. It was unlikely he'd escape detection. There'd be someone there who
would know his brother or his father and word
would get home. When that happened, there'd
be hell to pay.

It wasn't just his father's disapproval he
was risking—he'd risked that often enough
in the past. His father's disapproval was a private matter kept in the family. There would
be no hiding this. Society would know what
he'd done and that would bring shame to the
entire family. He, a captain in the military,
second son of a viscount, had taken up with a

billiards hustler and his daughter. Never mind that Lockhart was a celebrity. Playing billiards for a living was patently unacceptable. Flaunting Mercedes in the face of decent society was a direct slap in the face to all the eligible young girls looking for husbands. Mercedes could be his mistress and be kept discreetly out of sight, but nothing more. To be seen with her publicly at the gatherings of 'decent folk' was inappropriate.

It would send his mother swooning and his father might actually disown him this time for good. Mercedes was wrong when she'd accused him of having nothing to risk in this venture. He had everything to risk. What would happen if he lost the security of knowing the home farm waited for him? It was not a destiny he wanted, but it was there like a safe harbour should all else fail.

He'd joined the military to make his own way in the world. But that choice hadn't come at the cost of his family. Never before had 'making his own way' come with a price. His family had issues, but they were his family, the only one he'd ever get. If it came down to his own independence or them, would he give them up? He would need to decide soon. Even if he escaped Bath unscathed by recognition, it would be good to know where he stood. He couldn't plan a future without knowing.

Sleep started to settle on him. Mercedes shifted against him and he tightened his grip about her. Maybe she wasn't the only reason he'd got in the carriage in Brighton. Maybe he'd known this choice would push him to make the decision he'd put off for so long. It was time to face his future head on: home-farm manager, professional billiards player, half-pay officer waiting for a post, or something else altogether. Greer sighed. He wondered if there was a choice that could include Mercedes. That was the problem with options. They made one have to choose.

Chapter Ten

'It's time to work on your defence.' Mercedes tossed Greer an ash cue. They'd picked up the London-Bath Road and were in Beckhampton at an inn on the turnpike where her father knew the owner. At this pace, they'd be in Bath the day after tomorrow at the latest and the true work would begin—real games, real promotion of the tournament in Brighton. These early stops had been meant to be the warm-up for the real campaign; time to turn Greer's instinctive talent for the game into a more sharply honed skill, a calculated tool of intention without drawing attention to him until they were ready.

Mercedes arranged the balls in strategic clusters around the baize. 'We'll start with the group to the right.'

Greer grinned disarmingly. 'That's hardly fair. There's no direct line between my ball and the shot.'

Mercedes smiled back with feigned sweetness. 'That's why we have to work on your defence. So far we've been playing opponents who play like you do. They make great offensive shots. But what happens when someone *doesn't* play the table straight on you? Those men are waiting for you in Bath. You'll need to do more than pot balls; you'll have to know how to set up the table as well as setting up your shots if you want to impress them.'

Greer had a natural aptitude for the strategies. But she knew the real challenge would be whether or not he could pull each strategy out of his repertoire and use it at relevant points in a game.

They ran drills for an hour before her father came over to watch their progress, the perfect opportunity if she chose to seize it. If she didn't do something today, it would be too late. She didn't want to make Greer her whipping boy, but time was running out and so were her choices. She could only hope he'd understand.

Across the table, Greer raised an eyebrow,

questioning her hesitation. 'Are you going to rack them?'

She answered with a non-committal shrug. If she did this, Greer was going to hate her for it. A small part of her was going to hate herself too. She drew a deep breath. 'All right, if you think you're ready, Greer, let's play.' It was now or never.

That should have been his first clue something was amiss. Mercedes had opted out of lessons and drills far earlier than usual. His second should have been the way she'd chalked her cue. She held his gaze while she blew the excess chalk off the tip, a most seductive look that made a man think with a whole different set of balls than the ones of the table. 'I'll break.'

'Fine.' Greer was pretty sure most men would agree to anything with those eyes looking over a cue at them and those lips suggesting chalk wasn't the only thing they'd be good for bl—*that* was not worthy of him. But he was also pretty sure Mercedes knew exactly what she was doing. She'd done it with Mr Reed. Now she was doing it with him. Why?

Something sensual and wicked flaring between them was not new. Innuendo always lay just slightly below the surface with them. Why would she push this now when he needed to concentrate on the game on the table instead of the one in his head? His brain knew better; he just had to send that same message to his body and quell the early stirrings of his arousal.

Lockhart was watching intently and Greer knew Mercedes wasn't going to go easy on him. There was no need to. He was up to any challenge Mercedes might present. Greer bent to survey the table at cue level. No straight shot presented itself, Mercedes would be happy about that. He would be forced to select a skill from their lesson right from the start. Greer aimed his cue to hit the ball slightly off centre, using a slicing shot to send it to the pocket while sending the cue ball on ahead to safety, away from the hazard.

'No, wait.' Mercedes interrupted his concentration. 'You're still aiming too low. A slice shot is to be off-centre, not high or low. The shot you want to take will put your cue ball in the pocket too.'

'It's fine,' Greer said with a tight smile, not wanting to be taken to task in front of Lockhart. He was a man, for heaven's sake, not a sixteen-year-old schoolboy. He knew what he was doing.

Mercedes shrugged and let him take the shot, raising her eyebrows in an 'I told you so' gesture when his ball followed the other into the pocket. He blew out his breath. She briskly gathered up the two balls and set them back on the table. 'Try again. This time, let me show you.'

She stood close, wrapping her hands over his, positioning the cue. He was not unaware of her body pressed to his, the light floral scent of her soap or the womanly curve of her where her hips cradled his buttocks. The arousal that had sparked earlier was in danger of being fully achieved. This time the shot went in. She put the balls back into place one more time. 'Now, try it again on your own.' Greer lined the shot up carefully, thinking there might be something else he'd be trying alone if she kept this up. This time he sank the shot and the game was fully engaged.

By the second round, Greer was certain there was more than one game being played out. Mercedes was shooting out of her head. He'd never seen anyone make the shots she made, and he'd most definitely not seen *her* display this level of skill, which was saying something.

He'd thought her formidable before. Now,

there wasn't even a word in his vocabulary to adequately describe her talent. Phenomenal, stupendous—easy word choices, but inadequate. What did she think she was doing? But there was no time to contemplate hidden agendas. Greer played harder, his shirt sleeves rolled up, his jacket off. The intensity increased. He plied his skill tirelessly with slices, stop shots that careened on the lip of the pocket, bank shots that circumvented barriers to direct shots, but nothing would stop Mercedes.

Greer lost all three games, honourably and by mere inches to be sure, but in the end he'd simply been outplayed. When the last ball fell, Mercedes threw a triumphant smile in her father's direction. Greer expected to see Lockhart grinning at his daughter's success— perhaps he even expected a little scolding directed his way over having lost. But the scold that came was for Mercedes and it was not what Greer had expected at all.

Lockhart rose, fury on his face. He strode towards Mercedes and yanked the cue stick from her hand. 'What the hell do you think you're doing? Parading yourself like that? No man wants a woman who plays better than himself or even a woman who plays, for that matter, let alone one who has any skill at it. Act like a lady.'

Mercedes had a fury of her own. 'Act like a lady? What happened to "you've always understood the game"? You were happy enough to have me act any way I pleased as long as you could use it.'

Greer felt like an interloper. This was private, family business being aired in the midst of an inn. His family would not have dared to display their conflicts so openly. Then again, his family preferred to keep those sorts of things tucked away and ignored, pretending they didn't exist, like their financial deficiencies.

'You are not playing in Bath. That's final.' Lockhart's voice was terse, a tic jumping in his cheek.

'I'm better than any man,' Mercedes replied. 'Why are you so afraid?'

'It's not seemly. You've been raised to be a lady in bearing, if not in name. Is this how you repay me? Is this what your fancy dresses and fine education are to come to?'

Mercedes would not back down. 'You did that for yourself. *You* wanted that for me. You never once asked what I wanted. Why show me billiards at all if you never expected me to excel?' Mercedes's eyes glittered with wet, as of yet unspilled, emotion. Greer's heart went out to her in that moment. How brave she was. He'd been taught a man bore the decisions of the world stoically and without complaint. Never mind that he'd thought many of the same things Mercedes gave voice to now.

'That is enough, Mercedes.' Lockhart had gone rigid. 'If you don't like my decision, you are welcome to go home and await our return there.'

Mercedes shot him a look full of blazing discontent and stormed out of the inn, the door slamming behind her. She was nothing if not magnificent in her anger. Lockhart turned to Greer, his hands held out in a gesture of reconciliation. 'I am sorry, Barrington.' He sighed. 'She's emotional in spite of her pretensions to the opposite.' Lockhart gave a quiet chuckle. 'She's a woman, no? What can we expect? You have sisters. You know how it is.'

'Yes, two of them,' Greer said tightly. He didn't want to be corralled into taking sides against Mercedes, but neither did he want to offend Lockhart. Lockhart could send him packing as easily as he could Mercedes, and the ride had really just begun with the first big test looming in Bath if he embraced it.

'Two sisters—then you're used to their high-strung tendencies.' Lockhart made a shooing gesture with his hand. 'Go and talk to her. I don't like her on the streets alone, but I'm the last person she'll want to see. Maybe she'll listen to you.' He gave a fatherly sigh of defeat. 'The world is what it is; she can't change that, no matter how much she rails against it.'

Greer was more than glad to go after Mercedes. He didn't doubt she was safe, armed as she was with the knife in her bodice and her temper. No man with any intelligence would fail to read the signs of an angry woman. He could do with some air himself, some time to sort through what had just happened.

The more he thought about it, the more he couldn't help feeling that Lockhart, the consummate showman, had turned even a personal quarrel with his daughter to his advantage. If he was willing to do that with an issue of a private nature, what else would he stoop to use or who? Was there any sacred line in the sand?

That didn't make Mercedes the innocent party here by any stretch. It did occur to him as he walked down the street, replaying the quarrel in his mind, that she might have been using him to make her father angry, that he

was a tool for flaunting her own independence
in all ways. The realisation took the bubble off
the wine. He didn't want their kisses, their passion, to be part of some other game she played.
He didn't want to be another 'Mr Reed' to her,
someone she used for other ends. It was time
to confront her on that issue.

Mercedes saw Greer approaching out of the
corner of her eye. She flipped open the little
watch she carried. 'Ten minutes. Very good.
I win,' she said without turning from the window.

'I'm sorry, did we wager on something?'
Greer said coolly. He had his own issues to
settle with her. She'd used him in there.

'I wagered with myself that my father
would send you after me within ten minutes.
He wouldn't dare come himself. He did send
you, didn't he?'

'I was concerned for you.' Greer's answer
was evasive. But it confirmed her suspicions.

'If you've come to espouse his cause, forget it. Do yourself a favour and don't play his
messenger. I'd like to think you were a better
man than that.' She was being cruel on purpose, hoping to drive Greer away. She didn't
trust herself at present. If he touched her, if

he said anything kind, she might just go to pieces and she didn't want to. She wanted to be strong. Anger kept her strong.

'All right,' Greer said calmly, unbothered. 'I'll just stand here and admire the window with you.' Greer joined her in staring at the goods on display. There wasn't much to look at: a gaudy hat complete with bright purple ribbon and green feather and a few bolts of printed muslin. Beckhampton might be on a major road, but the town was still small.

'Maybe I'll just ask the questions. What was going on there? I don't mean the fight, I mean *all* of it; the blowing on the chalk, the bedroom eyes over the cue, the "let me show you how to line the shot up"? It was quite a show. Was it for my benefit or his?'

'Maybe it was for neither of you,' Mercedes replied succinctly. 'Maybe it was for *me*. Did you think of that? Or perhaps you've put too much construction on what it meant at all.' She tossed him a sharp, short glance.

'I could say the same about you. Did you roll up your sleeves and take off your coat as part of some grand flirtation?'

'Of course not,' Greer answered hastily. 'That's ridiculous. It's easier to play without my coat.'

'My point exactly.'

'Be fair, Mercedes, it's *not* the same thing. It's not like you were taking your *lips* off because they confined your play.'

Mercedes had to work hard to stifle a laugh. But it wasn't time to laugh yet. 'I'm sorry you were distracted—perhaps you should work on that. It seemed to be a problem the other night as well.' She turned to go, but Greer grabbed her arm, a *frisson* of warning and heat running through her body as she realised what she'd done. She could push the well-trained aristocrat in him only so far before she encountered the man in him too.

'You used me back there. I won't stand for that. Don't play with me, Mercedes. I think we've done that enough on this trip. We've been playing games since that night in the garden and most of those games you've started.'

'You haven't minded,' she shot back. 'It was *your* tongue in my throat in Bosham as I recall, your hips against mine in the alley.'

'You're right, I haven't minded.' Greer held her gaze, letting his own drop briefly to her lips. She licked them. 'I just want to know why. Are these kisses for business or pleasure?'

Mercedes gave a hard laugh. 'If I was using

you for sex, Captain, you'd have known it by now.' But she thought her words might be a lie. There was no arguing he was in her blood.

Greer smiled dangerously. 'Likewise. And if you're going to stand there contemplating how best to seduce me, call me Greer.'

'How do you know I'm thinking *that*?'

'Because we have unfinished business. Seduction between us is inevitable—I think the alley affirmed that. Don't you? It's just a matter of who will seduce whom.' He leaned close and whispered at her ear. 'If you're the betting sort, I'd put your money on me.'

Mercedes whispered back, 'If men's cocks were as big as their egos, I might take that bet, *Greer*.' The look on his face was priceless, part shock and part admiration. Now it was time to laugh.

Chapter Eleven

~~~~~~~~~~~~~~~~~~~~

It was a subdued group that pulled into Bath. He had no one to blame for that but himself, Lockhart mused. He shot a look at Barrington, who rode beside him. It was quite telling that the Captain had chosen to ride instead of his usual routine of sitting with Mercedes inside the carriage.

Clearly, words had been said between them when Barrington had gone after her. From the tension at dinner last night, Lockhart didn't think the words had solely been about the billiards game. There'd been a certain spark between Mercedes and the Captain from the start. Travel and close proximity had encouraged it just as he'd hoped. For that matter, *Mercedes* had encouraged it to their benefit. The

Captain's 'affections' for Mercedes, whatever their basis, had indeed kept him loyal. If this was a mere flirtation for her, a means to an end, fine. But if she actually developed true feelings for Barrington, there would be trouble ahead should either of them choose to rebel.

Mercedes's rebellion was of immediate concern. She'd been upset by his decision to not let her play in Bath. An upset Mercedes would need to be appeased before she did something reckless which could be disastrous for them all. Bath should go a great way in appeasing her once they got settled. He had a lovely house rented and he'd turn over the social calendar to her. She'd cultivate relationships for him that would be good for the tournament and she'd feel useful. She'd have gowns to wear and the handsome Captain at her side to act as an escort to balls and other entertainments. She'd forget she was angry.

As for Barrington, the Captain would be in his element, among people like him. And he was looking forward to making the most of Barrington's entrée. Bath would be most lucrative for him riding in on the Captain's coat-tails. He and the Captain would make a splendid duo in the clubs. He could feel the cue in his hand already. Between the two of them, they'd be unbeatable. Everything was working out splendidly and Mercedes would come around. He'd see to it with plenty of money and entertainments to keep her busy, and a few well-placed compliments.

Lockhart gave the coachman directions to the terraced house. This would not be an overnight stop. He planned for them to spend two, maybe three weeks in Bath, where the season was already under way.

The coach stopped in front of the Bath-stone town house with its neat wrought iron railings and large windows. Lockhart was pleased to note even the Captain was impressed with the lodgings and location—right on the Crescent and within walking distance of all the important places: subscription rooms, the assembly hall, the theatre and the almighty Pump Room, where the heart of Bath beat on a daily basis.

He dismounted and helped Mercedes down himself. She looked up at the house, a small smile on her face. Lockhart would take it as a good sign. 'Can you get us settled? I shall see you at dinner.' He drew her aside to let Barrington and the trunks head into the house.

'You've done splendidly with him.' Lockhart nodded to indicate the Captain as he passed. 'He's come a long way. His play has been refined. He has a sense of strategy now. Well done, Daughter.' He beamed at her. 'You should get some new dresses made up while we're here.'

'I may. I have plenty.' Mercedes didn't thaw any further.

'Well, it's up to you. A pretty dress might go a long way with the Captain. He wants to impress you. Make sure you keep him dangling. That can be a useful tool, a leash to keep him on.'

When Mercedes said nothing, he swung back up on his horse, calling down a promise, 'I'll see about tickets to the theatre while I'm about it.' 'It', of course, was arranging entrance to the subscription rooms where men would play billiards all day long, serious gentlemen like himself.

'How many should I expect for dinner tonight?' Mercedes gave him a half-smile. She knew very well he was plotting already. Good for her.

'None tonight, but the invitations will start rolling in by tomorrow.' Lockhart winked at the Captain as he came down the steps. 'Tonight will be the last night you're saddled with only my company.' Hopefully the Captain would take the hint. If there were any loose ends between him and Mercedes, Barrington had better tie them up quickly. In Bath the Captain might face competition for Mercedes. Not nearly so highbrow as London, Bath would be more tolerant of Mercedes's antecedents and he needed Mercedes and the Captain together for now. If Mercedes froze him out, he'd have to manage her through the Captain.

Her father would not manage her as if she were a little girl. He was *not* forgiven. He could dazzle and compliment and offer new dresses and theatre tickets all he liked, but he was not forgiven, not this time.

Mercedes stepped into the terraced house, her mind already whirling. Her father wasn't the only one with plans to set in motion. She'd had all morning alone in the carriage to adjust her strategy. Plan A had failed. Her father was not going to allow her to go public with her talent. The quarrel the previous day had shown her that very plainly and there was no longer any reason to hold out false hope things would change in that regard. But there was always Plan B.

She smiled to herself, surveying the luxuriously appointed drawing room, a place ladies would want to come and be entertained. This house was going to be perfect. With its location at the heart of Bath, it was well positioned to become a social centre to rival the Pump Room. She would see to it.

'Does it meet with your approval?' Greer had come up behind her, directing the grooms to take the trunks upstairs.

She turned to face him, hardly able to prevent her features from radiating her excitement. 'Absolutely.' To keep him from suspecting too much, she crossed the room with a brisk stride and pulled open the double doors, leading to the dining room. 'Very elegant,' she commented, running her hand down the length of the polished table. 'We can seat fourteen for dinner. That will do nicely.'

'Do you really plan on doing a lot of entertaining?' Greer queried dubiously. 'Do you know anyone in town?'

She tossed him a coy glance. 'Not yet. But we will, you'll see. We'll have tickets to the theatre by tonight and invitations will fill the salver in the entryway by tomorrow. That was no idle boast my father made. He knows how to play this game.' Mercedes smiled smugly. She knew how to play the game too and she could play it every bit as well her father could.

'You didn't go with him?' Mercedes said

as they made their way upstairs to see the private chambers. The downstairs had been perfect. Along with the drawing and dining room, there was a small office, a lady's parlour and, best of all, a room with a billiards table. She suspected the room was normally used as an informal dining parlour or second sitting room. But the table was Thurston's and fit the space admirably, and she would put that table to good use.

'I could tell he wanted to be alone,' Greer offered charitably. 'This is his town, isn't it? He grew up here?'

Mercedes nodded. That was something Greer would only have known from listening to bits and pieces of conversations, further testimony to the fact that he was a good listener, a keen observer. One had to be careful around people like that. 'He and Kendall Carlisle were boot boys in the subscription rooms until a gentleman noticed their interest and took them under his wing. He showed them the game and the rest, as they say, is history.'

They came to a large room done in dark, masculine greens, clearly designated for the master of the house. 'You can put my father's things in here,' Mercedes directed the grooms.

She would have to get staff hired this afternoon. She mentally added the task to her list.

Down the hall were two other rooms across the hall from each other, one in pale blues and the other in a deep gold. She stepped inside the latter and surveyed it, taking in the large, heavy four-poster bed and the clothes press. The room was simply done, but not shabby.

'Will it do for you, do you think?' It would be interesting to have Greer so close to her. On the road, most inns hadn't had three separate rooms available. He and her father had shared a room on those occasions. Having him alone and across the hall in a private home was far different. She wondered what he'd do if she were to slip into his room one night? She wondered if she *would* do it?

'Mercedes?' Greer was talking to her, *had* been talking to her.

'Yes?'

He shook his head. 'You haven't heard a single word I've said. What's going on in that head of yours? Your brain's been running a mile a minute since you got out of the carriage.'

Mercedes smiled sweetly and sailed towards him, running a hand up his chest. 'I was wondering what I'd find if I crossed the hall in the middle of the night.'

'You'd find me.'

'Yes, but which you?' Mercedes murmured, head cocked to one side, eyes on him. She watched desire flicker in his eyes as it warred with his sense of decency. 'Would I find the gentleman? The officer? The rogue? The gambler, even? I wonder what would happen to your wager then?'

'You coming to my room doesn't preclude my ability to seduce you first,' Greer countered.

'But it does make the waters murky,' she parried. 'One might argue I won because I opened the door. I started it.'

'You start a lot of things, Mercedes.' Greer's hand covered hers where it lay against his chest, his eyes going quietly blank, all desire pushed back for the time being. 'I thought we'd agreed yesterday it would be foolish to pursue this aspect of our relationship.'

'I recall no such thing.' Of course, it had been there in the subtext of their exchange. *If I was using you for sex, Captain, you'd have known it by now.* And his bold, *'likewise'*, with the candour of a rogue. But it was the gentleman she faced today and the gentleman was troubled.

'It could get complicated.' He raised her hand to his lips and kissed it—a gentleman's gesture. Almost. The press of his lips to her hand wasn't quite chaste in the same way her hands on him, helping manage his cue yesterday, hadn't been quite instructional.

'Complicated? How so?' She breathed, dreading his answer. Something had changed for him.

'People may know me here. Associating with me may make things difficult for you.'

That was the most polite way she'd ever heard it phrased before, but the meaning was still the same. 'Difficult for me or for you?' she questioned. 'I'm fine with it. I am proud to associate with you. I'm sorry you don't feel the same.' Tears threatened. She was not going to cry, not for him and *not* over this. This was an eventuality she'd known was coming at some point. Viscounts' sons were made for débutantes, not for the daughters of Bath bootboys.

She let anger come to her rescue. 'I'm good enough for a quick one in the alley, to push up against an oak tree when no one's looking, but heaven forbid people actually know we associate with one another.'

There was more she'd like to have said. She didn't get the chance. 'Stop it, Mercedes. That's not what I meant,' Greer hissed.

'It's exactly what you meant. You're a hard man, Greer Barrington,' she whispered, drawing her hand slowly away from him and stepping backwards towards the door.

'Yes, yes, I am.'

A swift glance south confirmed it. Mercedes smiled coldly. 'Good luck with that. Let me know when you get it all worked out.' Maybe bed wasn't a foregone conclusion after all. Her practical side offered consolation. Not bedding Greer avoided a number of extenuating complications, but her other side, the larger part of her, was extraordinarily disappointed. It was a small consolation to hear Greer's door slam moments later. Apparently he was disappointed, too. At least the issue of status was out in the open now. They were no longer dancing around it and all the ways it would define what could or could not be between them.

Being with Mercedes, or *not* being with Mercedes, was like a bad waltz: one step forwards followed by two steps back and a couple of missteps in between. This latest exchange was a definite misstep. He'd not meant to imply he didn't want to be seen with her, only that there might be people who would make it difficult for her, who might say cruel things because of her association with him, not the other way around.

Men could be fortune hunters and simply be called rogues. Women who did the same were grasping and desperate or considered licentious wantons. The grasping and desperate might be tolerated with pity, but licentious wantons were exiled. Whores had their places, after all. He didn't want that for Mercedes. He wanted her to be acceptable. *So that you can have her without cost.* It would be the easiest solution, or it would have been if he'd phrased his concern better. Now he had to dig himself out of this hole he'd dug. It was a shame. Things had been going well.

Greer wanted to punch the wall. It would serve Mercedes right if he broke his hand. But a broken hand did him no favours so he opted for pacing in the hopes it would subdue his temper and his erection.

He'd thought they'd made progress in their relationship in Beckhampton, building on their exchange in the park in the prior town and their wild run through the streets. They'd moved from flirting and testing the waters of their attraction to suggestive banter. That banter had become a contract. He thought it was fairly clear from their discussion in Beck-hampton where they were headed: into a relationship of sorts.

Of sorts. How was *that* clear? His logical mind laughed at him. Was all this about bedding her or having something more with her? Perhaps the whole problem was that they hadn't worked that out. Every time they seemed to make progress, one of them threw a roadblock up—a snapped comment, a shrewd insinuation, or a challenge, and then they withdrew until the next time. No wonder they were frustrated and reading things into conversations that weren't necessarily there. They had to stop overthinking this.

Greer stopped pacing and looked out the window of his room. He'd hurt her feelings today, inadvertently. It was up to him to make the next move and put things back into their proper orbit. It was up to him, too, to decide his future here in Bath, to stop thinking about what others wanted from him and consider instead what he wanted for himself.

Greer smiled. It felt as if a great weight had been lifted. Life had suddenly become simpler.

He knew what he wanted: Mercedes. And he was going to get her.

An idea came to him. He went to his trunk and pulled out his uniform, shaking out his scarlet jacket. Perhaps an association with him *could* work in her favour. Perhaps, if the need arose, he could make her acceptable.

Greer laid the jacket aside. One problem solved. Pacing had subdued his temper and given him clarity. There would be a price for this decision, but maybe it was time to pay it. He looked down at himself. There was still his erection to deal with, the problem pacing hadn't resolved. It was a good thing he hadn't punched the wall. He was going to need that hand after all.

Chapter Twelve

By half past six, Mercedes had the house well in hand; a cook, a housekeeper, one maid and two footmen-cum-valets, happy to act as men of all work, were established below stairs having performed their services for the evening with sufficient dexterity. Keeping busy had taken her mind off Greer. But she prepared for an evening at the theatre with a growing sense of trepidation. Either Greer would be downstairs waiting or he would not. Her father would have her neck if Greer had left and she would be vastly disappointed, but not surprised.

She'd not left things on a good note with him that afternoon. Perhaps she should have let him explain. But it had been easier to get angry, *safer*. She'd started that conversation with the intention of taking things further, of acting on the implicit contract they'd established in Beckhampton. But then, at the slightest hint of trouble—those ambiguous words about the consequence of their association—she'd retreated. Not only had she retreated, she'd thrown up a fortress. It would be no wonder if Greer left. Any other man would have. Men didn't like difficult women. Now, as she took a last look in the mirror, she was betting Greer wasn't like any other man.

She'd worn the oyster-coloured summer organdy and pearls and put her hair up in a simple twist. The effect was one of elegance and class. Tonight, she dared any lady to look better. Greer would be proud to have her on his arm if he was downstairs. Mercedes drew a breath to steady herself. There was no more waiting.

At the top of the stairs, that breath was taken away at the sight of Greer. He'd stayed! Relief swamped her, mingled with abject appreciation of his appearance. He leaned casually on the banister, one foot on the bottom step, his head resting on his hand as he looked up at her, his gaze hot and approving as he took her in. He was turned out in the full glory of his dress uniform, much as he had been that first night in Brighton.

'I'm sorry I'm late,' Mercedes said, taking the final step. The comment was *de rigueur*. She wasn't truly late, merely the last one downstairs, and the curtain didn't rise for another half hour.

Greer took the matching mantlet from her and stepped behind her to drape it. 'Beauty in any form is always worth waiting for.' His hands skimmed her shoulders, his voice low for her alone. 'I'm sorry about this afternoon.'

'I thought you might have left.' She drank in the scent of him, all citrus and sandalwood. His hands were warm where they lingered at her shoulders.

'Don't worry, Mercedes. I never leave until I get what I came for.'

'You mean me.'

'I mean you.' He offered her his arm. 'Shall we? Your father is waiting outside. He has rented a small victoria for the evening.'

'Greer?'

'Yes?'

She smiled mischievously. 'Nice buttons.'

The ride to the theatre was uneventful unless one counted the butterflies fluttering in her stomach. Greer had stayed *for her*. The realisation played in her mind like a litany. It didn't mean all their problems were magically solved, but it did mean they could move forwards to wherever they wanted to go.

The carriage stopped to let them disembark in front of the tri-arched Theatre Royale. Brighton had its culture, to be sure, but there was something distinctly exciting to be attending the theatre in Bath. The press of people and the buzz of a hundred conversations only made it more so. She put her hand in Greer's and he squeezed it as he helped her down, a shared look passing between them as if he knew what she was thinking and perhaps shared the feeling.

Inside, her father had secured prime seats in the box of his newest 'best friend', a Sir Richard Sutton, his wife, Olivia, and his daughter, Elise. Introductions were made, Sir Richard and her father acting like old friends instead of acquaintances who'd met only hours earlier. Seats were taken and the lights dimmed as Greer slid into the space beside her. She had not missed the fact that for the first time since their association, her father had introduced Greer as Lord Captain Barrington. Sir

Richard had been impressed. If the reference had bothered Greer, he'd made no show of it.

The play was a rendition of Shakespeare's comedy *As You Like It*, and the cast was good. There was champagne at the intermission, their box filled with the Suttons' acquaintances. It turned out Sir Richard was a prominent yacht builder with connections to the royal family and those in the exclusive royal set. As a result, he was quite popular with the titled families that had come to Bath before heading to London.

Mercedes smiled to herself. It was becoming clear why her father had ingratiated himself with this particular individual. But she liked Elise and thought Lady Sutton would serve her own purposes quite nicely. By the time the Lockharts and Suttons parted ways for the evening, Mercedes had an invitation to join them in the Pump Room tomorrow. They would have an invitation from her the day next for cards and afternoon tea, only they didn't know that yet.

Plan B was going swimmingly.

The next day set the pattern for the days to come. Mercedes slept late, dressed carefully for a promenade with Greer in the Pump

Room, during which she'd meet with her newly accumulated friends: Elise Sutton and her mother, and by extension of that, Lady Fairchild, Mrs Ogilvy, Lady Dasher, whom all her friends called Dash, red-headed and vibrant Mrs Trues and her friend Lady Evelyn.

After the gossip of the Pump Room, where Mercedes made an enormous effort to listen to everything that was being said and about whom, there were the afternoon activities. Most of these were organised or prompted by her. She talked Mrs Trues into arranging an 'historical tour' of the Roman ruins. She convinced Lady Evelyn, who loved painting in the countryside, to put together an 'artist's picnic' for the ladies. The event was such a success the ladies decided to do it once a week, weather permitting. There were the weekly card parties Mercedes hosted herself in the elegant drawing room of the rented terraced house.

Then it was on to the evening entertainments, the balls at the assembly rooms, nights at the theatres and private entertainments. Greer always escorted her and put in a lengthy appearance beside her before disappearing with her father to the elegant subscription rooms and gentlemen's clubs.

Greer proved to be a most able dance partner and by far her favourite time of day was in the evening when she could spend it on the dance floor in his arms. He was a popular partner with all the ladies, never letting any wallflower go unattended. On more than one occasion she'd been discreetly approached by the young ladies of Bath inquiring about her 'situation' with the Captain. To which she merely responded, 'He is a friend of my father's.'

'You should have told them we have an "understanding."' Greer gave a mock grimace as he swung her through a turn at the top of the ballroom one night.

She smiled up at him, flirting a little with her eyes. 'Do we? I wonder what that might be?' He'd made no obvious overtures since they'd reconciled after their quarrel and yet he'd not been inattentive. Just the opposite, in fact. He'd been her unfailing escort in the mornings to the Pump Room, to some of the afternoon activities to which she'd invited gentlemen, and every evening. Surely a man who invested that kind of time and energy in a woman wasn't unmoved?

'That pleasure awaits us when the time is right.'

'Pleasure, is that what it would be?' she challenged coyly.

He bent his mouth close to her ear. 'It's not always dismal, Mercedes.'

'For the man you mean,' she rejoined, but there was heat in her belly, conjured there by his words, breathed so seductively in her ear she thought she might collapse right there on the ballroom floor. They were not the words of a gentleman.

The dance ended and in the press of people leaving the floor, his next words were lost. But she thought his lips had formed the phrase, 'care to find out', before they broke into a most tempting smile.

Maybe she would. The time would be right just as soon as she got phase two of her plan underway.

Mercedes was up to something. It was a marvel Lockhart didn't notice it, Greer thought, leaning against his billiards cue in the subscription room. But Lockhart was too busy revelling in his fame. The billiards champ had been well received in Bath, everyone eager to hear his opinions on Thurston's tables. Everyone was eager to see him play, too, and to learn about the championship coming up in Brighton.

Lockhart was undeniably in his element and it was, admittedly, an exciting place to be. Lockhart introduced Greer to players who shared his seriousness about the game and to others who might be able to advance a second son's ambitions in other ways. The evenings were full of entertainments and then the gentlemen adjourned to the subscription rooms for games much like MPs would adjourn from dinner to a late-night session of Parliament. And with about the same level of gravity.

Lockhart had been right. In Bath there were serious games to be had and Greer was grateful for the hard work Mercedes had put him through in preparation for them. But since their arrival, Mercedes had backed away from billiards. True, she played him on occasion at home. But it appeared she'd meekly accepted Lockhart's verdict in Beckhampton and Greer didn't believe it for a minute. She'd become the epicentre of Bath with her circle of friends and whirlwind activities. For the record, he didn't believe that either.

Greer lined up a difficult shot and made it, using a gentle slice stroke. Lockhart nodded his approval. They were playing as a team against two other gentlemen, industrial princes from the north. But Mercedes was claiming a lot of his concentration. She was up to something, but what?

Chapter Thirteen

'I think the arrangement will be to your liking.' Mercedes fixed the woman across from her with a confident stare over the rim of her teacup. The woman in question was none other than Mrs Booth, proprietress of Mrs Booth's Discreet Club for Gentlemen, located just off Royal Victoria Park.

The attractive businesswoman smiled back. 'Twenty per cent of whatever you make?' she clarified the terms.

'Twenty per cent.' Mercedes nodded. There were only so many places in a town where a girl could make money, 'discreet gentlemen's clubs' being one of them.

'I have to ask: why here?' Lucia Booth took a bite of lemon cake.

'I like your clientele,' Mercedes said easily. She'd done her research in the last week. Mrs Booth's was a familiar destination for many of the husbands of her newfound friends. It would provide her a little leverage should she need it. Mercedes leaned forwards, giving the impression she was about to impart a juicier answer. She lowered her voice to complete the impression. 'I'm going to play in the All England Billiards Championship, if I can raise the entrance fee.' It was true, too. She'd made up her mind ages ago when the tournament was first announced, but she still had to raise the entry fee. There was no way to raise that money in Brighton where everyone knew her.

Mrs Booth arched her dark brows. 'That would be something, to see a woman play.'

Mercedes caught the approval in the woman's voice. She set down her teacup and rose, wanting to end the interview on a positive note. 'I'll start tonight. I'll come in the back around nine o'clock.'

Mrs Booth rose with her. 'I'll be happy to have you. The men need a new distraction, but I want to be sure you understand.' She paused for a moment. 'You do know this is not your usual gentlemen's club?'

Mercedes knew very well what she meant.

Mrs Booth's wasn't a club like White's or Boodles or even the subscription rooms. Mercedes smiled. She'd have to have been blind not to notice this club's main attraction was its women. It was not so much a club as it was a brothel. Classy and elegant, it catered to rich gentlemen with discerning tastes. 'I know very well what this place is.'

'All right then, because I won't be tolerating any trouble from an angry husband, father, or brother, who comes looking for you.'

Mercedes thought of the wig and gorgeously provocative gown she had stashed in her wardrobe, acquired from a 'discreet' modiste in town who probably catered to the employees of the 'discreet gentlemen's club'. 'It will be as if I'm hardly here,' she promised with the glimmer of a mischievous smile.

Mrs Booth smiled back and extended her hand. 'Call me Lucia. I think we shall get along just fine.'

Indeed, one would have been hard pressed to recognise Mercedes when she arrived at Mrs Booth's that night in a deep-red gown trimmed in jet beads and cut shockingly low. The gown was expensively done and Mercedes felt decidedly wicked in it. The wig, purchased from the theatre company, was a soft brown, much lighter than her usual dark tresses. It was styled with braided loops to give the impression that her hair was pinned up. Together, the wig and the gown created a most tantalising image of a proper lady behaving badly, a juxtaposition that was certain to distract the gentlemen, if not drive them a little mad.

And it did. The gentlemen flocked to the table, eager to play at first out of novelty, then, seeing her true skill, out of desire to prove themselves. They vied for her attentions, they bought her glasses of champagne, from which she sipped delicately, careful not to overindulge. As the night wore on, she recognised a great many of them as the spouses of her friends, who'd come to the charms of Mrs Booth's establishment after having done their duty with their wives.

She'd known the nature of those society marriages, but encountering it first-hand was more difficult, especially when Lord Fairchild, well in his cups, made an inappropriate overture after losing a large sum to her at the table. Louisa would just die if she knew her husband had propositioned the billiards girl at Mrs Booth's. Mercedes fended him off with a smile and turned her attention to the next game.

* * *

The first three nights had been easy. She was trading on novelty. But by the fourth night, word had got around about the 'new feature' at Mrs Booth's and curiosity over the unknown had blossomed into interest. Everyone wanted to know who she was. She had a ready fiction to hand, of course, prepared for such an eventuality. She was Susannah Mason, a gambler's widow from Shropshire, whose husband had met his death in a duel over cards.

'Really?' Mr Ogilvy, who'd become a shockingly regular customer and loser at her table, shook his head one night and studied her sharply. 'I could have sworn you looked familiar.'

Mercedes placed a light hand on his arm and gave a throaty laugh. 'Some people believe we all have a twin somewhere in the world. Perhaps you've met mine?' The court gathered around the table laughed along with her.

'Who is next, gentlemen?' Mercedes called out, eager to play. Her nest egg for the entrance fee was coming along nicely. In a few more days she'd have it, which was well enough since her father didn't plan to stay in Bath much longer. She won the break and began to play, bending low over the table, letting the gown do its job.

But Ogilvy was persistent, not nearly as distracted by her bosom as he usually was. 'It's the wrong-coloured hair, of course—the person I'm thinking of has dark hair. She's a friend of my wife's. I've met her a few times on outings,' he mused out loud. His musings chilled her. When he didn't stop, Mercedes fixed him with one of her hard stares. She needed him to stop before he figured out her secret.

'Does your wife know you're here, Mr Ogilvy?' she asked pleasantly, taking time to chalk her cue.

He chuckled, as did the men around him. 'She knows I'm at my club.'

'Does she know what goes on here? Or does she think we sit around and talk politics all night?' Mercedes blew chalk from the tip, deliberately seductive, a fleeting thought about Greer's comments flitting through her mind.

The men laughed heartily. 'No, she doesn't know. That's the best part.' Ogilvy laughed loudly.

Mercedes silenced him with a look. 'Then you'd better hope you're mistaken about the resemblance, sir. I'd hate to tell her what you've

been up to with her money.' Helen Ogilvy had
let it drop in a private moment on a picnic that
Ogilvy had married her for her money to save
his ailing estate. He was in line to inherit his
uncle's baronetcy later, but while he waited he
hadn't a feather to fly with.

Ogilvy looked properly chastised and there
was no further comment about her appearance.

The evening had ended well. Mercedes had
paid Mrs Booth her fee, put her wig and gown
away at the club and headed home, tired but
pleased. Plan B was working splendidly. She
let herself into the house and stifled a scream
as a large hand covered her mouth and an arm
dragged her against the rock-solid wall of a
man's chest.

'Where have you been?' a voice growled in
her ear. Then she could smell him, the familiar scent of oranges. Greer.

He dropped his hand.

'Not in my bed, as you very well know.
Been checking my room, have you?'

'I was worried. I came home and you were
gone.'

'So you thought you'd scare me half to
death. Fine idea,' she scolded in a loud whisper before going on the offensive. 'What are

you doing home in the first place? Aren't you supposed to be playing?' She'd thought her father had arranged a private party at one of the subscription rooms tonight.

He wagged a finger at her in the darkness. 'Unh, unh, unh. No questions from you just yet. *You* were supposed to be with Elise Sutton at Mrs Pomfrey's musicale.'

'I was.' *For a while.* Until she'd claimed a headache and left for more lucrative climes. Musicales were not one of the places a girl could make money.

Greer danced her backwards towards a chair, both hands gripped her forearms. 'What's going on?' He pressed her down into the chair and took the one across from it, pulling the chair up close.

'Nothing is going on.' Mercedes tried to sound outraged at the accusation. 'Is my father home?'

Greer shook his head. 'No, he decided to stay on with some old friends who've just arrived in town. Now, don't try to change the subject. I know you're up to something. Tell me what it is.'

Mercedes crossed her arms. 'What makes you think I'm up to anything? I had a headache and came home. Later, I decided to go for a walk. I thought the fresh air might clear my head.'

Greer laughed, leaned forwards and took a deep breath. 'Mercedes, you smell.'

She probably did smell of Mrs Booth's. Mercedes seized the lapels of his evening wear and drew him close. 'Nobody likes a nosy parker, Greer,' she whispered low and throaty before she slanted her mouth over his. She'd meant to distract him, a game only. But it had been ages since she'd kissed him and it was like coming home. He tasted of brandy and wine, and his body was strong against her when she slid from her chair onto his lap. She kissed him slowly, tasting, drinking him. She was hungry for this man who was so handsome and good, a definite departure from the groping hands and crass innuendo of the supposed gentlemen at Mrs Booth's. Surely he wouldn't become like those other men, forsaking their wives for the momentary charms of expensive whores.

Her hands moved to his cravat, exquisitely tied as always. She yanked, rumpling all that perfection in a single pull. She tugged his shirt from his waistband, aware that her own skirts were high on her thighs, provocative and inviting as if she rode astride. She slid her hands under his shirt, moving up beneath the fabric to caress him, to trace the muscled contours of him. His hands tightened where they gripped her thighs, a groan escaping him.

'Mercedes, be careful,' came the hoarse warning, uttered with great effort. She was sure he was as uninterested in caution at the moment as she was.

'Are you afraid?' She reached a hand between them and cupped him through his trousers. God, he'd be magnificent. She would have slid to her knees and parted his thighs right then if he had not restrained her, his hands tight over hers in a halting gesture that kept her on his lap.

'Damn right I'm afraid, Mercedes. If you had any sense, you'd be afraid too.' He drew a ragged breath, one hand pushing back a strand of her hair that had come loose. His fingers skimmed her cheek. 'What is this, my dear? Just when I think I have you figured out, have "us" figured out, and I've resigned myself to understanding this is a just a game to you, you go and make it feel real.' He shook his head, his eyes holding hers. 'I can't be a game to you, Mercedes. And I don't think it can be a game to you either, whether you know it or not.'

She rose from his lap and shook down her

skirts. She turned away and focused her gaze out the window, gathering her thoughts. She wanted to shout at him, but what was there to accuse him of? The truth? Her hand closed over the star charm she wore at her neck. She hardly ever took it off. It was a way of keeping Greer close. He was right, he should be a game. But one could only imagine what would happen if she took anything with Greer seriously. A game was the only way she could have him and still protect herself.

She could feel him behind her, warm and near right before his hands closed gently over her shoulders. 'Don't mistake me, Mercedes. I would welcome you. I have only one rule: when you come to me, you need to mean it.'

'Is that how a gentleman issues a proposition?' Mercedes snapped, shaking off his hands. She was suddenly tired and irritable. She was not used to having her advances foiled. Most men fell at her feet for the merest tokens of affections and there'd been nothing 'mere' about what she'd been ready to offer Greer.

'No, it's how I tell you I'm perfectly aware you were using the sparks between us to distract me from the true purpose of our conversation.'

Good Lord, he was like a dog with a bone. She huffed and said nothing, but Greer moved away. She could hear his footsteps at the door, halting before he passed into the hall. 'One more thing, Mercedes, your defence could use a little work.'

Her defence? Having her own words thrown back at her sat poorly. Mercedes stood at the window a while longer, staring at the empty street and letting his comment settle. He was right. She'd had only the dandies and the young, bright-eyed officers of Brighton to practise on for so long. She had to remember she was dealing with a man now and a suspicious one at that; possibly the very last thing she needed when she was so close to her goal. Well, he'd have to work fast if he meant to catch her. Two nights more, and Susannah Mason would disappear from Mrs Booth's for good.

Greer lifted his champagne glass in yet another toast. The private room Lockhart had procured for the night was filled to bursting with gentlemen who'd come for one last party, one last chance to hobnob with the former billiards champion. It was time to go. The Bath Season would officially close in little less than a month, sending its society to the country for the summer or, for those who could afford it, on to London where they could join that season under full sail. Already, Greer could feel the social whirl slowing down in anticipation of that shift.

'You'll be in Brighton for the tournament, of course?' Mr Ogilvy asked at his elbow.

'Absolutely.' Greer nodded. The tournament was on his mind a great deal more these days. The sojourn in Bath had been illuminating. For the first time he was starting to see the possibilities. If he could manage to win…he could what? Open his own billiards parlour? His family would cringe at the thought. But it would be a lucrative business, something he could support himself with, something he'd made from his own talent. He didn't believe this would occur without risk. His family might very well shun him, but perhaps that would be their problem, not his.

'It'll be deuce quiet around here with you and Lockhart gone,' Ogilvy said into his drink, looking mournful at the prospect.

Greer shrugged. 'It'll be quiet anyway. The Season's closing down.' But he knew Lockhart's parties would be missed. They'd been lavish, male-only affairs that had promoted jovial camaraderie amongst men who'd been bored beyond words at the predictable social rounds of Bath, a predictable whirl that went on for eight months, October to June. Lockhart had chosen just the right time to show up. Greer wasn't surprised. His arrival had been purposely calculated to draw maximum attention.

'How about a game, one final opportunity for you to beat me?' Greer gestured towards the table where the cues laid crossed like swords and waiting. Ogilvy was always up for a game.

Ogilvy shook his head. 'No, I'm afraid not. I'm cleaned out.'

Greer raised an eyebrow in disbelief. Ogilvy was a fair player, the kind Lockhart hoped to see in Brighton. 'Really? You were up a few games when you left here last night.'

Ogilvy shook his head again. 'I went on to Mrs Booth's, you know, the ole balls and stick.'

Greer laughed and clapped Ogilvy on the back good-naturedly. 'You're a fine billiards player, Mr O., but cards are not your thing. When are you going to learn?' Not much of a card player himself, Greer had watched Ogilvy lose large sums on more than a few evenings.

'Wasn't at cards,' Ogilvy mumbled, hastily taking a drink.

Greer elbowed him. 'Do tell, Ogilvy. It sounds like there's a great story there.' They edged away from the crowd towards a potted palm decorating the room's perimeter.

'Well, it's that billiards girl Mrs Booth's got. Susannah Mason? Haven't you heard of her yet? She's only been there about three weeks.' Ogilvy tossed a look towards the group beyond them. 'Lots of the men have lost to her. Most are too embarrassed to mention it.'

'That explains why I haven't heard about her.' Greer grinned. It was a good thing Mercedes didn't know about her. Mercedes would be over at Mrs Booth's with a challenge within minutes—another good reason he and the Lockharts were leaving. If Mercedes knew there was a woman playing somewhere, *anywhere*, she'd be impossible for Lockhart to manage. Greer could imagine the scene that would ensue.

'I can't figure out if it's her skill or her gowns that make her so difficult to beat.' Ogilvy was going on about Susannah Mason. 'There's something familiar about her, but I can't place it. She's a card player's widow from Shropshire, said her husband was killed in a duel. It's all very dramatic.' Ogilvy gave a wave of his hand in dismissal, but Greer could see the man was quite taken with Susannah Mason.

Ogilvy put a hand on his sleeve. 'Say, why you don't come with me tonight? You can win my money back. I dare say you won't be as distracted by her charms. Not when you've got Miss Lockhart's attentions.'

It was on his lips to deny that he had Miss Lockhart's attentions, but Ogilvy was already back to his favourite subject of Susannah Mason. 'Then again, the way she blows chalk off her cue tip does all kinds of things to a man's insides, if you know what I mean.'

'Yes, I do believe I know.' Greer said slowly. His earlier thought returned. *If Mercedes knew a woman was playing.* There was no other woman, Greer would bet on it. It was her.

All the little oddities of the last weeks came together: Mercedes's apparent acceptance that she should turn her efforts to more feminine pursuits, her absence last night which might have been one of many. Who really knew what she got up to after he and Lockhart left her in the care of the lovely but sharp-minded Elise Sutton? Elise and Mercedes were thick as thieves these days.

'Shall we?' Ogilvy said.

'Yes,' Greer said grimly. 'Let's go and win your money back.'

Chapter Fourteen

'Double or nothing, then?' Mercedes laughed up at the young heir to an earldom. He was so *very* rich, but he was going to be a few pounds lighter when he left. She ran a light hand down his chest. The poor boy blushed, obviously revelling in being treated like the man he thought he was by a very beautiful woman who'd seemed to have stepped straight from his fantasies. Mercedes moved closer to him and flashed him a come-hither smile. 'Be warned, good sir, I can make that shot all night long.'

'It's true, she can. Your money is safer in your pocket.'

The all-too-familiar voice made her freeze. Good Lord, Greer was here! Mercedes turned from the young earl and faced him, her stomach plunging to her toes when she saw Ogilvy too. Had Ogilvy just happened to bring a friend? Or was something more malicious afoot? Had Ogilvy sold her out after all? He'd be very sorry when Helen heard about it. There was nothing for it but to brazen it out and hope for the latter while believing the former. Greer's comment left her very little room to pretend he didn't know it was her.

Mercedes smiled sweetly and sailed around the table. 'Mr Ogilvy, have you brought a friend?' She linked her arm through Ogilvy's and stared up at Greer, giving him an assessing once-over.

'This is Lord Captain Barrington of the Eleventh Devonshire.'

'Enchantée.' Mercedes unlinked her arm from Ogilvy's and performed a delicate curtsy, the gesture and the French compliments of Mrs Bouchard's Academy for Girls.

Greer took her hand and raised it, pressing his lips to her knuckles, conjuring up memories of the last time he'd done that. *'Mon plaisir,* Madam Mason.' He made her name sound deliciously sophisticated, drawing out the Mason to Ma-sown. *'Est-ce que vous jouez?'* She retrieved her hand and shot him a narrowed-eye look. He knew very well her French was limited to about ten useful phrases and *that*—whatever it was he'd said—wasn't one of them. She hadn't exactly excelled at French. She regretted telling him that during one of their long mornings in the carriage.

'I believe Bonaparte lost the war, Captain. We speak English at Mrs Booth's.' That brought a round of laughter from her court.

Greer wasn't daunted. He selected a cue and began to chalk up. 'Mr Ogilvy tells me you play a good game.' He glanced around the room, smiling broadly. 'Good enough to beat most of the gentlemen present on more than one occasion. He has compelled me to come and defend men everywhere.' He gave the chalk on his cue tip an efficient blow, looking entirely likeable.

'Hear, hear,' came a few cries from the back of the room.

The dratted man was going to steal her crowd if she wasn't careful. Usually she admired Greer's ease, how people *wanted* to cheer for him. She wasn't admiring that trait at the moment. Beneath his aura of bonhomie, he was primed, a veritable powder keg and the fuse was lit. He was going to ignite this room and she'd get caught in the explosion.

He didn't wait for an answer. Greer gathered up the balls and stepped back. 'Your table, Mrs Mason. You may break.'

'Your heart or your balls, Captain?' came a voice from the crowd. Mercedes smiled at the crass comment, privately reassured. She hadn't lost the room yet. And she wouldn't. She'd beat Greer and give these boys a show they wouldn't soon forget. After tonight there would be no coming back. Susannah Mason would go out in glory.

Mercedes met Greer's gaze down the length of the table, eyes wide with secret laughter, her mouth a perfect, discreetly rouged 'O.' A gentleman or two sighed when she chalked up and raised the cue to her lips in her trademark gesture and blew, knowing Greer would get the unspoken message: *game on.*

She bent low over the table, wriggling her shoulders to advantage; she sashayed up and down the table with a sway of her hips; she flashed coy smiles and sipped provocatively from champagne flutes until most men in the room were worked to a frenzy. All but one. Greer remained most disappointingly unaffected. Unaffected or not, it didn't mean he won. He lost the first game and the third, and was on the verge of losing the fifth if she potted her next shot. He seemed unbothered by the circumstance. He matched her mad flirtation with his dry humour. The room was enchanted by the pair of them goading each other to greater heights.

Every eye in the establishment was fixed on them. Money changed hands. Mrs Booth came to stand beside her, watching her sink a shot with the cue behind her back to general applause.

The proprietress applauded, too, but when Mercedes stepped from the table, she pressed a wad of pound notes into Mercedes's hand and whispered fiercely, 'End it with your next shot. I don't care if you win or lose, just do it quickly. Your little duel with the Captain isn't doing business any good. The girls haven't been upstairs with a customer for an hour.'

Greer made his next shot, which would prolong the game. If he'd missed, she'd have had a clear path to victory in one shot. But now they were even and a ball of his blocked her play. Mercedes had no choice but to scratch. She recited the old gambler's mantra in her head: sometimes we win by losing. The wad of notes in her hand proved it. But pride made it deuced hard to swallow that reality. She didn't *want* to lose here or now or to Greer, who had somehow ferreted out her little gambit and had come to ruin her fun.

But she did it, hitting her cue ball too hard and letting it follow its target into the pocket. The crowd groaned. She groaned, too, but pasted on a smile as if it were a trifling thing and called for champagne all around. This got the girls circulating again, moving in and out of the press with trays of bubbling champagne, turning the gentlemen's attentions elsewhere.

Mrs Booth appeared at her side once more, ushering her and Greer into the hall. She was eager to be rid of them. 'Why don't the two of you settle up privately? Susannah, you can use Lisette's room at the top of the stairs.' Lisette had left yesterday for a more private arrangement with a well-to-do gentleman.

Mercedes understood it wasn't a request: it was a command. But she didn't relish facing Greer behind a closed door, especially if he had the upper hand. She made her choice in an instant. She was *not* going to let him take the offensive and berate her. No doubt he would view this latest behaviour as being entirely beyond the pale. A lady playing billiards in a brothel was almost inconceivable to one of his lofty birth. What he needed to understand was that she was as angry with him as he was with her. He could have jeopardised everything. The moment the door shut behind them, she faced him, hands on hips, and fired her salvo. 'What the hell do you think you're doing?'

'Isn't that supposed to be my line?' Greer crossed his arms. Her verbal offensive had caught him by surprise. He'd anticipated having the first words in this conversation. And the last. But he should have known she wouldn't play by the rules.

'Let's be clear, Mercedes, *you* are the one in trouble here, not me.'

'Me? I'm not the one poking his nose into someone else's business. You could have ruined everything tonight!' She flung an arm in a careless gesture that nearly knocked a pitcher off a delicate table. Greer reached out and righted the teetering vessel, taking a moment to get a grip on his vacillating emotions. He should be furious over *her* taking him to task in the middle of a French whore's boudoir, yet all he wanted to do was kiss her or spank her. At the moment, it was hard to decide which. Both held some appeal.

'Me? *I'm* not the one playing billiards in a brothel, dressed in disguise—' Greer ticked off her sins on his fingers '—and using a false name while emptying the pockets of your friends' husbands.' Lockhart would be furious if he knew she'd been stealing money he saw as rightfully his to win or if being beaten by a woman had scared the men away from the Brighton tournament altogether.

'It serves them right. They shouldn't be here to start with. They should be home with their wives. If they were, none of this would have happened.' Mercedes reached up her arms in a motion that brought her breasts into tight relief against the bodice of her gown and began to remove the wig. Definitely spanking, Greer thought.

Greer laughed. 'Only you would be able to turn *your* transgression into a moral judgement on your fellow mankind. You make it sound like you've been serving up matrimonial justice instead of simply fleecing them.'

She shook out her hair, a sensual gesture that put kissing back in the lead, but her lips tightened. Her eyes narrowed to blue slits. 'My transgression? I made money the only way I knew how.'

'By flirting with them? I saw what you were doing to that poor lad in there. He didn't know up from down with your hand on his chest.

You knew very well you'd have him at a disadvantage,' Greer accused. He knew he played the hypocrite here. He'd been as riveted as the next red-blooded male. She'd been intoxicating to watch. She'd commanded every man's full attention, giving them their fantasies in the flesh. There wasn't an Englishman in the room who wouldn't go home and dream about her tonight.

Greer's groin tightened at the memory of her leaning over the table, the naughty fire in her eyes indicating she knew precisely what he was thinking as she let the cue slide through the bridge of her fingers in erotic reference to other sticks that slid and sheathed themselves in other warmer, wetter portals.

Mercedes circled him, her coy half-smile flitting on her lips, one hand trailing idly over the shepherds and Staffordshire dogs littering the surfaces of the room. Apparently Lisette had packed in a hurry. Must have been a good offer, Greer thought wryly. Mercedes drew a long finger down the back of a pointer, causing him to repress a most male shudder. He could feel that finger on him, caressing, teasing, drawing its manicured nail ever so lightly down something much more worthy

than a china dog. At least he thought he had
suppressed it. Her next words confirmed he
might not have been so successful.

'Jealous, were you?'

It was an obvious gambit and she knew very
well what she was doing with her dog-tracing
act just as she'd known the effect she'd had all
night. He really should spank her. She was in
desperate need of a lesson. She was trying to
provoke him.

'Jealous? Of middle-aged men and boys
without beards? Hardly.' For a moment he entertained the notion that he should resist. Then
he thought better of it. No. She would expect
resistance. She was planning to lay siege to
him. Not tonight. If there was any mastering
to be done, it would be by him.

Greer picked up her trail, tracking her
around the room. He wanted her to know he
was coming, wanted her to anticipate the moment he would catch her. He reached for her
arm and spun her around to face him, drawing her to him. 'You should play with a real
man, Mercedes.'

Her breath hitched, her pupils dilated with
excitement. 'I suppose you think that's you?'

'Damn straight it's me,' Greer growled right
before he bore her back to the wall.

* * *

Mercedes stifled a gasp. She barely had time to wrap her arms about his neck before she found herself pressed deliciously against the pink-and-cream-striped wall, Greer's lips hard at her mouth, his hips grinding against hers in provocative invitation, his desire in rampant evidence where their bodies met. Her breath came uneven and excited as she let the thrill of excitement course through her. He wasn't the only one burning with need. He'd stoked fires of his own tonight.

Her hands made short work of his waist-coat and turned their attentions to the tails of his shirt, pulling them loose from his trousers in frantic jerks valued more for speed than efficiency. She wanted him naked—fast. He seemed to share her thoughts. In all her con-centration on his clothes, her own gown had found its way to the floor in an ignoble heap. She hitched a leg about his hip, her petticoat falling back to reveal a long expanse of leg. Greer's hand took the invitation, sliding up its length to cup her bottom beneath the fabric.

The act put her in intense proximity with the most male parts of him. She could feel the intimate swell of him at the juncture of her thighs. She nipped at his ear none too gently to convey her growing urgency. 'Magnificent' might not do it justice. 'Greer, these trousers have to go. Now.' She didn't wait for an answer. She pulled them down herself, swallowing hard when her hand met with the coveted length of his flesh, hot and rigid in her palm.

Greer wouldn't tolerate any play when she made to explore. 'Later,' came the gruff response. But he was right. They were both too far gone to enjoy any foreplay. What they wanted would be explosive and fast and it would happen against this wall.

He lifted her other leg and she wrapped them both about him, finding purchase between his strength and the unyielding wall. He took her then, in a fierce thrust that went straight to her core and wrenched a wicked scream from her throat. This was decadence and pleasure at its finest. She dug her hands into the thick depths of his hair and tightened her grip, holding him deep inside her as she moved her hips to his rhythm. She gloried in the intimate friction of his body inside hers. He shifted slightly, adjusting his position and thrust.

A gasp slipped her lips. She'd not been ready for the unexpected sensation it invoked. Her mind registered only one thought: more.

And yet more of such an exquisite glimpse of pleasure would surely drive her mad. But Mercedes was no coward; she'd risk it. 'Again!' she managed, her voice nothing more than a wispy tremble before that singular glimpse transformed into a wave of sensations that threatened to overwhelm her.

She rode that wave, bucking hard against Greer, vaguely aware that he was there with her too in this frenzied roil of rough desires. His hands were hard where they dug into her buttocks, his body heated with exertion as its very life pulsed against her, his voice hoarse with inarticulate need as they crested one final time and the wave broke, spilling them into a sweat-slicked oblivion of sated need.

Mercedes was boneless, useless in the dénouement that followed. It was Greer who brought them to the pink haven of the bed, seeing her settled before he gave in to his own, no doubt considerable, exhaustion. Mercedes felt the bed take his weight as he lay down beside her on the satin sheets. She snuggled into him, her head fitted to the curve of his shoulder, feeling the welcome strength of his arm gather her to him.

Within moments his breathing took on the soft pattern of one asleep. For a while she thought she'd sleep too. She was tired enough. But her mind would not comply. It was still too riotous, sorting through the images of what had transpired. Most of it she understood in an objective sense. Weeks on the road suppressing desires had come to a head, goaded in no small part by the circumstances of the evening and the reality that they'd been attracted to one another from the start. She'd seen it coming, and no doubt Greer had too for all his talk of honour. It had just been a matter of when. She could explain the 'when' and the 'why'. She couldn't explain the 'what' or the 'how'.

The 'what' that had passed between them had no comparison in her previous experience. She'd known such satisfaction was possible for the man, although perhaps not on such a grand scale as Greer's. But the same for a woman? She'd not known, not *imagined* there was anything more beyond the short-lived gratification of simply being physically close to another human being.

She laughed softly to herself, recalling Greer's words so long ago: *'Mine was better, much better.'* She might have to concede that it hadn't been mere male braggadocio speaking that day in the carriage.

The other unknown was the 'how'. How

did one go forwards with any normality after such an encounter? She would forever look at him over the dinner table or down the length of a billiards table and see not just Captain Greer Barrington of the fine manners but her *lover*, a man who had brought her unparalleled pleasure. The issue of pleasure raised another question altogether—how would she be satisfied with just the once? Pleasure like that should be tasted over and over.

She knew without being told it would become an addiction, one she'd have to find a way to live without when this tour was done and Greer Barrington went his own way. She was not fool enough to think such pleasure could be repeated with any man. Empirically, she knew it could not, which made what had happened all that more unique for its rarity.

Mercedes sighed, trailing a finger down his breastbone.

It was no wonder he'd said it couldn't be a game. She agreed whole-heartedly now, when it was too late and she was fully engaged. If the damage was already done, she might as well enjoy sweeping up. Mercedes moved her hand lower.

He awoke to her gentle cupping. She smiled up at him, pleased that his phallus stirred so easily to her touch even after a hearty bout of love-making. She'd feared he'd be spent. She should have known better. There was nothing weak about Greer Barrington. Mercedes reached behind his phallus and squeezed his balls, feeling them tighten. 'You're ready, Captain.' She looked at him from beneath coy eyelashes. 'Unless you need a bit more encouragement?'

Greer rolled to his side. 'I think that depends on what you have in mind.'

'A little equality.' Mercedes slid from the bed with a grin and stood before him, her arms crossed over her breasts in a provocatively modest display, her hands resting on the shoulders of her chemise. She slipped her thumbs under the thin fabric and pulled the garment ever so slowly over her head, letting it tease her nipples as it passed over her chest.

'Naked equality. I like it,' Greer managed hoarsely after the chemise had been discarded.

'Seductive equality,' Mercedes corrected, pulling the drawstring of her petticoat in a quick, decisive tug that rendered the item loose. She stepped out of it, aware of his eyes roaming her nude body with hot appreciation.

She came to bed and straddled him, letting him look his fill. '*I* mean to have *you* this time, Captain.' It was a wicked, selfish experiment she had in mind. Could the pleasure be repeated? Or had it existed because he'd been in charge? Did he control the pleasure or could she snare it for herself?

He raised his hands and filled them with her breasts, kneading in slow, delicious motions that stirred her fires. She could feel her control slipping away already. The effect he had on her was intoxicating, quite literally like drinking too much champagne, the world turning to a lovely place with blurred edges.

'You are more beautiful than I dreamed,' Greer murmured, raising himself up to kiss her, one hand leaving a breast to take up residence at the nape of her neck beneath her loose hair. The ingenuousness of his words was nearly her undoing. She'd been called beautiful before, but never with such sincerity.

'And you, sir, are a paragon of manhood.' She let the laughter dance in her eyes, as she raised herself up over his hips and then lowered, taking him inside as he'd taken her. 'It seems we are well suited.' A seductive smile played across of her lips.

'It seems we are.' Greer's eyes were dark with passion, his body tense beneath her as she began to ride. Slowly, up and down, she tight-

ened her inner muscles as she slid the length of
him, feeling him strain against her. Then she
began to rock, back and forth, and the magic
ignited.

Greer surged into her, arching in his need,
his body and mind wild at the sight of her atop
him, her hands cupping her own breasts. She
revelled in the thrill of Greer Barrington unleashed, unbound by his gentleman's code of
conduct in these unguarded moments, but the
madness was taking her too. The harder she
rode him, the more intense his response until
they were on that wave once more, cresting
and crashing and the amazing thing was happening again, sweeping her away, her wicked
experiment in shambles. Now she knew and
that knowledge cast a shadow over the future.
To achieve this pleasure, she needed him.

Chapter Fifteen

He needed her. That much was clear and nothing else. Greer would bet she was feeling something of the same. It was as good an explanation as any as to why Mercedes had elected to ride inside the carriage, *alone*, on a splendid morning as they pulled out of Bath. Lockhart had thought nothing of her decision. He'd dismissed the choice as female foibles. 'She wants to collect herself after saying farewell to all of her friends.'

To be sure, there'd been tearful goodbyes on the steps of the terrace house this morning. A large group of women had turned out to see Mercedes off. Mercedes had energised Bath. Her presence would be missed. Elise Sutton had hugged Mercedes tightly, whispered something in her ear and promised to see her in Brighton later in the summer. But Greer doubted such farewells had moved Mercedes as much as they had moved the women who gave them. *They* hadn't spent the night in a brothel 'settling things', to use Mrs Booth's phrase.

Settling wasn't the word Greer would use to describe what had happened in that room either. Unsettling was more apt. Bedding Mercedes had been an extraordinary moment out of time. If he could just leave it at that—an experience fomented by circumstance—things would be fine. But he couldn't leave it as a singular event and simply forget it. He'd had a few moments like that in his past, enough to know this wasn't one of them. Many officers did. Alone and far from home, he'd sought a night or two of temporary company from women whose names and faces had long since ceased to feature in his memory.

Such behaviour wasn't his usual habit, though, and he normally regretted it afterwards. Unlike many of his acquaintances, he'd never made a practice of treating sex as a mere physical exercise. He preferred more meaningful, long-term *affaires*. Although he'd had lovers over the years, he did not take just anyone to his bed for the sheer sake of a partner, which was why the incident with Mercedes last night had been so unsettling.

Those were poor choices of words. *Incident?* What had happened could not be classified as a mere instance. *Had been?* Still was. Once they'd returned home, he'd slept restlessly for the remainder of the night. From the dark shadows under Mercedes's eyes this morning, she had too. All of which proved that last night had meant far more to them than either had intended. It wasn't the culmination of a month's worth of flirtation. It was the beginning of something new.

Lockhart brought his horse up alongside, cheerful and oblivious to the dilemmas running through Greer's head. 'We're about three days out of Birmingham.' He was already planning the next stage. 'It's not a pretty city, but it's an interesting one. We'll only stay a few days, long enough to spread word about the tournament and whet a few appetites. There are adventurers in Birmingham—our kind of people, Captain.'

Greer cringed at the reference to 'our kind of people'. Lockhart was an intriguing man, to be sure, and there was much to admire about his journey in life. But it wasn't Greer's life and it wasn't Greer's journey. They had billiards in common and this brief interlude was a fascinating departure from Greer's regular patterns. But beyond that? The more he knew about Allen Lockhart, the harder it was to respect him. He and Lockhart operated by very different codes of ethics.

He'd watched Lockhart work the men in Bath, dining out on his celebrity status, entertaining in lavish style. It was a fascinating study in human nature. Lockhart had made those men believe they possessed a potential they didn't truly have and Lockhart *knew* it. Greer didn't want to be that sort of a man, a confidence man, a hustler.

'Do you think many of the gentlemen in Bath will come to Brighton?' Greer voiced his thoughts out loud.

Lockhart nodded. 'Yes. A few of them will play in the tournament. Perhaps Ogilvy will play. But most of them will come to watch, which is exactly what we want. The presence of peers will lend a certain cachet to the event and they'll bring money to town.'

He gave Greer a shrewd look. 'Money is good for everyone. All the businesses will prosper. There won't be an empty inn within five miles of Brighton. People need food and drink and subsidiary entertainment. *And...*' he paused here, drawing out the word for emphasis, 'those gentlemen might not play in the tournament, but they *will* play their own informal games in the subscription rooms around town. Everyone will benefit,' he repeated with a smile.

Lockhart lowered his voice although there was no one around on the empty road. 'Remember this—when the time comes, there's often more money to be made outside the venue than in. The tournament is just the draw, just the lure to bring in the money. The real money will be made elsewhere.' Lockhart laughed. 'I can see I've stunned you. It's not what you expected?'

Frankly, it wasn't. He'd taken this tour far too literally. He'd thought Lockhart had been looking for players when, in reality, Lockhart had been looking for spectators. Lockhart hadn't solely been out drumming up games when he went on ahead. He'd been drumming up business too. He'd probably been making arrangements for ale and food to be brought in. He'd buy it cheap from country vendors who had no way to get their goods beyond the local markets of their villages and then sell it high in Brighton, a simple case of supply and demand.

Lockhart laughed. 'Why would I need players, Captain, when I have you? You're my man. I'd back you against anyone in England, and in July I will.' He favoured Greer with a warm smile. 'You're one of the finest natural players of the game I've ever seen, Captain. You remind me of myself when I was younger, only you've got something I never had, something intangible that I can't name. But all the same, I know you've got it.'

It was elaborate flattery and Greer knew he should be wary of it, but it was nice to hear anyway, a type of reinforcement that he could make his own way if he chose. Lockhart was going on about Birmingham, the canals and the pioneering spirit of the city. Greer let him. Lockhart was good at one-sided conversation. He had other things to think about, like what to say to Mercedes when they stopped for lunch. There'd been no time to speak that morning amid the bustle of last-minute packing but they needed to talk, the sooner the better. A man didn't make love to a woman and then pretend it hadn't happened.

The northern roads towards Birmingham were well populated with villages and it was no trouble to find a promising inn for lunch.

The inn Lockhart chose had plank tables set up outside for guests to enjoy the weather and pretty flower boxes spilling with spring blooms, hanging from its windows.

Mercedes was reserved during lunch. Lockhart tried to draw her out with talk of her new friends. 'Elise Sutton's father has a new design for a yacht. I'm thinking of investing. He means to race the prototype next year. If it works out, everyone will want his plans.'

Mercedes smiled at her father's effort. 'Elise works very closely with him.' Greer could hear the carefully veiled barb.

Lockhart reached across the table and tapped Mercedes on the nose in a fatherly gesture. 'That gives us something else in common with them, my dear. It's a smart man who knows the value of a daughter. I knew I liked them. I'll definitely invest then, for the principle of the matter if nothing else.'

The look Mercedes shot her father was icily polite before she turned her attentions back to nibbling at the delicious meat pies. His own was nearly gone. It did amaze Greer that Lockhart with his commendable people skills could be so continually obtuse when it came to his own daughter. Mercedes had not forgiven him for Bath. But then again, people often missed what was right under their own noses.

Greer had just taken a healthy gulp of ale when Lockhart spoke again. 'I was so very proud of you in Bath, Mercedes.'

The man's daughter had been playing billiards in a brothel. Greer choked and Lockhart had to hit him on the back. All those outings and card parties had been a giant smokescreen for her clever little gambit. But for what? He still hadn't worked that part out. There'd been a table in their home. She could have played privately as much as she wanted. What had she needed that required such a venue as Mrs Booth's?

Across the table, Mercedes smiled, apparently finding the same ironic humour in Lockhart's comment as he did. 'I enjoyed Bath a great deal,' was all she said, but her eyes found his and he read a good deal into her simple statement, punctuated with the caress of a foot against his leg beneath the table.

'I enjoyed Bath greatly too.' Greer held her gaze for a moment, sending an unspoken message of his own. It was definitely time to get Mercedes alone. He rose before Lockhart could launch into a discussion of Birmingham. There would be days to talk about that. Right now, he just wanted to talk to Mercedes. 'I noticed some decent-looking shops when we entered town. Would you like to take a stroll before we depart?' He directed the offer at Mercedes, knowing Lockhart would be busy overseeing the horses.

They walked the short distance to the shops in silence, Greer rapidly assessing and discarding conversational openers: 'About last night…' No, too clichéd. 'We need to talk…' No. That sounded too dire. He didn't want her to panic. Good Lord, how hard could it be? He was an officer, for heaven's sake. He'd given more than one inspirational speech to his troops, encouraging men to make impossible stands on battlefields. Surely he could talk to one woman? It wasn't as if he hadn't talked to women before or even about things as delicate as the 'day after'.

But this was Mercedes he was talking to. She was bold and brash. She didn't need him to gingerly and correctly address the subject. She'd want him to be witty, perhaps even to attack the subject with a certain amount of insouciance regardless of the real, deeper feelings provoked by their night.

Greer smiled. He knew how to start. They

stopped to study the items in what passed for this little town's idea of an 'emporium'.

'It doesn't have to be a dismal, messy foray into curiosity.' *I enjoyed the pleasure we found with one another last night.*

'No, it certainly doesn't.' *I enjoyed it too.* They were getting quite skilled at this gambit of staring into store windows and delivering oblique words about important things. The word was not the thing. The subtext was.

'Experiences like that are not commonplace.' *I do not make a habit of one-night encounters. What happened between us was explosive and powerful and not to be taken for granted. Should we risk repeating it? Not just the sex, but what it implies—that there is a relationship of note between us?*

Mercedes turned from the window. It was her indicator that the gambit was over. 'I don't know how to answer,' she said softly. The admission was so entirely out of character for her that Greer was stunned. Mercedes *always* knew what to say, what to do. She was always so utterly in charge of herself and her situation. She knew how to use the lightest of touches, the smallest of smiles to her advantage. But he'd managed to render her guileless.

'I don't believe it. The great Mercedes

Lockhart is at a loss,' he cajoled, trying to fight back his own rising panic. What would he do if she said there could be nothing more? 'Is that good or bad?'

Mercedes shook her head. 'I don't honestly know.' She tugged at his arm and they continued their walk down the street to the end of the shops where the village gave into the countryside. 'What shall we do, Greer? Shall we become lovers? Is that what you want?' She was cool now that the empty countryside permitted free speaking. Maybe he'd been wrong to open with concealed wit. Maybe he should have cut straight to the chase: *I want you.*

'I don't think it's up to me alone to decide.' Greer matched her coolness. 'What do *you* want?' He thought about her foot under the table. It *seemed* obvious.

'I know what I *don't* want. I don't want an impulsive decision leading to a disastrous conclusion.' That sounded more like the Mercedes he had come to know: collected and in control. Her sudden lapse had passed. 'The fact is, Greer, we don't know where this *affaire* will lead and we have a lot riding on this trip. Perhaps it's not in our best interest to pursue a romantic attachment at this time. Perhaps we should wait until the tournament is over and assess our feelings then.' Then two steps back.

Greer stared at her in astonishment. She made it sound like a business contract. As for waiting until the tournament was over, that was almost a month away. He'd go mad by then. 'Do you doubt me?'

He could manage that. He could prove to her his feelings were genuine. Another more sobering thought occurred to him. 'Or is it that you doubt *your* feelings?' His anger was starting to rise. He sensed yet another of her exquisitely constructed smokescreens hiding true motives. 'Because if that's the case, I've got to tell you, your feelings were pretty clear last night.' He'd thought last night had been special to her too. Had he been that wrong? All this time he'd been thinking she was worrying over how to face him, how to delicately let him know what last night had meant to her. That hadn't been it at all.

'Is this what you've been sitting in the carriage all morning thinking about? How to put me off without endangering your father's little tournament? How to deter me without your father losing me?' In Bath, it had been her biggest fear—that he'd leave. He should have remembered. Instead, he'd given her womanly sensibilities too much credit. They'd come to a large spreading chestnut. He leaned against the trunk, arms crossed, daring her to admit to it.

'No, that's not it at all.' Something akin to genuine hurt flashed in her grey eyes. 'I was thinking of *your* best interests.' Her voice was sharp and low. She stood just inches from him, her colour high. His desire for her stirred. A woman shouldn't look so beautiful when she was rejecting a man. They'd have been better off standing in front of the store window with their masked conversation. This plain speaking exposed too much. No wonder society didn't recommend it.

'Listen to me, Greer. Last night was supposed to have been wild, a moment out of time fuelled by emotions.' She mirrored his earlier sentiments exactly. He supposed it was reassuring to know they'd started that spiral into passion with the same intentions. But what she said next transfixed him. 'Then it became...' she glanced down at her hands '...*more*.' She looked up at him, her soul evident in her grey eyes as she uttered the next, 'It wasn't supposed to, but it did.' *And if it keeps happening, we might both end up with far more than we sought.*

That's when the truth hit him. She hadn't

known. He'd been the first to show her true
pleasure, something beyond the physical.

'There *can* be more, Mercedes.' Relief was
swamping him. She wasn't rejecting him. She
was just nervous, on unfamiliar ground, which
he suspected happened very rarely to Mercedes Lockhart. He wanted to kiss her, to re-
assure her they could manage this. He reached
for her but Mercedes warded him off with a
nearly imperceptible shake of her head. 'Wait.
You have to promise me one thing, Greer.'

'What? Anything.' She could have asked for
a hair off the head of the Emperor of China. He
would have promised anything, too, in those
moments. Desire was riding him hard. But not
so hard that he'd forgot the lesson of last night.
Mercedes didn't play by the rules.

'That you won't fall in love with me.'

He wanted to laugh at the request but something in her gaze held him back. 'Would it be
so terrible if I did?'

'Disastrous. Promise me?' She was in deadly
earnest.

'All right. I promise.' But his fingers were
crossed, thank goodness, because he suspected
he already had.

What had she done? Mercedes was still
wondering that very same thing as she dressed

for dinner that night. She'd allowed herself
to commit to a relationship with Greer Barrington, something she'd vowed not to do
when this crazy adventure of her father's had
begun. It had not been her intention when
she'd started that conversation after lunch.
She'd spent all morning in the carriage re-
hearsing and reasoning.

She'd had her night; the mystique of him
had been resolved. She had her entry fee. She
needed to focus on the tournament, not a relationship that was bound to be short-lived. It
wouldn't last past Brighton. If she faced him
in the tournament, she'd have to beat him and
he would hate her for it. Until then, though, he
might love her, for a little while. It was hard to
convince herself it wouldn't be worth it.

Mercedes dug through her jewellery case
until she found a pair of small pearl earrings.
She laughed at herself as she put them on. It
was ridiculous, really, pearl earrings to dine
at an inn, albeit an upscale one. It was a sign
of how far she'd fallen. Being with Greer was
either the bravest or dumbest thing she'd ever
done.

In either case, it was definitely selfish. She'd
wanted him, had wanted him from that first
night in the garden. Even then the risks had

been obvious to her, and then, like now, she'd given them no regard. She'd brazened ahead, taking what she wanted and now here she was dressing for dinner at an inn as if it were a lord's manor.

Mercedes gave her hair a final look in the small mirror and smoothed the skirts of her pale peach gown—a perfect affair for early summer in light layers of chiffon, one of the Season's preferred fabrics according to the magazines out of London. She stared at her reflection a moment longer and took the opportunity to give herself a strong reminder. *Be careful.* This was how it had started the last time she'd got into trouble over a man. Luce Talmadge had been debonair and ultimately very persuasive to a young girl's heart. He, too, had been a special favourite of her father's and she'd ended up…well, she'd ended up in a very bad position with him. Enough said.

A knock on the door ended that bout of self-talk. Mercedes answered the door and smiled. Greer stood there, ready to take her down to supper in the private parlour. He, too, had taken care with his appearance, changing out of his travelling clothes into a jacket of blue superfine that did dazzling things to his eyes, buff trousers and a gold-on-gold paisley-patterned waistcoat with the popular shawl collar.

'I like the waistcoat,' Mercedes complimented appreciatively, linking her arm through his. 'Is it new?' She couldn't recall him having worn it before.

'I had it ordered in Bath. Tonight seemed like a good night to break it in.' Greer covered her hand with his where it lay on his arm. The gesture sent a shot of heat to her belly and a gambler's deadliest mantra to her head: *This time it will be different.* If gamblers didn't believe that, a whole lot more of them would walk away from the table a whole lot sooner and richer.

But Greer wasn't anything like Luce Talmadge. Besides, Greer had *promised* not to fall in love with her and a gentleman never broke his word. It was flimsy reassurance at best when he was looking at her with those hot eyes as if he would not only devour her right there on the stairs but would protect her from anyone else who tried to do the same.

Dinner was a festive affair with an excellent roasted beef, fresh vegetables from the local market and newly baked bread, accompanied by a good bottle or two of red wine. Luxurious by country standards, the meal was simple enough to be a welcome departure from the richer meals they'd eaten in Bath.

The three of them had the night off, her father declared with a flourish, pouring a second bottle of wine. There was no billiards table at this particular establishment, although her father had heard there was one in the assembly rooms down the street. He thought he might take a stroll in that direction but Greer needn't come.

'That is if you two are all right on your own?' her father asked solicitously. 'I could stay in and we could all play cards.'

'We'll be fine,' Mercedes assured him. Under the table, she kicked off a slipper and ran a foot up Greer's leg, attempting to finish what she'd started at lunch. 'Maybe we'll take a walk before the light fades.' It wouldn't be a very long walk. She knew exactly what she wanted to do with Greer and it did not involve walking or playing cards.

She found a sensitive spot on the back of his calf with her toe and watched him stiffen in response. She hid her laughter in her wine glass. Dinner finished quickly after that. Her father was eager to get to the assembly room and she was eager to get...well, frankly, to her room and do some assembling of her own, or dissembling as the case might be.

'You're a very naughty girl, Mercedes,' Greer said once her father had departed.

'It's not my fault you're ticklish behind your knee.'

'Truly, Mercedes, at the table? In front of your father?' He finished the last of his wine and set his glass down.

Mercedes could hear the evidence of humour in his voice. 'It wasn't in front of him. Technically. Besides, I'm twenty-three years old, far too old to be daddy's little girl.' *He'd want me to have you, anyway. It would be good for him*, came the unbidden thought. It was a most uncharitable idea and one she hadn't had for quite some time, at least not since their arrival in Bath.

On the heels of her quarrel with her father in Beckhampton, she'd been far too focused on raising her own stake for the tournament to give much thought to manipulating Greer. In Bath, she'd hardly seen him in a billiards context. Her contact with him, while extensive, had been limited to the social, and her needs had taken precedence. Now that her place in the tournament was secured and the whirl of Bath was behind them, the old thoughts had nothing to hold them back. It was a most un-settling realisation following the commitment she'd made today to Greer and a reminder that there was more than one way she could hurt him in all this. He would be devastated if he ever believed the passion between them had been nothing more than a means to an end. There were two things she hoped he would never find out about her. That was one of them.

'What are you thinking, Mercedes? You've gone quiet.' Greer's own foot was starting to caress a trail up her leg.

'I'm thinking we should take that walk. Then, when my father asks in the morning what we've been up to, we can tell him the truth.'

Greer laughed at that and pushed back his chair, feet games forgot. 'Ah, verisimilitude at its finest, the impression of truth. Perhaps we'll note a few minor landmarks on the way to add more credence to our claim.'

The evening was fair and other couples were out strolling the High Street of the small town. A warm tremor of satisfaction rippled through her at the notion; they were a couple. For a little while, she was Greer's. She should enjoy the moment and not worry so much how it would end. After all, she already knew it would and that was half the battle. It meant no unpleasant surprises.

'People are staring,' Mercedes noted as they made another pass down the street.

Greer seemed unbothered by it. He put his mouth close to her ear so as not to be over-heard. 'Of course they are, that's the purpose of all this, isn't it? This is their version of so-ciety. They'll go home and talk about who was with whom and what they wore and it will keep them busy until tomorrow night when they do it all over again. It's no different than London or Bath, just a smaller scale.'

'Much smaller.' Mercedes laughed.

'Italy has a similar custom,' Greer said, helping her over a muddy spot in the street. 'It's called *passeggiata*. Literally, it means a slow walk. Every night, people come out into the piazzas and stroll for hours, talking and showing off new clothes.'

'Showing off new loves too, I should think.' Mercedes said the first thing that came to mind. 'It would be the perfect way for a woman to say "stay away, he's mine now."'

Greer chuckled. 'My, my, my, what a cal-culating little mind you have, Miss Lockhart. Can't it just be for fun?'

She immediately felt guilty. It would be nice

to have part of her mind reserved to see things as 'just for fun'. 'It sounds lovely,' she said, trying to make up for her callous comment. 'I have to admit, most of my social experiences have been overlaid with a heavy dose of calculation: the right dress, the right information about a guest used at just the right time to flatter him.' She shrugged an apology.

'Like the night I came to dinner?' Greer asked softly, though there was an underlying edge to the question. They'd come to an intersection and Greer pulled her aside into a quiet street of closed shops. 'I was supposed to meet you that night despite your protests to the contrary. I remember exactly what you said: "My father doesn't need me to vet half-pay officers."'

He paused and searched her face. 'You wore a blue dress a shade darker than the dining room. You looked like you'd been posed for a portrait, so beautiful, so perfect. How much of that was for me?'

'I would have dressed well for the party regardless. My father wanted to sell tables that night.'

'Mercedes, tell me the truth.' His voice held the sharpness of steel in the gathering dusk. She hadn't come out here to fight. 'Your father knew I wouldn't be buying any tables and yet *you*, arguably your father's finest, most persuasive weapon, sat next to me.' A dangerous realisation lit his eyes and Mercedes opted for honesty. Greer would not tolerate a lie. Why did he have to ask these questions now?

Her chin went up. 'I watched you play at the club through a peephole. My father wanted my opinion of your skill.'

'And when I passed inspection, I was invited to dinner to meet you personally.' Greer finished for her. He gave a wry half-smile. 'You've been coaching me from the start, since that very first dinner.' He waved a hand in vague gesture. 'Is that why you don't want me to love you? You're afraid I'll discover I've been nothing but another Lockhart pawn?' Greer drew a deep breath. 'And when you wagered the road against the envelope?'

This was decidedly uncomfortable territory. She feared Greer was slipping away from her already, convinced she was in some conspiracy with her father, that she had used him, maybe was still using him. She had to act fast or her own little *passeggiata* was going to come to a screeching, disastrous halt. 'Your own chivalry worked against you. I didn't ask you to bet the envelope.'

'But you threw the second game, knowing I'd feel badly about beating you twice.'

'Your tendencies are not my fault,' Mercedes argued, thinking how much he'd changed since then. He was far less vulnerable to that strategy, thanks to her. That was one lesson he'd learned well.

Greer gave a self-deprecating laugh. 'I was a fool.'

'Why?' Mercedes slid her hands up the lapels of his jacket. 'Do you regret what has happened? This has been a fabulous opportunity for you and you've done well. I'm hard-pressed to say you've been "used." You've made money, you have new waistcoats to wear.' She smiled at her try for levity. It worked a bit. 'You've been travelling, meeting people and doing something you love.' She shot him a look from beneath her lashes. 'I don't think working the home farm would have provided the same. But perhaps I'm wrong?' she said with an innocent air.

Greer shook his head with a smile. 'Lucifer's balls, Mercedes, I swear you could sell milk to a cow.'

She smiled back; inside she sang a song of relief. She wasn't going to lose him tonight. It scared her just how glad that made her feel.

'Don't overthink things, Captain. Some things we should accept at face value.'

He gave a genuine laugh, loud enough to attract a few more stares their direction. 'Oh, that's rich, coming from the woman who has turned *passeggiata* into a calculated marriage mart.'

She looked up at him, her hands still twined in his lapels. 'It's not all calculation,' she whispered. 'This isn't.' She reached up and dared a soft kiss on his mouth. 'And this isn't.' She blew against his ear. '*Nothing* that has happened between us has been planned, Greer. That's why it's been so very difficult.' If he believed anything he had to believe this. 'I didn't bargain on falling for you.'

Then he nipped at her ear and said the words she so desperately needed to hear. 'I know.'

She ran a hand between them for a discreet caress. 'Let's go back to the room and do something just for fun.'

Chapter Sixteen

Fun turned out to involve the rest of the wine and a bowl of strawberries with cream the innkeeper had put out for dessert. Greer grabbed up the bowl and wine and climbed the stairs behind Mercedes, watching the sway of her hips and acknowledging that he was staking a lot of assumptions on the sincerity of her climax last night.

At the moment, a large part of his body didn't care, but he knew later an even larger part would—the part made up of his honour, his intelligence and self-respect, the core components of a man's pride. He would not stand for being duped, not even for a beautiful woman. In the military, one learned quickly to keep one's wits about them or end up dead.

Beautiful women were as dangerous as any-one else, just more distracting, which required double diligence.

At the top of the stairs, Mercedes slipped the key into the lock and turned to him with a secret smile. 'Won't you come in?'

He set the bowl and wine on a small table, taking in the room. It was bigger than his and far better appointed. A massive oak bed stood in the centre of the room covered in a cheery blue-and-yellow quilt, and a maid had been in to lay an evening fire. There was a dress-ing screen behind which the private essentials were delicately hidden from view. In all, the room was homey and inviting. Mercedes stood before the fire, pushing down the puffed sleeve of her gown.

'No.' Greer strode forwards, taking her hand gently away from the sleeve. 'Tonight, let me undress you.' Last night had been a hurried joint affair. 'I want to enjoy you, inch by inch.' Last night had been frantic, physical sex. *Fabulous* physical sex, but tonight would be different. It would be a slow feast of love-making or at least as close as one could get to such a thing without breaking his promise, or exposing himself unduly to heartbreak.

He removed her dress first, his hands skim-

ming the soft skin of her shoulders and following the gown down over corseted breasts and
slim hips, tracing the erotic silhouette of her,
thankful the gown hadn't required a petticoat.
He took off the stays next, luxuriating in the
feel of her breasts falling free into his hands,
their dusky nipples pressing against the thin
cloth of the chemise. He stroked them with his
thumbs, his own arousal straining and thick
in the confines of his trousers. But it was not
time for that yet.

'Sit for me.' He pressed her into the chair
and bent to her feet, removing her slippers and
sliding his hands up one leg and then the other,
searching for the hem of her silk stockings. His
fingers brushed the damp triangle between her
thighs, his erection surging at the evidence she
was absolutely ready for him, but he would
prolong this if he could, turn it into the most
exquisite of personal pleasures for her.

He knelt between her thighs, his face even
with hers. Her pulse raced at the base of her
neck, further assurance she was enjoying this.
He gave a wicked grin. His hands covered
hers where they rested on the chair arms. His
mouth bent to the top ridge of her chemise,
tugging with his teeth at the pale blue ribbon
securing it, and pulled it through its eyelet cas-

ings. Greer rocked back on his haunches, extracted a knife from his boot and severed the ribbon into two lengths.

'What are you doing?' Her voice was the merest of breathy whispers. She was riveted.

'You'll see.' He tied her wrists loosely to the chair and her grey eyes went gratifyingly granite-dark with desire. He'd not guessed wrong about his Mercedes; those who spend their lives in control sometimes like to lose it. His body didn't argue. Instead, it was encouraging him to take his own advice. *Not yet.*

Kneeling, he spread her legs wide and pushed her chemise back until she was exposed to him. It was a provocative sight: a woman revealed. More than that it was Mercedes revealed, her hair loose over one shoulder, eyes dark with knowledge of what was coming. Her wrists were tied, but she was not helpless. She understood the power she had by her very being to stir him. His blood began to boil.

He bent to her, his mouth at her core, tasting and teasing, suckling and surprising. He felt her buck and tense where his hands pressed back her legs high on her thighs, the delicious frustration of not being able to use her hands, to bury them in his hair, mounting. She would come for him soon and then they could slake their mutual pleasure together. With a last stroke, he wrenched a cry from her that spoke of utter ecstasy achieved. Her body went slack, her breathing coming hard and fast.

Greer slipped her ribboned bonds from her wrists and swept her into his arms. 'You're in no condition to walk,' he said when she would have protested.

'True. I guess it's a good thing we took our walk earlier.'

He laughed and deposited her on the bed, settling the bowl of strawberries beside her. He dipped one in cream and held it to her mouth. 'You're not worn out already, are you?'

'Never.' She took a bite. 'Get undressed and I'll show you who's worn out.'

Greer undressed quickly. The time for play had passed and his body was eager to join with hers. But she cried foul play at the speed at which his clothes fell to the floor. 'Unfair! Don't I get to look?'

Greer shook his head. 'Another night.'

Mercedes made a pretty moue with her mouth, more seduction than pout. 'You are going to pay for this.'

'With pleasure.' Greer stared down at her, marvelling at her boldness.

'Absolutely with pleasure.' Mercedes licked the cream off her strawberry with a provocative swirl of her tongue, looking entirely wicked. 'Is there any other way?' She pulled him down to her, her hand closing about his engorged length. 'Now, let's take care of this.'

Femme fatale. If they kept this up, she'd definitely be the death of him. And a happy death it would be. There were far worse ways to go.

They took their leisure heading into Birmingham for which Mercedes was grateful, grateful for the nights it afforded her in Greer's arms and for the days it offered her to figure out her feelings. Some of those feelings were easy enough. Greer excited her. His bold passions matched her own and in that regard the blossoming relationship was fairly straightforward. If it had only been about sex, all would have been well. But it would also have been missing a large part of what attracted her to Greer in the first place.

She peered at him over the top of her book. He'd gone back to riding in the carriage with her in the mornings. Sometimes they talked, sometimes they read. Sometimes they even read aloud to one another when they came across interesting passages. Today they were reading silently. As usual, he looked fresh. He shaved every morning and took great care with his *toilette* after he left her bed. She never got to watch that particular domestic intimacy. He always returned to his room for it, but in her mind's eye she had an enticing image of him bare-chested in front of a mirror and basin, running a razor down his cheek.

'Yes? You're staring.' Greer put down his book.

'I was just thinking sometimes a half-naked man is sexier than a completely naked one.'

'Perhaps we can put that hypothesis to the test later tonight.'

'We'll see.' She wondered if part of the attraction to this affair was the clandestine nature of it. There was no guarantee there'd be room arrangements conducive to a nightly visit. There was no guarantee her father would be out playing, although they'd been lucky that he had these last few nights. The unknown added a certain spice to their encounters, never allowing them to take for granted that the encounter would be one of many.

Outside, the scenery started to change. The bucolic countryside gave way to the more organised signs of civilisation Birmingham-style. Canals cropped up, full of the flatbed barges hauling cargo. In the distance, the smoke of factories loomed in a hazy grey sky. Mercedes dropped the curtain with a frown of distaste.

'Birmingham not to your liking?' Greer quipped.

'It's not one of my favourite cities. It's dirty.' There were other more personal reasons she didn't like Birmingham. A distasteful part of her past was here in this city too. It was where she'd first met Luce Talmadge.

'Your father thinks we'll find players here.'

Mercedes shrugged. 'I don't care what he finds here as long as we don't stay too long.' She could handle about two days in Birmingham.

Greer prodded her foot with his toe. 'Then it's the turn for home.'

She nodded. They would not head any further north. They'd turn east and take in Coventry and then south past Cambridge and London before making it to Brighton at the end of June with two weeks to spare before the tournament. The last part of the journey would go quickly. Her father would be eager to spend time in London now that the Season was underway. He'd spare little attention for the small villages and hamlets between Coventry and

London. It was the end of May. He would feel
time pressing. But that wasn't what Greer had
meant with his comment. There were three
weeks left of this magical journey with him
where everything existed time out of mind.
She tried not to think about it.

'London will be nice. You will see many of
your acquaintances, no doubt. Will you want
to stay at your own quarters there?' Since Bath
they'd not addressed the status issue again. It
didn't matter that they were together in these
nouveau-industrial towns full of men with new
money. Towns like Birmingham and Coventry
thrived because of men like her father, self-
made men who had parlayed skills and opportunities into fortunes. 'I do understand, Greer,
London isn't Bath. I won't be acceptable there,'
she said softly.

She couldn't say she hadn't been warned.
She'd known this from the start.

Greer shook his head. 'It's not you. It's what
I've been doing.'

Mercedes nodded, but in her mind she made
a check on her mental calendar. He would
leave her in London. The divide between their
two worlds would be painfully obvious. There
would be no buffer of the isolation of the road
to obscure it. Well, now she knew how it would

end. London would be good. It would mean the split wouldn't happen in Brighton over the tournament.

'Perhaps there will be word of a posting.' Mercedes changed the subject. It was the one topic he remained markedly closed on.

'I hope not.'

'Really?' It was the most insightful comment he'd made to date. But he offered nothing more and they returned to their books.

Although Mercedes hated Birmingham, she was glad it was a short day in the carriage. It was not a companionable silence that had sprung up between them. The coach pulled up to a new but elegant hotel in the city centre shortly after noon, and Mercedes was happy to have her feet touch the ground.

'A nice change from rural country inns, don't you think?' Her father took her arm and led her inside, pleased at his choice of accommodations. Luxury always pleased him. She could see why. The lobby sported a large crystal chandelier and twin spiralling staircases on either side of the spacious room leading to the floors above. To one side, Mercedes caught the clink of silverware on china, denoting the hotel restaurant. The clientele milling about were well dressed in the latest fashions. This was a place important people stayed and, above all else, her father liked to be important.

Upstairs, the rooms bore out the signs of luxury evident below. Her bed was wide and her window overlooked the street. She could catch a glimpse of the Birmingham shopping arcade just a few streets over.

A knock on her door distracted her from the view. Perhaps it was Greer, coming to apologise. But for what? London would be difficult. He didn't have to be sorry for the truth. Maybe for speaking it, she thought uncharitably. No one liked to be told they were second rate. Still, unspoken truths didn't make them less true, less existent.

It wasn't Greer at the door and her heart sank a little at the sight of her father. 'Is your room fine?' he asked. His room and Greer's room were right across the hall.

'Yes, it's lovely.' Mercedes put on a smile, but her father was too astute to be fooled.

'What's on your mind? Don't tell me you're thinking about things that don't bear mentioning?' He chucked her under the chin. 'What happened was a long time ago. You're free from all that. Luce Talmadge can't hurt you anymore.'

What if it's happening again? The words
nearly burst out. What if she was falling in
love with Greer? She couldn't tell him. Her father would either say, 'Well done, it will keep
him where we need him', or he'd do something
utterly stupid like march them off to a church.
After all, it was the kind of marriage he'd always wanted for her.

Her father loved her, but he didn't necessarily understand her, although he thought he did.
It was at times like this that she wished she had
a mother. Perhaps a mother would know what
to say. It was a foolish notion. She was twenty-
three, far too old to need a mother. Perhaps
a friend would do? She missed Elise Sutton
very much in those moments. They'd grown
close in Bath and had discovered they had a
lot in common with the way they'd grown up
as their fathers' favoured children.

'I know.' She nodded, knowing her response
would make her father happy.

'Good.' He drew out the thick wallet of
pound notes he carried in his inside pocket
and withdrew several. 'The arcade is nice.
Take the afternoon and go shopping. I'm sure
the Captain will accompany you. I don't want
you out alone in a strange town. Then, around
five o'clock, I want you to meet me at the bil-

liards lounge on this card. It's a subscription room, but you'll be admitted. Tell the Captain to pay the temporary fee.' He winked and she knew precisely what he wanted.

'You've been playing a lot since Bath.' The part of her that wasn't entirely distracted by Greer had noticed. Her father played privately at home, of course. But he seldom played in his own subscription room. He'd played nightly in Bath and he'd gone out since then even on the nights he'd given Greer off.

Her father merely smiled. 'I'm not so old as all that, Mercedes. A man has to have his pleasures. Who says I can't play when I want? I have to keep my game in shape.'

True enough. Her father was a handsome man in his late forties with dark hair lightly streaked with silver, and sharp grey eyes. Moderate in height and slender in build, he still cut an imposing figure at the billiards table. No one could doubt his acumen with a cue. Well dressed and well mannered, his presence was sometimes even considered daunting if one crossed him. Why shouldn't he be out playing? But it *was* out of character for him, and Mercedes couldn't help the suspicion that something else was going on. Perhaps she wasn't the only one living a double life, lately.

'Have fun. Shall I tell the Captain to meet you downstairs in half an hour?' He shut the door behind him and Mercedes set about changing her dress, something that would be appropriate for an afternoon of shopping and for pulling her father's little gambit later, maybe even something that might keep the attentions of *Lord* Captain Barrington, who worried London would be embarrassing.

Lord, that woman could wear a dress! Greer watched Mercedes descend the spiral staircase. Today it was a gown of figured-pewter silk with a fitted bodice and pristine white-lace trim at the neckline. The only adornment was a modest bow offset at her waist. The gown was meant to be lovely in a discreet fashion, but on Mercedes's curves it was an invitation to absolute and complete sin. He was already imagining how to get her out of it before he remembered she was angry with him. Well, maybe not too angry. He noted she'd strung his star-charm on a thin strand of grey ribbon and wore it around her neck.

Still, Greer wished he'd held his tongue about the London comment. She'd been far more sensitive about it than he'd thought. He was so used to her thumbing her nose at the world and its conventions; he'd not anticipated she'd take it so personally or even care. Her silence had spoken volumes.

He moved to the stairs and took her hand. 'You look lovely, but you always do.' He was proud to walk through the lobby with her. He was not oblivious to the subtle glances thrown their way by both men and women. He wondered, not for the first time, what his family would make of her. His sisters would adore her. He could already see them pestering her for fashion advice. His brother would be reserved, but she would win him over. Andrew never could resist a pretty face for long. His father? His mother? Hard to guess. His mother would be a polite hostess and not say anything outwardly offensive, as that was her way. His father would simply be dismayed.

At the doors to the lobby he surprised her with a waiting landau. She shot him a look of question as he handed her in to the open-air carriage. 'I thought it would be easier to drive than to walk, especially if you bought a lot of things.' He hopped in and took the seat across from her.

'Easier for you,' she teased. 'If we walked, you'd be the one who has to carry all the packages.'

The carriage lurched into motion, slowly merging with the traffic. Greer leaned forwards, encouraged by the teasing. 'Am I forgiven, then? We'll manage London somehow.'

She smiled at him and gave him the absolution of a single word. 'Yes.'

'Do you want to know a secret?' Her eyes danced like little silver flames. Of course he wanted to know. How could he not when she looked at him like that?

'I don't want to go shopping. Let's go to the botanical gardens instead.' A light breeze toyed with her hat and she reached a hand up to steady it, looking charming as she made the gesture.

The detour was a short one. The gardens were only a mile from their hotel and the weather, although overcast, was proving to be mild. Much to his delight, however, the overcast nature of the day had kept people from the gardens and the place was nearly deserted, all the better for having Mercedes to himself.

The manicured lawn leading to the four glasshouses containing different varieties of plants spread before them in verdant welcome, a most relaxing departure from the industrial bustle of the city. 'It's hard to believe a place like this is so near the centre of the city.' Greer held open the door to the subtropical glass-house for her, catching a delicate whiff of her floral scent as she passed, her skirts brushing his leg.

Mercedes looked about her, the expression on her face one of enrapt wonder, and Greer felt an unexpected surge of pride that he'd been the one to bring her here, even though it had been her idea. He often forgot that for all her worldliness she hadn't been past England's shores. Not that it mattered these days: England's empire was bringing the world here.

Mercedes bent to take in a particularly vibrant red flower with a large stem sticking straight out of its centre, inducing all nature of phallic thought which did not elude Mercedes. 'Oh my, this is certainly original,' she exclaimed with a naughty smile. 'I wonder what it's called. Too bad there aren't any placards.'

'I think my brief foray into botany is about to become useful.' Greer chuckled. 'My tutor would be gloating if he were here. This is an anthurium. It's in the bromeliad family.' He leaned close to her ear although there was no one to hear. 'It's also known as the "boy flower."'

She gave a throaty laugh. 'No further explanation needed. It's a very wicked-looking flower indeed.'

It was on the tip of his tongue to flirt a bit and say 'you've some experience with wicked things, do you?' but after this morning's misstep, he thought better of it. Mercedes clearly had some intimate experience beyond himself but she'd never brought it up beyond the game of questions they'd played, a certain indication the situation was as prickly as the long stamen rising from the anthurium.

They finished in the subtropical glasshouse and moved on to the other features. There were acres of lawn and shrubbery to explore and they conjured up images of home. He found himself telling her about his mother's gardens and all the time his tutor spent wandering him through them, teaching him all the names.

'English and Latin? I'm impressed.' Mercedes laughed up at him.

'Not that much of it stuck, though.' He laughed with her. 'At the time I didn't appreciate how inventive my tutor was. He could have had me read it all out of a book instead of letting me enjoy the outdoors.'

'Your mother's gardens sound beautiful. Our garden back in Brighton was already landscaped when we moved in. It's gorgeous, of course, but it doesn't have the thought or the scholarship of your mother's design.'

Her astute comment was disarming. Such a comment would charm his mother, Greer realised. Few people understood the aesthetic difference between a hand-planned garden and the generic but expensive urban garden like ones behind the terraced houses in Brighton.

'I wish you could see it. It will be in full bloom about now,' Greer ventured cautiously. He didn't want to stir up more dissension between them.

'Well, you know what they say about wishes.'

Mercedes smiled ruefully and he didn't pursue the argument. Instead he said, 'There's a teahouse up ahead. Why don't we stop? I think there's enough time before we have to meet your father.' But the thought of Mercedes meeting his family, which had taken root in the lobby of the hotel, was starting to blossom into a tangible fantasy, one that his overactive mind was starting to play with on a more frequent basis. There were other fantasies that were coming to life as he watched her pour out the tea at their little table, her gestures graceful and confident. His mother would say she could pass for a lady, but he didn't want that. He didn't want Mercedes to ever pass for something she wasn't. He wanted her just the way she was: bold and passionate, insightful and intelligent.

Today had proven to him his attraction to her went far beyond the passion. He'd suspected it had long before now, but he wouldn't be the first man blinded by the power of sex. Today, she'd listened to his stories about home, about his mother's garden and she *understood* what that garden meant on a fundamental level that had transcended the conversation. How would he ever give her up when the time came? Therein lay the burgeoning fantasy: maybe he wouldn't have to.

'Greer, I asked if you wanted the last scone?' Mercedes poked him with her finger, a most unladylike gesture.

'Let's share it.' Greer picked it up and broke the pastry. The scone crumbled into unfair halves and they laughed together. His heart soared from the simple joy of it. Never had it felt like this, *never. This* was good and he'd have to find a way to fight for it. He'd fought for England—surely he could fight for Mercedes.

Chapter Seventeen

The subscription room was sophisticated and avant-garde, allowing women to sit on the sidelines and watch the men play. It was a novel experiment and not necessarily one that was succeeding.

The women, Mercedes noted, were well dressed, but with a tinge of that inherent gaucheness often attached to those who are newly come to money. Their clothes bordered on garish, their jewels on gaudy. These women were not the fine ladies of Bath with their understated elegance and fifth-generation pedigrees.

The men were no better with their brightly striped waistcoats and colourful jackets. Expensive to be sure, but tasteful? One look at the room's population and Mercedes knew exactly what her father wanted to do. He wanted to run 'plucking peacocks', his favourite gambit.

'Are you ready?' she asked Greer quietly, taking up residence at the brass railing that separated the tables from the viewing section.

He rolled his eyes and consented before moving off to the bar to fetch them champagne. They'd done smaller variations of 'plucking peacocks' before. She knew he disliked it. He thought it was dishonest. She had laughed the first time, arguing that it wasn't their fault people were stupid. A smart man would *never* take the bet. It certainly wasn't her fault there were so few smart men in the world.

'Remember, Greer,' she prompted, taking her glass from him. 'We aren't making anyone do anything against their will. If they bite, they bite.'

They settled in to watch. Her father was playing very well. She'd not seen him play any of the newer versions of the game before where there was no longer any alternating of turns. Instead, players put together runs and shot until they missed, making it possible for a player to clear the table without the other getting a single turn.

Her father potted the last ball to a smattering of applause. She tossed Greer a quick glance. That was their cue. A little way into the next game, she leaned over and blew in Greer's ear. The public display drew a few looks their direction. Now it was Greer's turn. He started to heckle. 'Good shot, old man. I'm surprised you can see the ball well enough to hit it, let alone sink it.'

Mercedes laughed and kissed his cheek, earning them a few censorious looks. But her father had chosen this crowd well. It was before dinner, so 'crowd' was a relative term. The population in the club wasn't nearly as large as it would be later in the evening and these men weren't gentlemen, merely apeing them. A little action wouldn't be terribly amiss to them. It would be exciting.

Her father shot them a withering look and went back to his game, making a difficult shot. Greer gave a mocking round of applause. 'Bravo. I'd like to see you make that shot again.' His sarcasm was evident. He made an aside to Mercedes loud enough to be overheard. 'He's a lucky old bastard. I bet he couldn't do that again. It's one shot in twenty.'

They laughed and then she kissed him full on the mouth, becoming very distracting for everyone in the room.

'We're trying to play over here,' her father's opponent called over, pointedly gesturing to the money stacked on the table to indicate the game was serious.

Greer grinned and rose. 'Oh, there's money on this?' He took in the pile of pound notes. He withdrew a wallet from his pocket and pulled out some bills. 'You want to make some real money? I'll bet Grandpapa here misses the next shot.'

Her father's opponent leaned on his cue and gave Greer a look of disbelief. 'Are you joking? My opponent's had the devil's own luck this afternoon and the next shot is easy.' It was, too, Mercedes noted, just a soft straight shot into the side pocket. But she already knew just how her father would play it. It wasn't all that different from the shot she'd missed the evening she'd played Greer.

'Exactly. I'm betting his luck just ran out.' The room had gone silent, everyone watching Greer make his offer.

'Double it, darling,' Mercedes called out in sultry tones.

Greer gave a cocky grin. 'Seems my lady

wants me to sweeten the pot.' He tossed down another stack of notes.

That did the trick. The man fairly drooled at the sight of easy money. 'Well, all right, mister. If you're aiming to give it away, I might as well take it.'

Her father chalked his cue and gave a fair imitation of feeling the pressure. He even tried to talk the man out of the wager for good measure. Then he aimed, a soft rolling shot positioned a little too high up on the ball. It hit the edge of the pocket and slid away to the amazed groans of the room, no one more amazed than her father himself. His opponent paid up, begrudgingly, and not without a few deprecating words for Greer, who tucked the pound notes away and simply smiled before looping an arm around Mercedes and walking out. Only Mercedes sensed the tension simmering in the muscles beneath his coat. She didn't have to be a mind reader to know a storm was coming.

'I'm not doing it again,' Greer announced as soon as they sat for dinner in the hotel dining room.

Ah, the storm was breaking. Mercedes settled her napkin in her lap and looked steadily at her lobster. Her eyes drifted covertly between her father and Greer.

'You were absolutely brilliant.' Her father ignored Greer's comment by overriding it with a compliment. He turned to Mercedes, seeking to draw her in as a neutral buffer. 'And you, my dear, were a genius. "Double it, darling."' He chuckled. 'Brilliant. Couldn't have done it better myself.'

'It's not right,' Greer said again with more insistence. 'That man had no idea.'

Her father set his fork down. 'Of course he didn't. However, such is the nature of any gamble a person takes in any aspect of his life. No one made him take the offer. He considered his options and decided he would.'

'But his options were an illusion.' Greer laid down his fork as well. Eyes clashed across the table. 'There was *never* a chance to win.'

'You listen here, Barrington...' Lockhart took the challenge.

Mercedes drew a sharp breath. How many conversations had begun that way over the years? But Greer was a man and an officer. He could not be handled like a recalcitrant child. It was doubtful he could be handled at all.

'There was *nothing* illegal in what we did.'

'That doesn't make it right.'

The men were halfway out of their seats and Mercedes cast about for a way to divert the impending scene, anything...

'Why, Allen Lockhart! I thought that was you.' The masculine depths of the intruding baritone froze Mercedes in her seat. Anything but that, not *him*. It was what she'd feared in coming to Birmingham, although her father had assured her that in a city of thousands the odds were in her favour. She schooled her features and looked up into the chiselled features of Luce Talmadge. His arrival may have squelched the quarrel brewing between Greer and her father, but in the future she'd be more careful about what she wished for.

'Ah, Mercedes.' Luce grinned, flashing straight teeth. He took a lot of pride in those teeth. They were quite the luxury when one grew up in the rougher neighbourhoods of Birmingham. 'You're as lovely as ever. Lovelier even.' He pulled up a chair without being invited, audacious as always and just as tenacious. It was hard to believe she'd once found those traits attractive.

Luce sat and then half rose when it became apparent no one was going to introduce him to Greer. 'I'm Luce Talmadge.' He leaned over the table and offered his hand, but to her great satisfaction Greer merely inclined his head and offered nothing more than a glacial stare.

'Shall I order champagne for everyone? We should celebrate running into one another.' Luce pushed forwards, undaunted by Greer's snub. 'It's been ages since we've all been together, but I still recall how much you liked champagne, Mercedes.' He tossed her a wink that made her stomach curdle. How had she ever found him appealing? He was a boor, even if he was good looking. Greer would never have put a lady in such an untenable position, would never have insinuated himself into a conversation where he was not welcome, let alone someone else's dinner table.

'I hear there's a tournament in Brighton, an All England Championship. It's your doing, I suppose?' It was Luce's usual strategy—how it all came flooding back to her. He'd just keep talking, a rapid chatter filled with bonhomie until people just gave in and tolerated his presence or forgot they hadn't invited him.

Her father broke in and she could have kissed him. 'You're not welcome here, Talmadge. I must ask you to please leave.' Greer was tense beside her, ready to second her father's request, even though moments before

Luce's arrival he'd nearly been at her father's throat.

'Surely, Lockhart, you're not going to let the past keep us from friendship. That was nothing more than the foolishness of youth.' Luce waved a hand dismissively. 'Hardly worth carrying a grudge over. We've grown up and moved on.'

When her father didn't budge, Luce's smile turned mean as his attention focused on Greer. 'I was once sitting where you are. It's the good life, isn't it? Doing Lockhart's bidding? I think of all I learned on the road with him: how to win, how to lose, how to hustle, how to live the high life, which wine to order, which fork to use. Those were good years and they made me into the gentleman I am today.' He held out his arms to indicate the expensive suit he wore.

Mercedes gave a snort of disbelief. The suit was garish and he looked more like the peacocks at the subscription room than a subtly dressed gentleman. Greer would look like a gentleman dressed in a potato sack.

Luce glared at her and rose, finally understanding his welcome wasn't going to get any warmer. He was leaving. She started to breathe easier, thinking she might get out of this encounter unscathed. But Luce wasn't done yet.

'I think of those days with nostalgia, Mercedes. However, I see things have turned out for the best.'

He nodded in her father's direction. 'Best of luck with your new protégé and, Mercedes…' his dark eyes rested on her with the devil's own intentions, '…best of luck with your—what shall we call him? Your new lover? Your *husband*? Well, maybe not a husband. After all, I am fairly hard to replace and you aren't into long-term arrangements.'

How dare he! White fury gripped her. Mercedes seized her water glass and threw the contents straight into his face seconds before Greer's fist found Luce's jaw with a blow that made casualties of the dishes lying between them. The blow took Luce and most of dinner to the floor. Well, she hadn't had much of an appetite for the lobster anyway.

The bastard! Greer's blood was pounding by the time he was straddling Talmadge, the lapels of his gaudy green-checked coat in his hands. Some vague part of him was aware that his hand throbbed. He shoved the pain aside. Greer dragged Talmadge to his feet. Talmadge protested the brutality, looking entirely aggrieved as if he were the wronged party. 'We

are both gentlemen here,' he sputtered, trying
to simultaneously clutch his jaw and swipe at
the water running down his face.

'One of us isn't. You work out who that is,'
Greer snarled. He caught Mercedes's eye. She
was pale and her hand shook where it clutched
the stem of her empty water glass. 'Excuse
me for a moment, my dear, I have to take out
the rubbish.'

Greer roughly escorted Talmadge to the
door, pointedly ignoring curious looks from
the serving staff and the other diners. So much
for discretion, but he'd be damned before he let
a man treat a woman as poorly as Talmadge
had treated Mercedes.

'You can have her, you know.' Talmadge
tried to jerk free. 'She and that meddling father of hers will never mean anything but trouble to any man. They're users, both of them.'

Greer's answer to that was a hard shove that
set Talmadge staggering into the lobby. He
watched Talmadge disappear into the street
still reeling and off balance.

Certain the bastard was gone, Greer gripped
the door frame, finally letting Talmadge's
comments sink in. He was reeling too, albeit
in a far different way. Mercedes had been married and apparently divorced to the likes of

Luce Talmadge, a bounder on all accounts. Impossible.

Greer fought the urge to race back to the table and demand the truth in the hopes that Talmadge had been lying. But that was a slim hope indeed. The pallor on her face at the sight of him was proof enough. For a woman of Mercedes's remarkable steel such a reaction was telling in the extreme.

Racing back to the table would solve nothing if his emotions weren't under control. He needed to face Mercedes with a cool head. He'd punched Talmadge mostly for Mercedes's sake but also in part for himself. He was *not* Lockhart's protégé. He was nothing like that man, had no intentions of being like that man. But it did raise the question of guilt by association and it was high time he grappled with that particular dilemma. This evening in the subscription room, he'd glimpsed just how far he'd fallen and he hadn't even realised it.

By the time Greer returned to the table, Mercedes had gone. While he'd been marshalling his emotional troops, she'd been marshalling hers. It was just as well. Anxious as he was for answers, this was a conversation best held in private. As for the fantasies he'd harboured about showing her his mother's gardens, they'd just become a little more complicated.

Escorting her around London was the least of his worries. Now she wasn't merely the daughter of a celebrity billiards champion, she was also a divorced woman. Of course, she'd been that from the start. She just hadn't told him. He had to wonder what else she hadn't told him? What else was there to discover? What other reasons were being hidden behind the promise that he not fall in love with her? More importantly, did those reasons change how he felt about her? Her absence made it clear she thought they would.

Chapter Eighteen

Greer had found clarity by the time he reached the door of her room. The walk upstairs had given him time to collect his thoughts even if it hadn't provided him any answers, at least not answers he liked. Common sense would recommend he walk away right now. It is what his mother would advise. He could hear her voice in his head: there was a reason the classes didn't mix. Their values and lifestyles were too different.

But his heart was far too engaged with Mercedes to simply walk away because she wasn't a nobleman's daughter. Before he walked, there were things he needed to know. Hastily made decisions weren't always the wisest. He raised his hand to knock and heard permission to enter. The door was unlocked. She'd been expecting him.

'You hit him in my defence and now you've come for your answers, is that it?' Mercedes turned from the window, letting the curtain fall across the wide pane. Distress was evident on her pale features.

'I came to see how you are,' Greer amended. 'I won't lie and say I care nothing about answers, but neither did I come solely out of my own selfish need. I wanted to make sure you were all right.' He paused. 'Are you?' He flexed his right hand. It was starting to hurt now that his adrenaline had ebbed.

Mercedes noticed. 'Maybe I should be asking you the same thing. We need to get ice on this. I'll have the staff send some up.' She took his hand, feeling and flexing each of his fingers in turn. 'Father won't forgive me if you've ruined your hand on my behalf.'

'Stop fussing, Mercedes. My hand will be fine in a couple of days.' Greer covered her hands with his free one, but Mercedes would not be thwarted.

When the ice arrived she packed it around his hand. He insisted it was not necessary, but the colour had returned to her face by the time he was settled to her satisfaction on the little sofa in her sitting room, his hand in ice. The unintended distraction had worked, creating a sense of normality between them, elusive as it might be.

There was nothing left to do but return to the reason for his visit. 'Would you like to tell me about him?' Then he hastily added, 'Not because I am entitled to anything, but because you want to? Ghosts only have power when they aren't exorcised.'

He'd been wrong on the stairs. It wasn't the question of whether or not Talmadge's comments were true that mattered. It was this, right here. If she couldn't tell him, it would be between them always and there was no future in that. He held his breath. Everything hinged on this.

'I was young and foolish,' she began, sitting down on the sofa beside him. Greer began to breathe again. There was hope yet.

'I was seventeen and my head was easily turned by the attentions of a good-looking man.' Her throat worked and it was clear it was hard for her to say the words. 'I was stupid, so headstrong when it came to Luce Talmadge.' She gave a short, deprecating laugh. 'Forgive my hesitation. Saying it out loud makes my mistake much more real.'

'Everyone makes mistakes,' Greer offered. He meant for it to be encouraging, but the words sounded empty even to him.

She raised a dark brow. 'Mistakes aren't usually of this magnitude. My father was already a renowned champion in our circles when Luce took up with us. If I'd been smarter, I'd have seen that Luce was using me as access to my father. Luce was, and is, a consummate user of people, only he's not very subtle at it, which makes falling for him that much worse.'

She shook her head and traced a pattern on the sofa cushion, unable to look at him. 'I mistook his lack of subtlety for boldness and tenacity. When we're seventeen, I suppose we don't make those distinctions. My father tried to warn me, but I was too stubborn to listen. Anyway, my father took Luce on a short tour to advertise the Brighton room. He was good at billiards and even better at separating people from their money. I went with them and it was heady stuff for a girl fresh out of boarding school.'

Much the same as it was now. The comparison between the two situations was not lost on him. It was the second time in as many hours he'd been cast in the role of Lockhart's protégé, and the label did not sit well with him. He was about to protest that this time was different, but Mercedes read his mind. 'Now that I've started, you have to let me finish.' She put a soft finger to his lips.

'Luce convinced me he was in love and that he wanted to marry me. He painted a compelling picture. We'd be the most dazzling couple in Brighton and I was not immune to the images he conjured. They were exciting and I entirely overlooked the reality that all of Luce's dreams were built on my father's subscription room. He'd assumed I would inherit the club. It was only one of many assumptions Luce made about my connection to my father's wealth.

'We married three days before we returned to Brighton, a secret wedding in the morning in a church in a tiny sea-coast village. Luce told me I was the most beautiful thing he'd ever seen. He wooed me with kisses and a solid gold ring. He'd even been a bit misty-eyed when he slipped it on my finger.'

Mercedes shrugged. 'In truth, I was having misgivings before we married, but in my stubbornness I shoved them away, blaming it on my father. I wouldn't let myself be influenced by him. I was going to make this decision on my own.'

Greer wanted to punch the man again. He knew men like Luce Talmadge, who preyed on the susceptibilities of young girls. Fortune hunters existed at all levels of society. It just proved that 'susceptibilities' came in all forms; her own inherent stubbornness had been as lethal to Mercedes as a weaker woman's belief in false flattery. But he could well imagine an obstinate Mercedes, a formidable force even at seventeen. Words would not have stopped her once she'd set her mind.

'We didn't tell my father until we got back. He was furious. He said a real man would ask permission, a real man wouldn't slink off behind his back and marry a man's daughter. We were in my father's study and I remember very clearly how my father looked at me and said, "He's only after your money, Mercedes."'

Greer's gut clenched in anticipation of what would come next: a deal of the kind Lockhart loved to make, the kind where no man was forced to do anything other than what his nature motivated him to do, like the greedy man in the club tonight. The only difference was that tonight, the man had been his own victim. In this scheme, it had been Mercedes.

'Of course, Luce made all the requisite noises about being offended by my father's brash assumptions. Then my father stood up and went to his safe. He pulled out a stack of pound notes and a document. He set them on his desk. He opened the document and showed it to Luce. It was his will, in which he left the subscription room to Kendall Carlisle. In the event that Carlisle preceded him in death, it comes to me in the form of a trust to be overseen by my father's solicitor. It's never mine directly.'

'Let me guess—Talmadge didn't like that arrangement?'

Mercedes gave a sad laugh. 'At the time, I thought he was going to faint. It's rather funny now, at a distance. But I assure you, it was not humourous then to look the man you thought you loved in the face and see quite clearly that your love was a one-way thing.'

Promise me you won't fall in love with me. Was that because she didn't feel the same way? Had she extracted that promise in order to protect him? 'What did your father do next?'

'He tapped the pounds notes with his hand and said, "There are a thousand pounds in this stack and I'll write you a personal cheque on my account in London for nine thousand more if you take the money, declare the marriage false and walk out this door today with the promise that you will make no further claim on Mercedes." I don't think it took Luce even a minute to make up his mind. I had not seen him in six years until this evening.'

Tears threatened. Greer could see them swim in her grey eyes. She swiped them away with a dash of her hand. But they weren't tears for Talmadge. 'It's embarrassing beyond words to know you were sold for ten thousand pounds. In my girlish dreams, I'd thought for-ever would cost a bit more.' She shrugged and tried for a smile.

'I think you have it backwards.' Greer said thoughtfully, his eyes on her. 'You weren't sold. Your freedom was bought.' Whatever he might think of Lockhart, the man had done this one good deed.

She nodded. 'I'll always owe my father for that. He'd warned me. I didn't listen and yet he was still there, in his own way, to pick me up.'

It was one of the ways in which Lockhart had a nobility of his own. Greer saw that. But he also saw the prison it created for Mercedes and he liked that even less. Lockhart was not above using people, even his own daughter. Greer had seen him do it on two occasions.

Lockhart knew precisely what he was owed by others, Mercedes included.

Greer pulled his hand out of the ice and flexed it experimentally, slowly. 'I'm glad I hit him.' He knit his brow. 'Is this the reason you didn't want me to fall in love with you? You didn't want me to find out about Luce?' He hoped it was as superficial as that and not his earlier supposition.

'Something like that.' Her answer was not reassuring.

'But not quite? Talmadge and I are not the same. I'm not using you, not looking to trap you. You've said you're not using me.' He could not make it any plainer without breaking his promise to her. He *would* break it, but not yet. An inspiration struck him.

'Why did you come on this trip?' Based on what she'd revealed, coming made very little sense, especially if she saw too many similarities between these circumstances and the previous ones.

He could see this question bothered her more than anything she'd told him about Luce. She rose and paced the room, going back to her curtain at the window and looking out. So he couldn't see her face when she lied to him? He didn't want to believe that.

'Well, Mercedes?' he prodded. 'What is it you wanted badly enough to put yourself through this?' The pieces were coming fast and furious to him now. This trip was a proving ground for her, a chance to claim…something… The fight in Beckhampton… The madness of the Bath brothel. Yes. He had it.

'You…' Greer began, grappling with the reality that flooded him. 'You wanted to be the protégée.' She had coveted what he would throw away, what he felt distaste for. He had unwittingly stolen something from her that she cherished.

She turned back from the window, her face fierce. 'Yes, I wanted to be the protégée. I wanted to show him I could not only train you, but beat you. I did and it still made no difference.'

Because she owed Lockhart. Perhaps he'd been too hasty in suggesting Lockhart had bought her freedom. He'd merely transferred it from one gaoler to another. This was the side of Lockhart that Greer could not countenance. Everyone had a purpose. Greer wondered what his was. He was not naïve enough to think he would be the one singular individual to escape Lockhart's machinations. He wondered, too, if he could free her. Would she ever leave her father? Tonight was not the time to put the question to her.

'I should go.' Greer stood. He needed time to think, time to sort this all out and his place in it as well.

She came to him and ran a finger down his shirtfront. 'I think you should stay.'

Greer trapped her finger with his good hand. 'Not tonight. We both have too much on our minds. I don't think there would be room in bed for all of it.' Not when she was vulnerable, not when she might be tempted to use sex as a way to bind him to her. He kissed her lightly on the forehead. 'Goodnight, Mercedes. I'll see you in the morning.'

But he couldn't help wondering as the door closed behind him if things would ever be the same between them. His mind was far too restless for sleep. A walk would do his body good and the gaslights of the city centre made Birmingham safe enough if a man was careful.

The irony of what occupied his mind, however, was that his thoughts were not on Luce Talmadge and the brief, ridiculous marriage. *He'd* been the first to show her true pleasures. In his more fantastical moments he hoped to be the last and only man to do so some way, somehow.

Knowing about Talmadge made it far easier to understand Mercedes and her reticence to admit this relationship between them was anything more than sex. But that would also be the easy answer. Did she return his feelings or was she using him? Was he still merely a tool to get what she wanted from her father? Was she so determined to wrest it from her father that she was willing to sleep with the enemy? Did she still hate him for being the protégé?

The real issue that occupied his mind as he walked Birmingham was what to do about Lockhart. The longer he thought about it, the more convinced he became that Lockhart was the villain of the piece and he wanted no more part of it—no more inns, no more days on the road, no more nights watching Lockhart trade on his celebrity in big towns or adopting false aliases in small towns in order to 'pluck peacocks' or some other game. Lockhart liked toying with people, determine their price.

Greer felt shame that he'd let Lockhart toy with him for so long. Lockhart had been in his element in Bath, introducing him as Lord Captain Barrington. And Greer had let him, convinced that such a use of his title could buy

Mercedes acceptability. In part, he'd begun to believe in his own mystique, charmed by his own growing celebrity as he won game after game, as he danced with Mercedes in his arms, distracted by beauty, lust, and money.

It had been a glorious life for a few weeks. He wanted to be angry at Lockhart for leading him into such iniquity, but there was no one to be angry with but himself. Lockhart had simply dangled the carrot—something the man was very good at doing. No one had made him take it. No one could make him stay.

Birmingham had a direct train route to London. He should be on it first thing in the morning. But truly, he didn't want to go to London. He wanted to go home, to the rich fields of Devonshire, fields he hadn't seen in three years. There would be sense in Devonshire, equilibrium, even if there was a reckoning to go with it. But he couldn't go, not without Mercedes. If he left her now, he would not get her back. If there was one thing he didn't regret about this madcap trip, it was her. Could she say the same for him? Would she come? There was only one reason to come and many reasons to stay. Would she refuse because of Luce?

Only the densest of people would fail to see

the parallels there in his request. Or would she refuse because it meant choosing another man over her father, who had rescued her once before and to whom she felt indebted? Or would she refuse because she'd been using him all along? If he was gone, she could be the protégée just as she had planned.

He did not figure well in either scenario. But maybe would she choose him for the simple reason that she was Mercedes Lockhart, a woman possessed of a boldness unequalled? Greer turned back to the hotel. He wouldn't know unless he asked.

Chapter Nineteen

Mercedes could muster no enthusiasm for the sausages and eggs piled on her plate for breakfast the next morning. She'd decided around three that sleeping alone was not conducive to a good night's rest. Around four, she'd concluded neither was a restless mind. Both of which had resulted in having very little appetite for breakfast. A pity, really, when the breakfast looked quite fine. She was certain it looked better than she did. She didn't need a mirror to show her what she already knew. Her appearance was drawn, and dark shadows created purple circles beneath her eyes. She could practically feel the bags.

She was not alone in that regard. Greer, who always looked fresh, looked haggard in spite of his impeccable clothes and polished boots. He must have sent them out after he came back from his walk—his very long walk. She knew. She'd seen him leave the hotel from her window and she'd stood sentinel until she'd seen him come back, safe and unharmed, although the exercise had not resulted in a restful night.

She caught the faintest whiff of the sandalwood soap he preferred as he sat down. But all the grooming in the world couldn't hide the tiredness in his eyes and she felt a twinge of guilt over having been the one to put it there.

'How's your hand?' she asked quietly before her father reached them. He was across the dining room, finishing assembling his plate from the buffet.

'Much better.' He smiled and flexed the hand to show her. 'We need to talk.' He spoke in low, urgent tones, aware that their time alone was limited. 'I've made some decisions.' Ah, so that was what he'd been doing on his walk. Thinking. Deciding. Weighing all things in the balance. There was no time to hear more.

'Good morning, everyone.' Her father smiled broadly and took a seat, effectively interrupting. 'Did we sleep well?' Mercedes gave him a critical stare. He wasn't fooling her. For all his apparent zest, he had not slept particularly well either, but it hadn't diminished his appetite.

'I've decided we should have a slight change of venue,' he said between bites of egg. 'The new railway line runs up to Manchester. I think we should go. We couldn't have hoped to reach Manchester and get back to Brighton in time by coach, but a railway makes it possible. We can take the railway straight to London from Manchester and then—' he snapped his fingers '—we're home from there in plenty of time, just like that. What do you think? I can get us tickets on the eleven o'clock. The coachman can drive the team back to Brighton.'

It wasn't really a question. She knew her father too well. He'd already decided. They were going to Manchester.

Greer pushed back from the table and set his napkin aside, his eyes serious as they darted her direction in a quick glance she couldn't quite interpret. 'I will not be coming. I told you last night that I was done and I meant it.'

Beneath the table, Mercedes's fingers clenched around her napkin. Greer was leaving. He'd finally had enough of the manipulating Lockharts. This was the decision he'd alluded to. She'd known it would end. But she'd thought she'd have until London. Just yesterday they'd been walking in the botanical gardens, dreaming impossible dreams, and now it was over. Her heart sank with the sudden realisation she'd never wanted anything as much as she wanted Greer Barrington.

Her father took the news with his famous equanimity. If he was upset over this announcement, he didn't show it. He took out his wallet and began counting out pound notes. 'We can meet in London. You can take the coach to Coventry and carry on with the tour.'

'No, thank you, though the offer is generous.' Greer was all courteous politeness, but there was firmness as well. Whatever came next, her father wasn't going to like it. 'I will be ending my tour here. All of it.' Translation—he was ending his association with them. 'I think it is time for me to move on. I thank you for the experience. It has been illuminating.'

She shifted her gaze to her father. What would he make of that? He smiled and dug into his proverbial bag of tricks. 'Is it more money you're wanting? You've been playing well and you're not an unschooled apprentice any longer. How does twenty per cent of the take sound, and a slice of the profits in Brighton? You've earned it.' It was a generous offer. Her father must be desperate to keep him.

'I must decline,' Greer said solemnly. She knew it must be killing him to refuse the money.

Her father's eyes narrowed at the last refusal. 'Is my money not good enough? You think you can simply walk away whenever you want? After all I've done for you? After all Mercedes has done for you? Don't think I don't know what the two of you have been up to.'

Mercedes blanched, embarrassed. Of course her father would make her private business his own if he thought he could use it. But Greer was not cowed and Mercedes silently applauded him. When it came to knowing his own mind, no one knew it better than Greer Barrington. Watching a man be true to his principles was a gratifying experience. So much of her life had been lived around chasing the money, convictions be damned if they got in the way. Principles were easily trampled by pounds.

Greer dropped his voice to a dangerously low tone. 'After all you've done for *me*? I think the accounts are settled. I have earned my keep, sir, and then some. You've done very well with me by your side. You've used my skill and you've used my name to great advantage. Whatever I've owed you has been well and truly paid and you know it.'

Greer rose and offered his hand to her father. There would be no further negotiation. She'd never seen her father so utterly silenced. 'Will we see you in Brighton?' her father asked with a hint of his earlier Lockhart smile.

'If *you* do, it will be as my own man, not as your protégé,' Greer replied. There was an odd emphasis in the sentence. He had said 'you' in contrast to her father's 'we', and it had a singular tone to it. She was still puzzling out his intent when she felt his gaze on her, his hand outstretched.

'Mercedes, will you come with me? My train leaves slightly earlier than your father's.' It was not a choice she wanted to make and certainly not in such a bold fashion. She would have railed at him if she hadn't been so keenly cognisant that he was giving her a choice. He hadn't assumed she'd follow him. He was letting her decide. He wanted her still.

The enormity of his question and all it denoted, all it stood for, overwhelmed her. She fought to master the sensation in the seconds she had to make her choice. She forced her mind to dissect her options with a gambler's assessment of risk. Greer knew her most scandalous secret and he'd chosen her anyway. Because he loved her, although she'd asked him not to? Or because he didn't intend to keep her long enough for it to matter? *He's not Luce, and he's not your father. He doesn't think like that. What he feels for you is genuine.*

Would it be enough? Did it matter? She wanted Greer Barrington and Mercedes Lockhart took what she wanted. She set aside her napkin and stood. She put her hand in his and felt the strength of his grip close around her, warm and reassuring.

'Mercedes, think!' Her father rose, disbelief etched on his face. 'Don't do anything rash. You know how it worked out the last time.' It wasn't a plea, but an accusation, a thinly wrapped threat.

She focused on the feel of Greer's arm at her waist, ushering her towards the door. He was already gesturing for a runner to fetch her trunk and get it to the station.

'Mercedes, stop and listen!' Her father was at her other side, refusing to let them leave without saying his piece. 'This is madness. What do you think will happen? He'll use you like Talmadge did and then he'll throw you away. You don't think he actually loves you, do you? He could never marry you and eventually you'll come crawling back to me, begging me to bail you out. He's a lord, Mercedes, and you're the daughter of a bootboy.'

Hearing her worst fears spoken so blatantly did nothing for her nerves. She had notoriously bad luck in love. For all her bravado, she'd never stood on her own. She thought of the stake money she'd won in Bath, neatly hidden in her trunk. She'd earned money once—she could do it again if need be. 'This is not about Greer. This is about me.'

'Taking her home, are you?' Her father turned to Greer, ignoring her outburst altogether. 'Devonshire, is it? That will be lovely.' His gaze swung back to Mercedes, his features calm as if this was a usual conversation. 'Home to meet the Viscount? Really, Mercedes? How do you think that will go? I know how it will go, but if you need to find out for yourself, so be it. I give it two weeks and you'll be begging me to save you.'

He shuffled through a pile of cards he'd taken from his coat pocket until he found the one he wanted. 'Here it is. There's a gentleman from Bath who's from that area. He invited me to come for a visit. I think I'll change my travel plans and do just that. I'll be there until the twentieth of June.' His eyes softened. 'You can come to me and all will be forgiven.'

'I won't.' She met his eyes evenly. He was calling her bluff. But he didn't understand all the potential that waited for her if she would just embrace it. This time she finally understood no one was going to give her a chance unless she gave one to herself. This time, he would lose.

'I'm going with Greer,' she said firmly.

It was a final declaration of independence. She turned, stepped out the entrance into the bright morning light with Greer beside her, and walked into the busy streets of Birmingham, into her future.

They spoke little on the drive to the station. Her mind was still reeling with what she'd done, acknowledging what she'd done. This time it *was* different. Walking out with Greer was about taking charge of her life, of deciding she wasn't going to be one of her father's pawns any longer. She wasn't going to hide away in his Brighton mansion playing hostess, ignoring her talent and hoping to be noticed some day for what she was. When she'd accepted the offer to come on the road, she'd seen Greer as her chance. She'd not imagined in what way that chance would come. But here it was and she was going to seize it.

Greer settled into the plush seat across from Mercedes. He'd paid extra for the private accommodation. It would be worth it. There were things that needed settling and there was no time to wait. He'd seen their trunks boarded and they'd had time to settle their turbulent emotions. Now, with the sliding door shutting out the aisle, they needed to talk. The morning had not been without its share of drama.

'I hope your decision is a little bit about me.' He crossed his legs at the ankles and folded his arms over his head in a casual pose. She'd come. He told himself not to get greedy. Last night his goal had been to free her. He'd done that. He'd made the opportunity available and Mercedes had taken it.

'Of course it is. You know it is.' She gave him a small smile that assuaged his male ego.

He understood. She didn't want him to feel any pressure, to feel any sense that she was under his protection now. She was, though. She would protest if he ever said it out loud. But he would protect her, care for her, as long as she would let him. He would have to be subtle about it. She wouldn't tolerate any blatant chivalry.

He also understood that for Mercedes, getting on the train wasn't entirely about him, although for him, asking had been entirely about her. He'd have to change her mind, but for now it was a start. She was still smiling at him, the colour returning to her face as the train pulled out of the station. 'So, we're on the train. Where exactly are we going?'

He laughed the first real laugh he'd had in a while. 'Shame on you for getting on a train with a strange man without even knowing where it goes.' But it was exactly the kind of thing she would do, the kind of thing that made her Mercedes Lockhart, the woman he loved.

'That's nothing.' She gave a wide smile, her eyes lighting up. He shifted his position slightly to accommodate the beginnings of an arousal. He'd have to address that in short order. 'I once heard of a man who went on the road with a woman he didn't know simply because he lost a billiards bet.'

'Probably the best adventure he ever had.' Greer grinned and reached for her. She came willingly, straddling his lap.

She reached up and flipped down the curtain that covered the small window of their sliding door. 'It's about to get better.'

It most certainly was. Her mouth was on his, her hand between their bodies, stroking his cock through his trousers. He groaned, his nascent arousal growing in full force. 'I see great minds think alike,' she murmured against his mouth.

She slid down to the floor and worked the fastenings of his trousers, pushing them down past his hips. 'I believe it's my turn?' They'd not done *this* yet and Greer's breath caught in anticipation.

'I hope that's a rhetorical question.' Real thought, real response beyond the physical was becoming an increasing impossibility. Greer gave a soft moan as she touched her lips to his phallus, kissing, licking, building him to a frenzy with each wicked stroke of her tongue, until she took him in his entirety into her mouth.

Her hand found his balls, and she squeezed ever so gently, just enough to increase his pleasure to nearly unendurable limits. Greer moaned and arched against her, his hands tangled in the silky expanse of her hair. He'd never been touched so sensually before, never experienced such depths of eroticism as the ones summoned up by her hands, her mouth, caressing him in tandem. And yet, when he arched against her, spilling himself in the achievement of his pleasure, the core of him knew that it wasn't the eroticism of the moment alone that had conjured such ecstasy.

She looked up at him, a veritable Delilah with her hair falling over her shoulders, looking for all the world like a very happy cat who'd licked the cream, which of course she had.

Chapter Twenty

Pride was all well and good, but it couldn't feed you, which was why Greer found himself at a billiards table an hour after getting off the train. Still, he wouldn't have taken Lockhart's money for anything. He was going to do this ethically and on his own.

Greer studied the lay of the table. He'd need to use a bank shot to get around the mess of balls blocking his access to the pocket. He bent, lined up his shot and halted in mid-strike, distracted by movement in the open doorway—a glimpse of a coral-coloured gown, of long dark hair curled into a single thick length, the sound of a sultry voice full of unwavering confidence.

'Good evening, gentlemen. Care for a game?'

Mercedes. It was hardly worth the effort to ask what she was doing here. He knew what she wanted before she began to move from the doorway. She wanted to play. Her eyes met his ever so briefly before sliding away. She was wondering what he'd do. It was something of a shock to realise she wasn't certain of his response—would he support her bid for acceptance or would he usher her straight back to the inn with a scold?

This would be the first test of their togetherness. If he did the latter, he'd prove himself no better than her father and that would be anathema to their relationship. Mercedes didn't want a man who would chain her to rules. Even for her own good.

Greer stood, gauging the reactions of the other men in the room. They were slack-jawed in amazement, as well they should be. Mercedes was stunning. Like many of her dresses, this one wasn't given to excessive trims and bows, relying instead on the curves of her figure for its adornment. The faintest hint of lip-colour highlighted her lush mouth and drew one's gaze upwards towards her eyes as a subtle reminder of where a gentleman *should* be looking when he addressed her. Most of the

men in the room were having difficulty re-
membering that rule.

She strode towards the table, surveying the
game. Greer followed her with his eyes, wary
and waiting for her to signal what she was
up to. This was a test for her, too. He'd been
clear that he wouldn't run any of her father's
crooked gambits. He would play fairly and
without artifice. He needed Mercedes to accept that as much as Mercedes needed him to
accept her right to play.

'Is it your shot?' She looked at him for the
first time since she entered the room. 'You'll
need to use a bank shot to get around that
mess.'

Greer smiled in hopes of easing the tension
that had sprung up. The men didn't know what
to make of a female presence in their male-
dominated milieu. He could help them there
and he could help Mercedes. He nodded and
held out his cue to her. 'An excellent assessment. Perhaps you'd like to take the shot for
me?'

A few of the men snickered, thinking he
asked out of sarcasm. He quelled them with
a look. Mercedes was not daunted. She took
the cue, bent to the table and made the com-

plicated shot with practised ease. Appreciative murmurs hummed around the table.

'Would you like to join our game?' Greer offered. The invitation had to come from him. No one else would dare go that far. They had to live here after tonight with wives and mothers who would never let them forget their one lapse in solid country judgement. But he could tell they were impressed.

'I would love to.' Mercedes chalked the cue and blew the lingering dust lightly over the tip in his direction. A few of the men sidled away to join card games in other rooms, but most remained, intrigued by the woman in the coral dress who would be gone in the morning, leaving them with a night they'd long remember.

'Were you surprised to see me?' Mercedes asked as they made the short walk back to the inn well after midnight.

'No. You wouldn't have got on the train this morning if you'd meant to hide away in inn rooms.'

'You're very astute for a man,' she teased.

'That's quite a compliment, coming from you.' Greer laughed into the mild summer darkness. In moments like this, laughing with her, walking with her, he felt alive as if he needed nothing more than Mercedes and enough money in his pocket to make it to the next town. Those were *not* thoughts worthy of a man raised to be a viscount's son, but they were his thoughts and he'd been thinking them more and more often—one of his many fantasies when it came to Mercedes. She provoked the impossible in him.

'You really weren't surprised?' she pressed. 'I wore this dress just for you.'

'Nothing you do surprises me, Mercedes.' He drew her close and stole a kiss, and then another, a slow spark beginning to ignite. Why not? There was no one out that late to see.

'*Nothing?* We'll have to work on that,' she whispered between kisses.

What happened next would always remain blissfully fuzzy in his memory. He was fairly sure it was Mercedes who danced them back into a shallow alley off the main thoroughfare and hitched her leg about his hip. But it was him who rucked up her coral skirts and took her wildly against the brick wall of a building just like he'd wanted to on a prior occasion, both of them aroused beyond good sense by the eroticism of the encounter and the exhilaration of the night. Climax came fast, a blessed, thundering release.

'*Nothing?*' Mercedes sucked at his ear lobe. 'Really?'

'All right,' Greer panted, exhausted. 'Maybe that.'

'*Maybe that?*' Mercedes echoed softly. 'I'll try harder tomorrow.'

Greer caught his breath and arranged his trousers with a laugh. Good Lord, if she tried any harder, he'd be worn to a stub before they reached Devonshire, which might not be an unpleasant experiment.

Mercedes hoped Devonshire would not prove to be an experiment in unpleasantness. Devonshire was close to nothing, least of all Birmingham. It had taken a week's worth of travel to reach this south-west corner of England. The week itself had been extraordinary, made up of billiards games and trains, and coaches, when the rails ran out. Every night was spent in Greer's bed. Every day was spent believing this could work. They could be to-gether—weren't they proving it?

But now that they were here, Mercedes's stomach was an inconveniently tight ball of nerves. By the time Greer's home came into view down a long winding drive lined with ancient oaks, her rampant thoughts had coalesced into one singular concern: what had she done? She was miles from anywhere with a viscount's son, about to meet a family that couldn't possibly welcome her, but who could quite possibly throw her out of their home.

The sprawling estate loomed over a horseshoe-shaped drive, an overpowering sandstone testament to good breeding that dwarfed the Brighton terraced homes and she *knew*. She'd overstepped herself this time, reached too high. On the road it had become easy to forget all that Greer had been born to. There would be no forgetting here, for her or for him. Greer reached over and squeezed her hand, reading her thoughts with alarming accuracy. 'You'll do fine.' He pulled the gig they'd rented in the village to a halt and he moved around to help her down, his hands resting at her waist. 'I would say "they're going to love you..."' he murmured.

'But they're not.' She gave him a smile. They were here for Greer. He needed to make decisions and put ghosts to rest and that could only happen here where they could be confronted.

Do you love me? She hated herself for the traitorous thought. She'd asked him not to love her and now she found that was the very thing she craved. *You don't need him*, her mind rallied. Didn't need Greer? What a lie. She didn't want to need him, but she did. When he'd held out his cue to her, when he'd punched Luce Talmadge, the countless times he'd made her laugh, or divined her thoughts before she'd voiced them—all proved it.

Worst of all, she suspected she more than needed him. She *loved* him. What else could explain why she'd risked coming here where there wasn't only his family to face? There was also the possibility Greer might never leave. He might take a look around and decide to stay. There was no guarantee he'd go on to Brighton. But she would. She had to. Her ghosts had to be exorcised there.

'Don't borrow trouble, Mercedes.' Greer squeezed her hand reassuringly. 'It's just my family, not the Spanish Inquisition.' He led her up the curved stairs to a front door which opened before he could knock, a footman bowing with a gracious, 'Milord, welcome home.' For a second it was all very formal, then chaos broke loose.

'Greer!' Two blonde girls rushed at him from the wide staircase in the foyer, and more people materialised from doorways. There were hugs and handshakes for Greer. It was not a moment for intrusion. Mercedes stood back, giving Greer the moment to drink in his family. After the initial onslaught of familial affection had ebbed, Greer drew her forward.

'Everyone, this is Miss Mercedes Lockhart. Mercedes, these are my sisters, Clara and Emily.' They were charming, blue-eyed and blonde. Clara was perhaps fifteen, Emily seventeen and on the brink of womanhood. She'd be going to London soon and breaking hearts with a smile that looked so much like Greer's there was no doubting the resemblance.

'This is my brother, Andrew.' The heir, the brother who wanted Greer to take over the home farm. He had Greer's looks, but not Greer's graceful build. He was solid, sturdier, not unattractive, but lacking Greer's magnetism. He was a practical man, a reliable man who'd probably never entertained a risky thought in his life. It was no wonder he couldn't understand Greer's reticence to embrace the home farm.

'This is my mother, Lady Tiverton.' *Viscountess Tiverton*, Mercedes thought. She had a kind smile for Mercedes but Mercedes was reluctant to trust it. Such a smile wouldn't last, not when she discovered the type of woman her son had been fraternising with. It wasn't self-pity or a sense of inadequacy that led to the thought, just honesty. She'd lived in Brighton, after all. She'd seen plenty of nobility and she knew where the lines were drawn. Rich billiards players and their daughters were fine when it was all fun and games. They became *de trop* when blood was on the line.

'And this is my father, Viscount Tiverton.' Greer completed the introductions. The Viscount was tall, having passed on his lean physique to Greer, and his more reserved personality to his older son. Mercedes thought Greer had got the better portion of the genetic deal.

Lady Tiverton ushered them all in to the drawing room and rang for tea, giving the staff time to recover from the surprise of Greer's arrival. Tea would give Lady Tiverton time to arrange for rooms to be prepared. Mercedes had used the ploy more than once when her father had brought home unexpected visitors. For the first time since she'd left her father, Mercedes felt a twinge of loss. She'd had a week to let her anger cool and in the absence of that anger, she missed him.

Tea was a polite interlude. There was nothing more than small talk exchanged. If there was to be an interrogation, it would occur in private. Well, there was no 'if'. Mercedes knew there *would* be an interrogation. She was aware of Andrew's eyes on her, studious and discerning. The next time she caught him watching her she looked him straight in the eye and smiled. He looked away hastily, nearly spilling his teacup and earning a short scold of caution from Lady Tiverton.

Greer nudged her covertly with the toe of his boot as if to say, *play nice*. She'd try, but she'd decided after the second cup of tea she could be nothing other than she was and Mercedes Lockhart didn't tolerate insolence in any form, not even from viscounts' heirs.

When rooms were ready, Mercedes found Emily and Clara at her side, insisting on accompanying her upstairs. They chattered the whole while, pointing out aspects of the house as they passed hallways and closed doors.

'What's down there?' Mercedes gestured to one corridor the girls didn't mention.

'That's all storage. It's where we keep the nice things for special visits.' Clara shrugged as if such an area was commonplace. Mercedes didn't comment, but the corridor intrigued her. It might be worth a visit. She'd noticed a change in the house as they'd moved up the stairs. The public rooms had been exquisitely done up, but the private areas lacked that same veneer.

The runners on the hall floors were clean but worn, having seen generations of Barringtons. The long curtains at the hall windows were faded from years in the sun. Tables that should have been cluttered with knick-knacks were bare.

The room she was given was lovely, done up in light yellows and pinks with a view of the south lawn and gardens, but by no means sophisticated. The old, solid oak furnishings would have suited a well-to-do farm house. Her rooms in Brighton far outclassed them.

The girls made themselves comfortable on the wide window seat, watching in wide-eyed amazement as she unpacked her trunk.

'Don't you have a maid?' Emily asked.

'No. We've been travelling and it's been faster not to be burdened with one.' Mercedes shook out the blue dinner gown she'd worn the first night she'd met Greer. She hoped he wasn't being interrogated downstairs. She'd felt awkward leaving him after a week solely in his presence. Since Birmingham it had just been the two of them. That would all change. Now there were others vying for his time. She'd have to learn to share him.

Emily's eyes widened further. She was old enough to take in the implications of such a statement. 'You travelled *alone* with my brother?' Mercedes wished she'd worded it more carefully.

'He'll have to marry you!' Clara chimed in with a worthy amount of adolescent fervour over the scandal.

'No, he doesn't.' Mercedes turned away, putting a chemise in a bureau drawer scented with sweet lavender. Would *she* marry *him* if he asked? It was an academic question only. They'd never talked of any future beyond Brighton and even that future had become uncertain lately. Would they go on to Brighton? Or would only she go on? Greer had not mentioned the tournament since leaving Birmingham and it was highly possible, once he saw the benefits of home, he'd simply stop here. He didn't need Brighton, not like she did.

'How did you meet my brother?' Emily asked. 'Was it at a ball? Did he sweep you off your feet? Greer's a great dancer.' Of course, she would think they met at a ball. Where else did nice girls of Emily's background meet nice young men? It was another reminder of how far apart their two worlds were.

The girl would have to be redirected before the questions became more awkward. She wouldn't lie to Greer's sister, but the truth might see her expedited from the house. His parents wouldn't like her telling impressionable Emily that she'd been travelling the countryside playing billiards with men and masquerading in brothels.

'I met him in Brighton. He had business with my father.' It was true, but it wouldn't hold up for long. It was time to redirect. 'Have you been to Brighton?' She didn't expect they had. Young girls didn't travel further than the distance between the schoolroom and the dining room. 'The Prince's pavilion is a sight to behold. I've danced there once.'

She went on to describe the oriental palace with its spirals and domes, the seaside and the bathing machines that took people out into the ocean. The girls were enrapt and soon questions about their brother were forgotten.

'You have lovely clothes.' Emily looked longingly at the oyster organdy. 'I wonder if Mama would let me wear something like this? She only lets me wear white. She'd never let me have a colour like *that*.' She gestured at the coral gown hanging in the wardrobe. 'But oyster, maybe. It's almost like white, only creamier. White makes me look so pale.'

Mercedes picked up the gown and held it against the girl. 'Yes, oyster becomes you—see how it gives you a little glow?' Emily beamed. Mercedes felt encouraged. She could use a friend in these environs. *Pick someone who is open to your advances.* She pushed the hustling rule aside. She was *not* hustling Greer's family into accepting her. She was merely cajoling them.

'White can be helped along with ribbons.' Mercedes dug through her personal items and pulled out a handful. She sorted through them until she found the one she wanted. It was a gentle aquamarine, not too bright. Lady Tiverton couldn't complain. It would look light but fresh against a white dress. 'Why don't you try this? I think you'll like how it looks.'

'Really? I can keep it?' Emily was thrilled at the impromptu gift.

'If it's all right with your mother.' Mercedes smiled. It wouldn't do to alienate Lady Tiverton. 'Now, how about you, Miss Clara? What kinds of colours do you like to wear?' She would conquer the Barringtons one by one and hope it would be enough. Tea with the family had set a nice tone, but Mercedes was not fool enough to believe that meant her worries were over. The other shoe was going to fall. It was a given.

Chapter Twenty-One

The other shoe was, in fact, falling in the gardens right then. When an unsuitable woman showed up on one's doorstep, action must be taken immediately before word spread. Still, for Andrew such speed was most impressive, Greer thought uncharitably. Mercedes had barely been whisked upstairs before Andrew had asked for this interview on the premise of wanting to show him new plans for a fountain.

Greer eyed a much-folded sheet of paper Andrew withdrew from his inner coat pocket and rethought his analysis. He might be wrong about the speed. His brother might have had a week or two to compose his words. Not even the army moved as slowly as his brother.

'Miss Lockhart is a most improper lady.'

Andrew handed him the folded sheet. 'My friend, Mister Ogilvy, wrote to me from Bath. Would you care to read it?'

'I take it we're not going to discuss the fountain?' Greer could feel his temper rising. He didn't like hearing Mercedes maligned so casually. He'd come home to sort through his thoughts and regain his perspective. He'd thought he'd have a little more time before he had to defend his choices. Apparently he was only going to get an hour.

'It's going over by the roses. There. We've talked about the fountain,' Andrew said tersely.

'I haven't been home in three years and the first thing you can think to do is berate me for my companion.'

'We're all glad you're home. We're glad you weren't killed in some meaningless action. But...' Andrew gestured with the letter in his hand, urging Greer to take it '...you've been home for some months. Instead of coming here where you belong you've elected to cool your heels in Brighton and head off to Bath with a billiards champion and his daughter.' He looked at Greer sceptically. 'Half-pay officers must make considerably more than I thought. I know an expensive woman when I see one.'

Greer's fist tightened at his side. 'I should hit you for that. You don't know a thing about her.'

'I know she's got you spinning so fast you can't see straight. Ogilvy says the pair of you were inseparable in Bath and that you had rooms in her home.'

'Her father's home.' Greer corrected. Andrew made it sound as if they'd been living in sin. Greer yanked the letter from Andrew's hand and scanned the page. He'd known something of this nature was bound to happen. England wasn't that big and the peerage even smaller. Everyone was connected in some way and news travelled. Still, *Ogilvy and his brother*? It seemed an unlikely connection. Ogilvy was so gregarious and his brother was, well, *not*.

'How the hell do you know him, anyway?' Greer asked, passing the letter back. It hadn't been nearly as damning as it could have been.

Andrew shrugged and put the paper back in his coat. 'I've only met him a couple of times in London. We are both members of an agricultural society and have exchanged letters about crop rotations over the years.' And now they were exchanging letters about him. Great.

'Ogilvy wasn't even sure you and I were related,' Andrew added. Too bad he'd decided to mention it at all, Greer thought. In all fairness, though, if it hadn't been Ogilvy, it would have been someone else. He couldn't have kept the last two months of his life a secret forever.

'We're getting away from the subject at hand.' Andrew stopped on the garden path and faced him squarely, arms crossed. 'I must ask what your intentions are in bringing Miss Lockhart here. Good Lord, she's upstairs right now with our sisters. Who knows what she's teaching them?'

Probably how to blow chalk off a cue. It would almost be worth it to voice the irreverent thought out loud. Andrew looked so serious, as if the fate of the world rested on this. Greer supposed it did. Andrew's world was considerably smaller than his. 'Father put you up to this. You sound just like him.'

Andrew didn't bother denying it. 'Yes. He thought you'd take it better from me. You and he haven't always been close. He thought you might think he was being heavy handed, as always.' Andrew softened, reminding Greer of the brother he'd grown up with. 'Besides, I volunteered to do it willingly. I'm worried about you. I don't expect you to be excited about the Devonshire life, not after all you've seen. But it's a good life, Greer.'

'It's not the life I want,' Greer answered simply. If he'd learned anything on the road with Lockhart, it was that he'd not be happy isolated in the country doing the same thing every day. There was a tedium to country life that had never quite suited him even when he'd been young. Greer shook his head. His plans were starting to take on a new importance. They had to succeed or it would be the home farm for him.

'What do you mean to do?' Andrew asked when there was no response from him. 'Have you received a new posting?'

'No. I'm thinking about selling my commission.' His family would not like it, but he knew with absolute clarity what he'd do. 'We mean to go on to Brighton. There's a billiards tournament I'm going to play in and then I'm going to open a subscription room. People in Brighton are always looking for entertainment.'

'We? You mean with her?' Andrew was more agitated about Mercedes than the subscription room.

'Yes. If she'll have me. We haven't talked about specifics yet.' He couldn't imagine returning to Brighton without Mercedes, couldn't begin to contemplate launching this new enterprise without her. They'd have to contend with Lockhart, of course, but he might be more amenable to reconciliation once his anger cooled.

'If she'll have you? I'm sure there's no question of it. You're a good catch for a girl like that.' Andrew's tone bordered on derisive, the moment of softness gone.

'A girl like what?' Greer went on the defensive.

'Well, just look at her. She's the kind of woman who makes a man think with his wrong head.' Implying, of course, that Greer was doing just that.

'Will you accept her?' Greer asked point-blank. He was really asking if the family would accept her.

'Your mistress is your own business, you don't need the family's approval on that. But a mistress isn't to be flaunted in your family's face. You knew better than to bring her here.'

'No.' Greer cut him off before Andrew could begin a sanctimonious tirade about a gentleman's ethics. 'Will you accept her as *my wife*?' It was an admittedly madcap idea, marrying Mercedes. He wasn't even sure she was up for it after her *débâcle* with Luce. But once the idea had taken up residence in his brain it wouldn't be evicted. *Lady Mercedes Barrington*.

Andrew shook his head. 'You need to think this through. This could be a scandal for all of us and with Emily's Season next year it's an enormous risk.'

'I don't think the risk is all that great,' Greer countered. 'She's a celebrity's daughter and I'm a second son. I doubt the scandal would last long enough to do Emily any damage.'

'Then there's Father to consider. He won't forgive this, Greer. You will have crossed him for the last time. Think of all you'll be giving up.'

He tried not to think of that. Grandmother's inheritance, left specifically to him. Twenty thousand pounds to be his upon his marriage to a suitable bride.

Andrew dropped his voice. 'That twenty thousand would go so far here. We wouldn't have to live like we do. You know what I mean.'

He did know what his brother meant: keeping up appearances. 'There's money for a new fountain.'

'We're entertaining this autumn. We had to do something.' Andrew sighed. Yes, Greer thought, something to distract the eyes from what was really around them—a tired, worn-out estate.

'With your twenty thousand, we could invest and draw on returns. We could fix the roof.'

'You mean *you* could,' Greer broke in coldly. 'You've been dreaming of the inheritance, haven't you?' He was starting to see where this was all headed. Andrew lacked the sophistication of Allen Lockhart when it came to manipulation, but the end game was the same. He saw his brother's plan. Give Greer the home farm to run, find him a nice baron's daughter to marry and keep him and his twenty thousand here.

'No,' Greer said firmly. 'I will not be emotionally blackmailed into this or threatened into it.'

Andrew's face turned red. 'You'll never see a penny of it if you marry her.'

'Not unless you use your influence with Father to convince him to release the funds.' Greer smiled coldly. He didn't relish what he was going to say next, but it had to be done if he wanted to know Andrew's true colours. 'What if I promise you half of the money if you can get it released?'

The anger left Andrew's face almost immediately, replaced by a calculating glint in his eyes. 'Well, that would be something to consider. Ten thousand would certainly help.' His words were slow as he thought out loud, already imagining how to spend the funds.

Greer wanted to hit him. 'You bastard. This isn't about money.' At least it shouldn't be about money.

'Of course it is, Greer. It's always been about money.' Andrew sneered. 'Don't be naïve.'

'You disgust me.' Greer turned on his heel and headed back to the house. It was something of a setback to discover he'd traded Allen Lockhart's shenanigans for his brother's, and that the two weren't all that different. This visit might turn out to be shorter than planned, but he couldn't leave it, as much as he wanted to. He wanted to spend time with his sisters, to show Mercedes his home and he needed to talk with his father, even if the outcome of that discussion seemed obvious and futile.

Five days in, Mercedes could sense things were going poorly. Not that anyone was going out of their way to be cruel. She almost wished they were. Then she could meet trouble head on. In fact the opposite was true. Dinners had been unfailingly polite, as had the game of cards afterwards. The girls and Greer's mother had shown her around the gardens the next morning. They'd spent a companionable afternoon on the back verandah enjoying the sun and their individual arts. Emily worked with her watercolours while Clara read aloud from a novel while she and Lady Tiverton stitched.

On the surface, it all looked perfect. Like the public rooms downstairs. But underneath there was a very rotten core. She noticed it in the way no one asked her anything personal. There was no attempt to get to know her in any meaningful way. She was included enough to make it clear she was excluded.

Today she was left to her own devices, another reminder of her ultimate exclusion. The girls and Lady Tiverton had gone to the village for a meeting at the church. She'd notably not been invited. It would have required public acknowledgement. Greer was nowhere to be found, as he had been for the better part of the visit.

She saw very little of Greer and they were never alone when she did. Out of respect for the home and his parents, there was no question of a clandestine visit to his rooms or hers. She sorely missed his presence in her bed.

It was the perfect strategy: divide and conquer. She wondered if Greer saw it, this attempt to keep them apart while reminding him of all he had, of who he was, maybe even of what he stood to lose if he defied them. All the while the clock was ticking. She had to think about getting to Brighton.

Mercedes wandered into the storage corridor. Today was a perfect day to check it out. It was intriguing enough to have a storage corridor. Most people used attics. What in the world did they keep in here? She gave the first door a tentative try. It gave and she pushed it open. The room was the size of a bedroom and full of boxes.

Mercedes studied the labels: linens, tablecloths, bed sheets. Curious, Mercedes pulled down one box and opened it. The scent of cedar and lavender wafted from it. She dug her hands into depths past layers of tissue paper. Whatever was in here had been stored with the utmost care. Her hands made contact with the softest of linen and she pulled out a pristine set of white sheets trimmed in expensive lace and exquisitely embroidered. She held them to her nose and inhaled. It brought a little smile to her lips.

'Now you know our dirty little secret.' A voice behind her made her jump. She felt terribly vulnerable. She'd been caught red-handed at snooping.

'Andrew, you startled me.' Mercedes replaced the sheets and rose, brushing dust off her skirts. 'I thought everyone was out.'

'Obviously.' His blue eyes were cold, lacking any of the mischief and warmth she found so often in Greer's. He moved into the room, crowding her between the boxes and his body. 'What do you think of us now? We keep our best things packed carefully away, bringing them out only on special occasions like state visits.'

One look at the sheets and she'd guessed as much. 'It doesn't matter one way or the other to me,' Mercedes offered, stepping past him into the hall.

He grabbed her arm. 'It matters to me. We need him to marry well. He can do much better than you and he should.'

Mercedes jerked her arm free, tempted to go for the knife in her bodice. 'If you'll excuse me, I think I'll see if Greer's returned.'

* * *

But she didn't see Greer until that night at dinner, another polite affair even though the bubble was officially off the wine after her unpleasant encounter with Andrew. She knew where the family stood. Did Greer? He looked immaculate in evening wear appropriate for the country, his blond hair momentarily tamed back from his face. He was tanned from riding and radiated strength and health. Her heart nearly cracked in two at the sight of him. Did he understand he'd have to choose between her and his family? How could she force him to make that choice?

Dinner dragged on interminably. Emily talked about the watercolour she'd painted today. Everyone laughed when Clara told a funny story about the new kittens in the barns. But there were subtle tones of tension that underlay the table tonight. Greer's father was more taciturn than the norm and Andrew was not trying at all to disguise his dislike of her. She wished desperately for some form of escape. She was just about to fabricate an illness when Greer rose right before dessert was served.

'If you would all excuse us, I need to steal Mercedes away. I promised her on the way here that I'd show her the gardens, but I've been remiss so far in carrying out my word.'

'Thank you,' Mercedes breathed once they were outdoors. The gardens were cool and dark in the summer night. They weren't lit like her garden in Brighton. The only brightness was the light thrown haphazardly from the house. 'I didn't think I could stand another moment.' There was so much they needed to discuss. 'We need to talk, Greer.'

'Hush. We'll talk in a while. For now, just enjoy. Look at the stars. There aren't stars in town like this.' Greer tipped his head back to the sky and she did the same, gasping a bit at the brilliance overhead. The stars had come out in multitudes, diamonds against the black silk of the sky.

'Stunning,' Mercedes offered.

'Like you.' Greer traced a finger along the curve of her upturned jaw. 'You're like the sky tonight, all those brillantes in your hair, your gown like a moonbeam. I think I like you in silver best. You're my very own star fairy.' He placed a kiss at the base of her neck and she shivered.

'I must apologise for leaving you alone so long. I had hoped some time with my father

might help us resolve some of our differences.'
He shrugged to indicate that he'd not been successful in that regard.

So this was it. He *did* know he'd have to choose. How many more times would he touch her like this? They'd resumed walking the open pathways through the knot gardens. The heat of him radiated through his coat, warming her.

'Your brother doesn't approve of me,' Mercedes began.

'Maybe you'll grow on him.' Greer tried to dismiss the concern with humour. 'It might take a while though. Andrew is a slow learner.'

'Do you think there will be time for that?' she ventured, veering carefully towards the conversation they needed to have. Would he stay or would he come to Brighton?

Greer stopped and turned towards her, his eyes taking on a serious cast. 'I certainly hope so.' Something in his demeanour put her on alert. Her hands were in his, flat against his chest. He held her with those deep blue eyes and she waited, unable to form the questions pelting through her mind.

'There is much I need to talk to you about, Mercedes, but I felt I couldn't until I was sure of things. I had arrangements I needed to make, conversations I needed to have. Now all is settled and I can come to you.'

Her heart began to race. She'd understood the first part. There was much to talk about and she could imagine most of it. It was time to say goodbye. But the rest made no sense. Arrangements he needed to make…? A pit formed in her stomach, the roasted fowl threatening to come up. He wanted her to be his mistress. For him it would be the perfect compromise. He could have her without separating from his family.

No, oh, please not that. To have him, but not have him, would be worse than not having him altogether. It would cheapen everything they'd shared. Was that all he'd seen her as? Even if it was all she could expect from a nobleman's son, she wouldn't take half measures. It wasn't the offer that turned her stomach so much as the realisation that she'd thought he'd known her better than to ask.

She tugged, trying to free her hands. Greer held tight. She lashed out with cold words. 'I will never be any man's mistress, Captain Barrington. Not even yours.'

He gave a slight shake of his head. 'Not that.' Then he laughed. 'This is not going quite as I had planned.'

She realised her mistake with a dawning fear that replaced the horror over being his mistress. A man like Greer didn't bring a mistress to the family seat. A man like Greer would only bring home a woman he meant to… Mercedes felt her legs go weak. Oh Lord, Greer meant to propose.

Chapter Twenty-Two

Greer sank to one knee on the stone pavers in front of her and she wished she could do the same. Her hands were still tightly gripped in his. She let their warmth and strength sustain her through this terrible, beautiful moment. She was cognisant of it all—how carefully he must have planned even if it had gone awry; this lovely, private setting, his family home on display at its summer finest with the moon and stars overhead, the faint call of the night birds in the distance.

'Mercedes, will you do me the honour of marriage?' There was no great speech, no listing of her attributes and the fixing of his affections, no protestations of undying love. Yet it was all there in the single line, in the touch of his hands, the dark mirrors of his eyes. 'You would make me the happiest of men.'

That galvanised her into action. 'I would make you the most miserable of men,' she said softly. She didn't want to be cruel. Clearly, this moment meant much to him. It meant much to *her*. Any girl would be flattered to receive such a proposal from such a man. Men like Greer didn't grow on trees for the picking. 'Why now, Greer?'

The romance of the moment passed. Greer sighed and rose. He sat down on a stone bench, arms balanced on his knees, head down. She regretted her practical questions. She'd bungled this. What had he said to her once? *You really know how to cut a man down to size.* She'd done that tonight most assuredly. *This moment will pass and I'll be glad I saved him from this grievous mistake.*

'Why now? Isn't it apparent?'

'Not really,' she answered truthfully. 'Unless it is a strategy of yours to keep me here with you instead of going on to Brighton.'

He shot her a cold look. 'A strategy? Is that how you saw this? Is it how you see everything?' His tone was not kind. This is it, she thought. *This is where I lose him.* After all, this was where her father had lost him. It had been the games, the manoeuvres, and the strategies that Greer could not tolerate about him.

'This was an honourable proposal of marriage, given, I think, with the sincerest of emotions,' Greer ground out. 'Brighton is our watershed. We can't keep piece-mealing our relationship together. We need to decide what we shall mean to each other. I have decided, but apparently you haven't.'

Her mind had latched on to one word. 'What do you mean "Brighton is our watershed?"'

'We're going back, aren't we? Back to where this all started and for the reason it started. We're going to play in that tournament and, after one of us wins, we need a plan.'

This nearly reduced her to tears as the proposal had not. *We.* 'How did you know I meant to play?' she whispered.

Greer laughed, his anger dissipating a little. He wasn't gone from her just yet. 'You haven't cornered the market on deductive powers yet. There was only one reason you went to Mrs Booth's. You needed money and there was only one reason you needed it. Then, when you confessed in Birmingham the reasons you'd come on the road, I knew my assumption wasn't wrong. You meant to play. Besides, you got on the train with me and I knew at the time, you didn't get on the train for me. Not solely, anyway.'

Mercedes blushed. 'It was more about you than you think.' How could she tell him she lived in fear of losing him? That she wanted nothing more than to accept his proposal. 'But I don't see how it's going to work.'

'I'll sell my commission. We'll have a little money to start. One of us could win the tournament. The purse will definitely help.'

Mercedes put a finger to his lips. 'Just like a man.' She laughed softly. 'We can survive on our own. Didn't we prove it on the road? That's not what I'm worried about. There are more important considerations than money.' She made a gesture to encompass the grounds. 'There's your family and all of this. You have everything to lose and I have nothing.' *Except my heart.*

'They will accept you, Mercedes, given enough time.'

'You don't know that and you have no reason to believe it. I will not have you throw away your family. No matter what you think of them, they're the only family you've got.' She paused. 'I know what you'll be throwing away, Greer. I miss my father.' She had to make him see reason, see all the things he might be jeopardising.

He kissed the column of her neck, his voice low against her throat. 'Stop thinking of questions, Mercedes, and start thinking of answers. How do we go to Brighton?' She understood—separately as Mercedes Lockhart and Lord Captain Greer Barrington, occasional and unconventional lovers, or did they go as Lord and Lady Barrington, bound together forever by the bonds of matrimony?

Mercedes swallowed. Did she dare reach out and claim her heart's desire, to be with Greer always? The road would not be easy no matter how certain he was of his plans.

'Please, Greer, give me time to think.' The gambler's motto came to mind: know the rules, know the stakes, know when to quit. She'd broken the rules; they were of no help to her now. She knew the stakes, her heart against the odds. As for quitting, was this the time? She simply didn't know.

He kissed her one more time, a slow lingering kiss meant to last. 'While you're thinking, think about this. I love you, Mercedes Lockhart.'

She reached up and twined her arms about his neck. 'I know. That's why I have to think for both of us.'

Predictably, she couldn't sleep. She wondered if Greer had managed to sleep. He'd taken her request with equanimity, if not disappointment. She didn't doubt Greer cared for her. But would such a sacrifice be worth it for him? Would there come a day when he'd regret his choice? When he'd wish he'd married a pale virginal beauty of the *ton*? When he'd wish he hadn't resigned his commission or that he had stayed in Tiverton?

Mercedes got out of bed and put on a simple dress. It would be morning soon enough. Even now, grey light pierced the darkness. Perhaps some exercise would be enough to clear her thoughts. Not surprisingly, her feet found their way to the billiards room. The Barrington table was well worn in the style of the house but solid. Perhaps she might shoot just a few balls to relax.

No. There was light coming from the room. Drawing closer, she could hear the very quiet snick of balls against one another. Someone was playing. She almost turned back and then laughed at her foolishness. Who else would be up besides Greer?

She stepped into the room, realizing too late the blond hair and form bent over the table wasn't Greer, but Andrew. He looked up, pinning her with his gaze like an insect in a display gaze. She felt about as small, too, not that she'd give him the satisfaction that he might be able to intimidate her just a teeny bit. Mercedes met his gaze.

'My brother has proposed. Have you accepted?' Andrew made an angry shot. He was adequate, but not especially good.

'That's none of your business.' Mercedes picked up a cue stick. 'Shall I play you for him? Will that make you feel better? I win, I get him.'

'Do you really think you can beat me?' He was all smug disbelief over the idea of a woman playing.

'Let's find out.' Mercedes racked the balls and they chalked up in taciturn silence, each of them consumed by their thoughts. She played hard, her concentration absolute. Mercedes lowered her cue, catching the ball slightly below the centre, and executed a neat split, putting one ball in a pocket and the other effectively in Andrew's way.

'I wish my father had never taught him to play,' Andrew said, forcefully potting a ball. 'It's been nothing but trouble.'

'It's a gentleman's game. He was honour-bound to learn.' Mercedes struck back with a slice.

'Is it?' he said meanly, missing his next shot. 'You seem to suggest otherwise.'

Mercedes ignored the gibe. 'Greer will never truly be happy here. He has a great gift.'

Andrew leaned on his stick, surveying the table. She'd made it hard on him and he didn't know where his next shot was coming from. 'A gift? And he should use that gift to be a billiards sharp in some club with you?' He gave her full scrutiny. 'Why do you want him? You're not pregnant, are you?' He took a poor shot.

'No, not that it's any of your business,' she answered sharply, making her own. Greer had been careful, but she'd taken precautions too. A child at this point would complicate things even further. Mercedes made her last shot. 'I win.'

'But at what price?' Andrew laid his cue on the table. She could see he wasn't finished with her yet. 'Do you understand? He's got nothing of his own. You were going through the boxes, you know how we live. It's all smoke and mirrors around here and what there is will come to me.'

'I understand perfectly,' Mercedes replied.

Andrew shook his head. 'You must be fabulous in bed, absolutely fabulous. It's the only answer I can come up with. Do you do it all? You must, for twenty thousand. I almost wish I could have a taste of it so I could better comprehend how my brother could give up so much.'

Mercedes's temper surged. 'You're a very crass man, and I haven't any idea what you're referring to.'

Andrew gave a malevolent smile. 'You don't know? Our grandmother left him twenty thousand, available to him upon his marriage to a suitable young lady. He marries you and he won't see a penny of it. And yet he seems determined to pursue that course.' His eyes raked her in an uncomfortable perusal. 'Again, I do wonder.'

Mercedes did not dignify his remark with a response. All she could think of was getting out of the room. He made her feel unclean.

Once up in her room, the guilt came. How many times had she taunted Greer about risking nothing? How he always had the security of the home farm waiting? In truth, he'd risked scandal, both private and public. Now, he risked his future. Twenty thousand would see him set for life if he lived within his comfortable means. But Greer had said nothing about it and was apparently ready to throw it away for her.

She wouldn't let him. Her answer was clear now. She had to refuse him for his own good. Her heart started to rebel. *But you love him.* No, don't think, just do. She would pack and be gone before he rose. She'd leave a note. She wouldn't survive facing him.

Mercedes had packed in record time, fearing to stop for a moment lest she start thinking about what she was doing. At last the note was scribbled, the room clear. A carriage stood waiting at the front door for her. It had been no problem to summon one even at this early hour. The footman had asked no questions when he'd come for her trunk. Apparently if Miss Lockhart wished to leave, everyone was to comply. At the last, she reached up and took off her star necklace and set it on top of the note in the salver in the front hall. Greer would understand this was for the best. And eventually she would too.

Mercedes climbed into the coach.

'Where to, Miss Lockhart?' the coachman asked.

Her throat was tight as she handed him a worn card. 'My father.'

Andrew Barrington watched the carriage pull away into the dawn from the front room window, the note clutched in his hand. Good riddance—the bitch was gone. Greer's twenty thousand was safe. He had every confidence his brother would forget the brazen hussy soon enough. There was a nice baron's daughter a few miles from here who would turn his head. Very soon this dalliance with the fiery Mercedes Lockhart would be nothing more than a bachelor's last fling.

Andrew scanned the note. The hussy claimed to have loved Greer. Too bad. If she hadn't told him already, it was too late. He crumpled the note and threw it into the grate. 'Molly,' he called to the early-morning maid in the hall, 'set a fire in here. There's a bit of chill in the air.'

Chapter Twenty-Three

A chill ran through Greer as he came down the stairs, full of nervous energy. A slice of silver gleamed in the front-hall salver, further compounding his feeling that something was wrong. He'd gone to Mercedes's room that morning wanting to talk, decency be damned, only to find it extraordinarily neat the way a room is after someone has left it. Of course she hadn't left, he'd told himself. It was nine o'clock in the morning. No one went anywhere until noon.

His reassurance slid away as he approached the salver, his worst suspicions confirmed. His hand closed over the necklace. His stomach clenched with confirmation. She was gone. Greer rummaged through the salver, looking for a note. Surely she wouldn't have left without any word? Questions bombarded his mind as he tried to make sense of it. Was this her idea of 'time to think'? Or was this outright rejection? Perhaps something else altogether? Had someone said something to her that had scared her off? She was acutely sensitive about their differences in station and after the proposal she'd feel any jab about her status keenly.

All he knew was that he hurt, physically hurt, at the thought that she was gone. She'd left *him* and he wanted answers.

Muffled voices from the estate office drew his attention. Ah, his father and Andrew were up early. Perhaps they knew something, or, came the sinister thought, had done something to drive her off. It felt good to have his hurt transform into anger he could use. He let it propel him into the office.

'Where is she?' Greer burst in, the necklace dangling in accusation from his fist.

'Ah…' Andrew gave a sad smile at the sight of the charm. 'Miss Lockhart has left us, so I was informed. She called for a carriage early this morning.'

Greer's anger ratcheted up a notch. 'And you let her go without question? A woman calls for a carriage at dawn and you, who just happen to be up, oddly enough, let her drive away?'

'She's not my woman,' Andrew sneered. 'She left you, not me.'

'You knew how I felt. You knew my hopes.'

Exactly. Andrew knew and Andrew hadn't approved. Andrew had been awake far earlier than usual. He'd never wanted to do violence to his brother as he did this very moment.

Greer gave in to the base urge. He grabbed Andrew by the lapels, hauling him against the wall. 'What did you do to her? What did you say?'

'It has to be me?' Andrew struggled to free himself, but Greer held fast. 'Can't you accept the fact that she's had her fun and now she's done? She decided she didn't want you. I caught her yesterday going through our storage room. She knows you haven't a feather to fly with. She's decided she doesn't want to be poor Lady Barrington after all.' Andrew's face was turning red.

'I don't accept lies,' Greer growled. 'Again, what did you do?'

'Boys, that is enough!' His father rose from behind his desk and Greer let Andrew go. 'Miss Lockhart is gone and I say good riddance if she's going to cause this kind of turmoil in our home. It's further proof she's not acceptable.'

Andrew sat down in his chair, smoothing his rumpled jacket. 'Trust me, it's better this way.' He made a conciliatory gesture.

Greer looked from his brother to his father in disbelief. They were simply going to dismiss Mercedes as if she were a bill to settle, and move on. 'Better for you,' he replied. Had he always been a pawn to them? Had it taken all this time away to see the truth? They were not much better than Allen Lockhart, with their schemes and manipulations. He was better off on his own.

Greer exited the room. His direction was clear now. He was halfway up the stairs when his father called up to him.

'If you go after her, you won't see a penny of that money, my son.'

Greer turned on the stairs. 'Neither will you. As for me, I'd rather have her.' It was true, every last word of it, and saying it out loud was a bright spot in a dismal morning. He knew exactly where he'd find her. He was going to Brighton to claim her and to claim his future. He was done here. Devonshire could offer him nothing more.

No distractions! Mercedes chided herself as she bent to the table and lined up a shot.

Greer wasn't here. She had to stop seeing him in every blond head that passed. She focused and made the shot. Those gathered around the table applauded.

The tournament began tomorrow and Brighton was bustling with business and tourists. Players and spectators alike crowded the subscription halls, none more so than Lockhart's, to watch potential contestants play. Spectators interested in wagers assessed the odds while players sized one another up.

She'd played every game she could get. Her father hadn't the heart to gainsay her. It was a convenient way for him to bow to the inevitable. In the weeks since leaving Devonshire, billiards was the one activity that took her mind off Greer, off the sinking sensation she felt every time she thought of him and what he'd been willing to give up for her. *Willing.* He'd chosen her and she'd not allowed him that choice. Her current misery was her own fault.

She collected her winnings and racked the balls for another set. There were plenty of men lining up to play Lockhart's daughter for the sheer newness of it, if nothing else. She didn't care what their motives were. She only cared about buying herself a moment's peace from Greer Barrington. If anyone had told her in

March she'd feel this miserable about playing in the tournament she'd have laughed and wagered against such an outcome. She'd wanted this opportunity. Now she had it and it was not enough.

'Are you playing in the tournament, Miss Lockhart?' someone in the crowd called out.

'Absolutely. Are you?' she called back while the crowd laughed.

'What happens if you draw your father? Can you beat him?' someone else chimed in. She'd become something of a celebrity since returning to Brighton. Everyone was interested in what she did and she always gave them a show.

'We'll cross that bridge when we come to it,' Mercedes said with a saucy smile. The scenario did unnerve her. She hoped they would avoid each other in the pairings. It had been something of a surprise to discover her father had entered his own tournament until she'd sorted through the pieces, the little clues that hadn't made sense at the time like all the playing he'd done in Bath and afterwards. He'd used Greer as a smokescreen for launching his own career. The hard truth was, she had too. Only she'd fallen in love with her own mark, something she was willing to admit too late.

'Who's next?' she called out, pasting on a

smile. Men liked to play a pretty woman and
any woman was prettier when she smiled.

'I am.' A broad-shouldered man parted the
group from the back. Her breath caught and
she had to remind herself that Greer wasn't
here. He wasn't coming. She had left him and
he wasn't going to chase after her once cool-
headed logic set in.

'Hello, Mercedes.'

'Hello.' Her heart raced. She gripped the cue
for support. Not every man was Greer Barrington, but this one was. He looked a bit tired
around the eyes, but it was him.

He smiled. 'Shall we play for dinner? I win,
you take me. You win, I take you.'

'Take me where?' She chalked her cue, eyes
not leaving him.

'I'll take you wherever you like.' There were
some whistles and catcalls to that answer. Her
crowd was in a good mood.

'It might be worth losing just to find out.'
Mercedes gave the tip of her stick a naughty
blow. 'Your break.'

In the end she won, although she suspected
Greer's inadequate slice might have had something to do with it. But she was more than willing to live up to her end of the wager. She had

questions, and dinner would be the perfect opportunity for answers.

They chose the restaurant at Greer's hotel, a lovely place on the promenade where they could eat outside and watch people as they passed on their evening strolls along the water.

'What brings you to Brighton?' Mercedes asked once they were settled at their table.

Greer gave a short laugh. 'What do you think? The woman I proposed to fled my home in the middle of the night without any word.'

'I left a note,' Mercedes said defensively. Inside, her stomach was doing flip-flops. She wasn't sure how she'd manage to eat anything. *He'd come for her.* Not for the tournament.

His face registered some surprise. 'It did not reach me. But this did.' He pulled out the silver charm. 'I'd like for you to take it back.'

Mercedes took the charm and studied it. It gave her something to look at besides his handsome face. 'I've regretted how we parted, but the reasons I left haven't changed, Greer.' She looked up briefly. 'Your brother told me about the inheritance. I can't let you give that up. Or your family. You will come to hate me. You don't think so now, but you will.'

'Have you missed me, Mercedes? I've missed you and in the weeks it took to raise my own stake for the tournament and come here, I realised that being with you was all that mattered.' He reached for her hands and she let him take them.

'I won't change my mind, Greer.' She hoped he wouldn't call that bluff. Her mind was a malleable pudding at this point. Just seeing him again had reduced her insides to jelly. To have him touch her, to look at her with those eyes, was ambrosia.

'Come with me.' He grabbed up the bottle of champagne from the ice bucket and took her hand.

'What are you doing?' People were starting to look at them.

'Changing your mind. If you won't change it, I'll have to change it for you.' He grinned wickedly as he guided her through the dining room. 'Never say you're afraid?'

'Never.' She smiled back, but she knew this was sheer madness. One more night with Greer would only remind her of all she was giving up because it couldn't be any other way.

Upstairs in the privacy of his room, he stripped for her, seducing her with his movements as he took off trousers and boots, shirt and coat until he stood in front of her, gloriously and unabashedly nude. He would convince her any way he could tonight, with any tool he possessed.

At least she was willing to play along. Mercedes propped herself up on a pillow and licked her lips. 'You certainly know how to give a girl a good show. What do you have in mind for act two?'

She let her skirts fall back and parted her legs ever so provocatively, making her expectations for 'act two' quite clear. He nearly spent himself right there. Act two would be a very short one, leading directly to the main event.

He covered her then. There would be more time for talk later. For now he wanted the desperation of his body to speak for him. His need for her had reached a fever pitch after weeks of enforced celibacy. It had been almost impossible to concentrate on billiards that afternoon. All he could think of was this.

Mercedes drew him down to her, her legs embracing him, urging him, and he took her in a swift claiming thrust that wrung a gasp from her. He thrust again, establishing their rhythm, aware of the feel of Mercedes's long legs locked about him, aware of her body clenching about him, the tight warmth of her sheath as she took his length again and again.

Had anything ever felt this good? This right? Then of course, something did. His own release was upon him, pounding and furious, obliterating all else but pleasure in its path until he was spent.

There was champagne then, but not in the usual way. He saw to it even that was an exercise in decadence. He drank champagne from her navel. He licked the juice of strawberries from her lips and her breasts, watching her grey eyes go black with desire, feeling her body arch to him, wanting the pleasure as much as he wanted to give it and he came to her again as a lover complete, until they were too exhausted for more.

It was well after midnight before they found the strength to talk. She lay in his arms, her head against his shoulder, the light floral scent of her hair in his nostrils. 'I'm staying in Brighton, Mercedes, after the tournament.' Greer began laying out the plans he'd formed since leaving Devonshire. 'I am going to sell my commission and open a subscription room. I have a lead on a property not far from here. It's small, but it's a good location. I'm hoping the tournament will help build a clientele for me.'

She laughed softly in the darkness, a throaty sound he'd missed. 'In other words, you hope to finish high enough in the tournament to win both money and attention.'

'Yes. I'd forgotten how good you are at seeing to the heart of a matter.' Greer ran a hand down her arm, revelling in the feel of having her beside him again. 'My proposal still remains between us. My desire to marry you has not changed. Come run my subscription room with me. You can play. Perhaps you can even have a women's club. Wouldn't that be something? We'd be the only place in Brighton with one.'

'Have you forgotten your family, your inheritance? Those things remain as well.'

'I will not be their pawn, Mercedes. They can acknowledge me or not. That's their choice, not mine. My choice is you. I wish you would trust that.' He sighed, more than a little frustrated in her obstinate reticence. How else could he show her?

'On one condition, Greer.' She was all business, and his mind quickened at the prospect of one of her challenges.

'Name it.'

'Play me for it. Play me for our future.' She rolled out of bed and dressed, while he watched, pondering the request. This was starting to feel like the twelve labours of Hercules.

'Why?' Greer asked.

She came to the bed and kissed his cheek. 'Trust me, Greer. Stay alive in the tournament until you can get to me and you'll see. You have to keep your promise this time.'

'What does that mean?' Greer answered, half humoured and half perplexed. He always kept his word; surely she knew that by now.

'It means you broke your word once before when you promised me something.'

'I don't recall...' Greer hesitated.

'When you told me you wouldn't fall in love with me,' Mercedes prompted.

'Oh, well, then I had my fingers crossed,' Greer argued.

Mercedes shook her head. 'And now? There can be no crossed fingers on this, Greer.'

From anyone else, he would have laughed at the melodramatic nature of the request, but not with her. She was serious and in earnest. He might never get used to the intensity she had for billiards, but he could not doubt her dedication. 'Yes, Mercedes, I promise.'

Mercedes Lockhart took Brighton by storm, as she had fully intended to do. The gown she'd chosen for the tournament was black with a moderately full skirt to facilitate easy move-ment, but not nearly as full as common fashion dictated and it was most certainly being worn *without* a petticoat—only the gored folds of the skirt kept it from indecency. But nothing kept the bodice from earning such a label, what there was of it. There were no sleeves or neck, only the heart-shaped torso of the bodice, leaving her *décolletage* entirely bare save the single piece of jewellery she wore on a thin black ribbon: Greer's star, shining and silver. Her hair was worn in her customary drape over one shoulder. She smiled at the nearly quieted crowd, only to have it go wild again. Kendall Carlisle, the tournament's designated master of ceremonies, let it. Mercedes Lockhart was good for business. She sailed through the preliminary rounds, her luck and skill holding unchallenged. But in the quarterfinals her luck failed. Her father was still alive and playing spectacularly well.

So be it. Mercedes studied the table, steeling herself for the upcoming match. If she meant to win the tournament, facing her father was inevitable any way. She *did* need to win this game for her plans to advance. Beyond the match with her father lay the semifinal bracket in which she'd face Greer, just as she'd hoped and intended. But first, she needed this game to prove herself to her father once and for all. Mercedes chalked her cue, bent to the table, and broke with a smile. She could do this.

And she did, sweeping the match in three straight games to thunderous applause. If her father had deliberately thrown the match or lost on purpose out of some misguided effort to apologize, she couldn't tell, nor did she want to know. She could no longer feel responsible for his private agendas. She only knew she had what she wanted, a chance to send Greer to the finals and a chance to secure his inheritance in a roundabout way. She couldn't actually claim the trust for him but she could secure the amount he'd given up by coming after her. All he had to do was keep his promise.

Mercedes studied the semi-final brackets on the pairings board. The winner of her semi-final match with Greer would face a flirty rogue of a player from York, Alex Cahill. She'd seen the man play. He was devastating and attractive—an absolute showman. She smiled to herself: Greer would know exactly how to beat him. Mercedes fingered the large roll of pound notes she'd accumulated and went to place a bet.

Greer met her at the table for the semi-finals,

his voice low. 'All right, Mercedes. I stayed alive long enough to face you. Will we survive it?'

She turned and smiled at him. 'We will.' There wasn't time to say more. The games would start very soon. Tonight would decide everything. 'Remember what you promised me?'

'I remember. Do you remember what you promised me?'

'Absolutely.' Mercedes picked up her cue and began to chalk with a smile.

She made sure they gave the crowd a show. She was mesmerising and deadly with her splits. Greer was dominating with his slices. She smiled and dazzled, he laughed and charmed, brushing his hair out of his eyes every so often. People would long remember that match. She won the first game. He won the second and when the third game looked like it would somehow end in a dead heat, Mercedes caught Greer's gaze over her cue and bit her lip, sending him the only signal she could. Then she took her decisive shot, deliberately too hard, and the cue ball followed the other into the pocket. The crowd groaned and Greer shot her a thunderous look across the table. There was going to be hell to pay for this.

Kendall Carlisle grabbed Greer's arm and

raised it high, declaring him the winner amid applause, but that only delayed the inevitable.

'What the hell do you think you're doing?' Greer seized her none too gently and guided her to a private room the moment they could escape. 'Have you forgotten I've seen that shot before? You forfeited that game.'

'Have you forgotten you promised to trust me?' Mercedes answered. 'You are the one who has to advance.' The words rushed out. 'Please listen, Greer.' She gripped his lapels. She'd known he would be mad, but the reality was far worse than the theory. 'You promised you'd play for me. I am holding you to it. I need you to play for me now.'

Greer paused, his eyes past her in his anger. 'You're the one, Greer, who has the best chance to beat Cahill. I've already secured my reputation by making it this far, but you need that money and you need *your* reputation.' Mercedes held his gaze, willing him to believe her.

'And what do you need?' Greer asked gruffly.

'I need you, Greer.' She kissed him hard on the mouth, then. 'And I need to go pick up my winnings.'

He arched his eyebrows. 'What winnings would those be?'

'The money I placed on you.' She smiled

mischievously. 'The odds were more lucrative on you to win.'

Suspicion crossed his face. 'How much did you wager, Mercedes?'

'How much do you think? Enough to make sure you won't miss that inheritance you're giving up,' she said softly. 'I couldn't let you give it all up, Greer. I promised myself I'd make it back for you. But now is not the time to get emotional about money. Lesson number one, remember? Don't get emotional about money. Yours or anyone else's.'

Greer protested, 'At least you should have told me.'

'And risk having you throw the game first?' She shook her head. 'I know you, Greer Barrington, and you would have meddled if you thought for a second it wasn't my best game. Besides, tonight I wasn't betting on you, I was betting on us. Go out there and win this, Greer.'

'You've taken an enormous risk, Mercedes,' he began.

'Of course I have. But you're worth it.' She twined her arms around his neck and drew him down to her. 'For better or for worse, isn't that how it goes?'

'I thought a good gambler knew when it was time to quit?' Greer quizzed sternly.

'If there is such a time, I haven't found it.' She kissed Greer hard. She'd learned her lessons well and knew that sometimes it paid more to lose than it did to win. Just look at what she'd gained when she'd lost her heart.

Three days later, Mercedes Lockhart married the newly crowned All England Billiards Champion at St Peter's Church, the closest thing to a cathedral Brighton had. The church was filled with flowers and friends, and even strangers who'd been caught up in the drama of the tournament. Mercedes had very little attention to spare for those details, though. All of her focus was spent on the man at the altar. Was there ever a more handsome man than the one waiting for her or did every bride think that on her wedding day? No, surely not.

She concentrated on every detail of him: how the filtered sunlight hit his hair, firing it to a platinum sheen; the clean-shaven strength of his jaw and the piercing quality of his blue eyes as they found her; the square set of his shoulders in the red coat of his uniform, every last button and brass polished; his legs long and lean in the pristine white trousers, a ceremonial sword hanging at his side. It would be one of the last times he wore it before giving up his commission. But the uniform had been chosen to send a message, perhaps for her as much as for the crowd, Mercedes thought. Here stood a man who knew and did his duty—his honour was not in question nor should be his choice of bride. She would have his protection and his devotion all his days and let no man gainsay him—not his father, not his brother.

He took her hand, giving her father a short bow. 'Thank you, sir.'

She could feel the covert squeeze of his hand as they turned to face the vicar, a happy round-faced man. He began the service and she let the words flow around her, aware that they were nothing more than a pleasant sound. She was riveted on Greer, on this man who'd pledged himself to her, who stirred her to a passion so great she'd defied her father.

Greer bent close to her during a prayer. 'Your father spoke to me this morning. He has given his blessing.' Her father had been slow to forgive Greer for deserting him in Birmingham.

'I know. I played him for it.' She kept her eyes straight ahead, fixed on the cross above the altar.

Greer chuckled, drawing a moment of censure from the vicar who shot him a reproving look over the prayer book. 'Of course you did. You know, you can't settle everything with a billiards game, Mercedes.'

'Not everything,' she agreed. 'But those things that can be, should be.' She elbowed him. 'Look reverent. It's a prayer, after all.'

'I should have guessed sooner. He said you'd talked to him last night. I couldn't imagine what you might have said.'

Mercedes shot him a quick look as the vicar closed the last prayer. 'I did talk to him. I told him I loved you.'

'Was that before or after you ran the table?'

'After, of course.'

The vicar intoned the closing words of the ceremony, pronouncing them man and wife.

'It just so happens,' Greer whispered, his mouth hovering above her lips ever so briefly, 'that I love you too.' Then he kissed her so as to leave no doubt that all parties approved of this match, no one more heartily than the groom himself, and her heart sang with the knowledge that Greer Barrington loved her even though he'd promised not to.

There was a wedding breakfast hosted at her father's club to accommodate the many guests. By the time they could decently take their leave, Mercedes was exhausted, her mind riddled with names and faces. Who would have guessed weddings could be so tiring?

She was more than eager to slide into the closed carriage that would take them across town to their property. They would live above the subscription room for now. Greer joined her with a firm slam of the door and sank into the seat.

'Alone at last! Are you as hungry or as tired as I am?' His blue eyes sparkled. 'I never realised how little time the bride and groom have to actually eat at their own wedding breakfast.' He laughed and reached under the seat. 'Fortunately, the cook packed a few extra victuals for us.'

Her stomach rumbled and she smiled. 'Fortunately. We have to keep your strength up, after all.'

Greer uncorked a bottle of champagne, slopping a bit on his trousers when the carriage hit a bump. 'I must apologise—it's not your father's carriage.'

'I don't care.' They were on their own now, wanting to build their life from the ground up. She took the glass, more bubbles than wine in it. She sipped carefully. 'I don't think I've ever drunk champagne in a carriage before.'

Greer gave her a most wicked grin that warmed her to her toes. 'What else haven't you done in a carriage, Lady Barrington?' He slid onto the seat beside her. 'Have you done this?' He blew gently in her ear, nipping the tender flesh of her lobe. 'Or this?' His hand cupped her jaw, turning her face towards him for a soft kiss on the mouth. She sank into it, revelling in his touch. She had missed this!

'How about you, good sir? Have you done this?' Mercedes reached for him, finding him hard and ready. He laughed into her mouth, tasting faintly of champagne, letting her unfasten his trousers.

'You are most shocking, madam. I do not think I've ever been undressed in a carriage before.'

'Ha, and you said nothing I did surprised you.' She shot him a flirtatiously sly look. 'I bet I could "surprise" you a little more.' With that her hand began to move. 'Maybe after this, you could "surprise" me.' But, in truth, he already had.

* * * * *

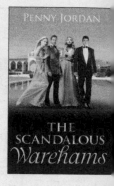

oin the Mills & Boon Book Club

Subscribe to **Historical** today for 3, 6 or 12 months and you could **save over £50!**

'Ve'll also treat you to these fabulous extras:

- 🌹 **FREE L'Occitane gift set worth £10**

- 🌹 **FREE home delivery**

- 🌹 **Rewards scheme, exclusive offers…and much more!**

Subscribe now and save over £50
www.millsandboon.co.uk/subscribeme

Where will *you* read
this summer?

#TeamShade

Join your team this summer.

www.millsandboon.co.uk/sunvshade